i promise to be better

Written by Erinn Keala
Edited by Lottie Hayes-Clemens and Azure Hall
Cover design by Maryn Lain

ISBN 979-8-218-39772-2

www.erinnkeala.com

i promise to be *better*

erinn keala

To Sam, my best friend and canine soulmate,
for loving me unconditionally through my lowest moments, providing
comfort in times of bitter loneliness, and being my reason to never give up.

And to my dear friend Gabi for blessing me with deep, honest, loyal
friendship and inspiring me to be the best version of myself.

I miss you both immensely.

*"When you are not fed love on a silver spoon,
you learn to lick it off knives."*

LAUREN EDEN

intro

I was 15 years old the night I lost my virginity in the back of a Chevy Tahoe on a Sunday night in December.

I had been hooking up with Carter for a year, but he wasn't my boyfriend. From my first kiss, to my first for everything else leading up to this moment, Carter was the closest thing I'd ever had to a boyfriend… except for the painful reality where he wasn't.

We talked everyday – text messages, phone calls, private meet-ups – but he ignored me at school as if I were a stranger. Blinded by desperate hope, I believed things would change after we had sex. Carter was a virgin, too. The moment our bodies united, he'd realize he loved me – at least that's what I told myself.

The anticlimactic event lasted all of three minutes. He put me on top and I didn't know what to do, so I let his hands guide me up and down until the look on his face told me he was finished. When it ended, I waited for him to pull me into his arms, look me in the eye, and finally say those three sacred words.

"Time to go home," he said instead.

He pulled up his pants and made his way to the driver's seat, motioning at me to do the same. The short ride to my house was silent. When we arrived, I looked over at Carter from where I sat.

I longed to kiss him.

I ached to tell him I loved him.

Carter looked back at me vacantly. "Bye, Emily."

Reluctantly, I unbuckled my seatbelt and got out of the car.

I went straight to my room and collapsed on my bed as my mind attempted to catch up to the thrill my body had experienced. The most anticipated moment of my teenage life. He chose me. It really happened. What would Gina say?

My phone vibrated with a text from Carter. I fantasized about what it might say before opening it – "*Thank you for tonight. It was everything. You mean so much to me.*"

I tapped open the message, my heart racing.

Carter: *This doesn't mean I like you.*

MY PARENTS SEPARATED when I was seven years old. Although my father remained physically present, his emotional absence left a void no number of court-ordered visits could fill.

My earliest childhood memory was my father's temper. As a toddler, I spilled a cup of juice, leaving a mess on the floor. This threw him into a fit – yelling, spanking me, and sending me to my room to cry alone.

When he left my mother some years later, I tiptoed to her locked bedroom door and placed my ear against it to listen to her sobs. A small part of me felt grateful that we no longer had to deal with his unstable moods, but in the face of her sadness I was ashamed of my relief.

The pain inflicted on my mother was palpable. She clung to the hope of salvaging our family, waiting patiently for him to be ready to be a husband and father again. But he never did. He came and left sporadically over the next few years, giving me glimpses of what having a father could be like while withholding any permanence.

When I was ten, he surprised me with a weekend trip to Disney World. I overflowed with excitement at the rare invitation to a special father-daughter adventure. But that weekend, I watched him and a strange woman bask in each other's company – holding hands, sneaking kisses – and I trailed behind like an afterthought. I came home feeling stupid, angry at myself for expecting more, and crushed by guilt as my mother questioned me about the woman.

In the wake of their separation and eventual divorce, my mother became a ghost of the woman she once was. Creases formed between her brows and at the corners of her mouth. Each day I searched her eyes for joy, but they were devoid of it. She was cloaked in a thick fog of heartbreak. It was difficult for her to shower me with the love I needed when her own heart was bleeding.

I fed myself cereal for dinner most nights and sought solace in the homes of friends whose family dynamics were better. I yearned for the warmth of a complete family, for the laughter and togetherness that seemed foreign in my own household.

As I grew into my teenage years, I deeply desired a boyfriend. Aching for connection, for someone who would cherish and adore me, I was drawn like a moth to the first flickering flame of attention: Carter.

Carter kissed me one night at a football game. My friend had recently started going out with one of his friends. The four of us got together for the game, and eventually the couple split off to go make out. Carter, his mom's car keys in hand, brought me to our own private spot where he gave me my first kiss. It was a kiss that held the promise of something magical, a moment that etched itself into the depths of my soul.

As days passed by, I found myself entangled in Carter's perplexing desires. He craved more of me but was uninterested in having a girlfriend – or he was uninterested in having *me* as a girlfriend.

We grew close in private, though. Rarely would a week go by without us indulging in late-night phone calls, texts and inside jokes. In those moments, I allowed myself to believe that he was my boyfriend, despite the agonizing truth that he wasn't.

No matter how close we grew, Carter refused to acknowledge me in public. We had classes together at school, but he avoided eye contact with me during them. Yet when those same classes brought us on an overnight field trip, he quickly conspired a way to spend the night together.

It was tantalizing. He made me feel wanted, and simultaneously he made me feel worthless.

During the spring of my junior year, two years into hooking up with Carter, he suffered an injury playing baseball that required surgery. We talked nonstop during his recovery, including hours-long late-night phone calls where his heavy painkillers combined with a sleepy state of mind had us flirting and telling deep secrets.

"Emily," he drawled into the phone. "I need to tell you something."

"What?"

"I'm afraid to tell you."

"Tell me! What is it?"

He paused. "I love you."

I love you.

Those three words made my heart stop. It was the first time anybody had ever said them to me; and it wasn't just anybody – it was *Carter*. I was suspended somewhere between disbelief and euphoria, grappling with the weight of the words.

"What?" I asked, afraid that I had somehow misheard him.

"I love you. I've always loved you, Emily. So much." He laughed, and it sounded like he was releasing a breath he had held in for so long. It was happy laughter.

I laughed in return. "I love you, too. But seriously? Do you mean it?"

"I do. Go to prom with me."

I closed my eyes to let it sink in. Everything I'd dreamed of was falling into place. Each time he hurt me was worth it for this moment. It was as if a million stars had aligned.

"Yes, of course. I'd love to."

BUT I SHOULD have known it was too good to be true.

Once Carter came off the pain meds and recovered from his surgery, there was never a mention of love again.

He came back to school and the loving reunion I'd fantasized about was instead a vacant stare. A prettier, more popular girl needed a prom date and asked him to go with her, and he blew off the arrangement he'd made with me, leaving me dateless for my junior prom.

I couldn't even act surprised. This is how it always went with Carter. I would never be enough for him, and I would never understand why he put me through the cruelest emotional rollercoaster I could imagine.

A couple months later he graduated and moved away to college, and our relationship ended as quietly as it began – and nobody knew the impact it left on me, except for me.

part one

chapter one

The summer Carter moved away, I was driving through our small town on the California coast when I passed Shane in the opposite lane and he waved. A minute later, he called.

"Hey!" I answered.

"You'll never believe what just happened," he said dramatically.

"What?"

"The most beautiful girl I've ever seen just drove by in a silver Toyota."

I laughed. Shane had always been a flirt – with everyone. During my freshman year of high school, he dated my friend Sarah. She was 14 years old compared to his 20, but the age gap didn't feel unusual. Freshman girls often dated senior guys, and being old for his grade he was only one year past graduating. Still, they kept their relationship secret due to what her parents might think.

One night, Sarah got caught sneaking out to be with Shane. Her parents were furious. They forbid her from seeing him again, took her phone, and grounded her indefinitely. But being young and in love, Sarah wanted to continue their relationship despite her parents' wishes – and that's where I came in.

While Sarah and I were together at school, she and Shane would text and call each other through my phone. I listened to them talk about how hard it was to be apart, and I ached to experience that profound love for myself.

But after six months, they ended their relationship. Sarah had a high school life to enjoy and couldn't continue keeping this secret from her family and friends.

"How have you been?" Shane asked.

"I've been okay, how about you?"

"I'm doing well!" he chimed, before his tone shifted to concern. "Just okay? Who do I need to beat up?"

I laughed again, fondly recalling this protective side of Shane. We had spent a considerable amount of time talking while I played middle woman in his relationship with Sarah and developed a friendship of our own. He'd listened to my complaints about Carter and always jokingly threatened to beat him up for me.

Reluctantly, I answered, "Carter."

"Holy shit, Emily! You're still hooking up with him?"

"Don't be mean about it," I warned. "I'm already upset enough."

"I'm not going to be mean about it. I just don't know what you see in him."

I sighed, glancing at the waves moving in patterns along the oceanside highway. I didn't know either. "It doesn't matter anyway. He just left for college."

"Well, maybe now you can finally find a better guy," he joked.

I chuckled. "Yeah, maybe."

"We should get together soon. It's been way too long since we caught up."

I pondered it. The year after Shane and Sarah broke up, she relocated to a new city and school. Since then, Shane had dated more girls than I could count. Although he and I remained friends, we sparsely interacted without the common thread of Sarah tying us together.

But catching up could be fun. I'd always enjoyed his company, and I could bring Gina along to avoid any awkwardness. "Sure!" I agreed, and we made plans to watch a movie at his house Friday night.

SHANE TOOK THE middle seat between Gina and me on the couch. We cozied up together, the three of us sharing a blanket as if our sexually-charged teenage hormones weren't enough to keep us warm.

Throughout the movie, Gina checked her phone every five minutes, noticeably irritated to see no new messages. "He's such a dick," she snarled. "I don't know why I'm even checking." She had recently ended a relationship and agreed to come to movie night because she needed the distraction, otherwise she might end up calling her ex.

Gina and I had been best friends since we were three years old. Although alike in many ways, she had a confidence I lacked. She was gorgeous and exuberant, and guys lined up to date her. She always saw the good in people, and she was fiercely loyal to the people she loved. But even a girl like her could attract jerks.

She set her phone down on the couch and faced us. "Let's do something fun."

"Like what?" I asked.

She raised an eyebrow. "Truth or dare."

"Oh my god, that's so high school!" Shane laughed.

Gina turned her focus to him. "Then you can go first, Shane. Truth or dare?"

Shane rolled his eyes. "Fine. Dare."

Gina gave me a rebellious smirk. "I dare you to make out with both me and Emily."

My jaw fell open. It was not the dare I was expecting.

"Alright," Shane said casually, and my cheeks heated. Of course it wasn't a big deal for him – he'd probably kissed more than a hundred girls while I could still count the number of guys I'd kissed on one hand.

He turned first to Gina. Their lips met, and they kissed for only a few seconds before Gina erupted in laughter. "Your turn!" she shouted at me.

Shane turned to me next. While I was caught somewhere in between feeling embarrassed and unprepared, he went right in for it. His lips met mine and immediately his tongue pushed into my mouth. A surge of electricity pulsed through my body. As his hand moved down my back, I fought the strange desire to push my body into his. Something about him felt so… good.

I pushed the feeling aside and followed our kiss with laughter as well, chalking it up to excitement to be kissing someone other than Carter.

"Okay, who's next?" Shane asked, his interest piqued.

"I feel like nothing else is going to be that exciting, so we can just stop playing," Gina said, prompting laughter from Shane and me. She got the distraction she needed, and the three of us resumed watching our movie.

GINA AND I were at the mall shopping the next day when a text from Shane came in.

Shane: *I felt something last night when we kissed. I'm not sure if you felt it too, but if you did, we should explore it.*

My stomach fluttered as I read the message a second time. I showed my phone to Gina. "Did Shane send you this, too?" Maybe he was messing with us – a silly prank to see if he could get us both to admit to wanting him as a way to feed his ego.

Gina's eyes widened as she read the text. She checked her phone.

"No, I don't have any texts from him. How are you going to respond?"

"I don't know." I bit my lip. This wasn't something I wanted to get involved in – Shane had dated one of my friends, he had a reputation for getting around with a lot of girls in our hometown, and I didn't want to complicate our friendship. "What should I say?"

She shrugged. "If you felt something, maybe you should see where it goes." She picked out a dress from the rack and held it up against her body in the mirror.

"But what about Sarah?"

"What about Sarah? It's been two years since they broke up." She turned to face me. "Besides Em, you really need someone other than Carter to focus on. This could be good for you."

I loved newly-single Gina's attitude and fearlessness. She was right. What I felt wasn't something I could ignore – I'd been thinking about our kiss from the moment it happened. Could there be a deeper connection between us? What did I have to lose by exploring it?

I typed my response to Shane.

Emily: *I felt something too.*
Shane: *What are you doing later?*

chapter two

The next time we hung out was the first time we had sex.

"Hello, gorgeous," Shane purred as I walked into his house.

I laughed, looking down at my Half Moon Bay High School Class of 2008 sweatshirt and matching sweatpants. With my hair pulled back in a messy bun and no makeup, I was anything but gorgeous. But I didn't feel the need to impress Shane. His presence – dressed down in his own baggy hoodie and basketball shorts – exuded a comfortable confidence that spilled over onto me.

We settled in beside each other on the couch, Shane resting his arm across the cushion behind us. As the movie played, his leg pressed into mine and I could feel the heat radiate from his body. I replayed our kiss from the night before in my head.

As if reading my mind, Shane's arm migrated from the cushion to my shoulder, pulling me closer to his body until I could feel the sturdy muscles of his chest against my cheek. He leaned down and planted a kiss on my forehead. I looked up, craving his lips on my mouth.

"I want to kiss you," he said, his eyes studying my lips.

"Then do it," I taunted.

He took my face in his hands and angled it toward his as his tongue parted my lips. Just like the first time, his kiss made me feel like I was on fire. As his tongue explored my mouth, his hands moved everywhere – up my shirt, down my pants – and my skin burned under his touch. His hands tugged at my waistband and I lifted my hips to allow my sweats to slide down.

He stopped kissing me and pulled back to look at me. "I don't want to do anything you're not ready for. I know you've only been with Carter."

I frowned at the mention of the name, then took a steadying breath. "I'm ready."

"Are you sure?"

I was inexperienced compared to Shane, and he knew that. It was a big deal to take this step with someone other than Carter, but it didn't feel like one. Somehow, doing this with Shane made sense – an unfamiliar territory that felt oddly like coming home.

I nodded confidently.

We began kissing again and moments later he entered me. As our bodies melted into one another, something inside us connected, too. I felt a wildfire of emotions consume me, as if every nerve ending had burst into a symphony of ecstasy.

When it ended, I stared into his blue eyes as he held my gaze. He leaned in and kissed me with an intensity that resonated through my body. In my head I played back the times Carter and I had found ourselves in the same vulnerable position, and how he'd always pulled away.

Now, Shane looked at me with a longing adoration. Never had I felt so wanted, desired and accepted. In that simple moment, he awakened a dormant part of me.

"You have no idea how long I've wanted to do that," he said.

"I do know." Apparently, I'd wanted the same thing.

"Who would've thought?" He looked up at his ceiling. "Thank you, Gina!"

We both laughed.

We finished the movie before he drove me home. When he dropped me off, he pulled my face in for a kiss. "Thank you for a really good night. Do you want to do it again soon?"

"We'll see." I smirked and he eyed me curiously. "Goodnight, Shane."

"Goodnight, Emily," he said, and he watched as I got out of the car and walked toward my front door. I felt his eyes on me as I unlocked it and stepped inside. It wasn't until I closed it that I heard him reverse out of the driveway.

I *absolutely* did want to do it again soon.

THE NEXT DAY I met Gina for coffee and told her I slept with Shane.

"*Emily!*" she shouted, causing several people in the cafe to look at us.

"Shh!" I scolded her.

She lowered her voice. "Tell me *everything*."

I recounted the night in a hushed voice, not leaving out any details as she gleamed with excitement.

"You like him, don't you?"

"I do." I grimaced. "But I don't want to!"

"Why not?"

"His reputation." I sighed. "He's dated so many girls. His relationships never last and he moves on quickly. I don't want to be just another name on his list."

"Well…" Gina strummed her fingers on her coffee cup. "It's a little late for that," she joked.

"I know." I put my face into my hands. "He might not even want to hang out again. But I swear, it really feels like there's something between us. Don't tell anyone, okay?"

Gina used her finger to zip her lips closed.

Later that evening, I was working on homework in bed when my phone lit up with an incoming call. My mouth curved into a smile as I accepted the call.

"Hey, Shane."

"Hey, how was your day?"

"Good, I hung out with Gina. How was yours?"

"I thought about you all day." His smooth voice sent a chill down my spine.

"Really?"

"Really."

"I thought about you, too," I admitted.

"When are we going to see each other again?"

I considered my response. *Fuck playing hard to get.* "Is tomorrow too soon?"

He chuckled. "I don't think I could wait a minute longer."

WE STARTED SEEING each other regularly and I stumbled through the unfamiliarity of being someone's girlfriend, my every move filled with awkwardness. I took my cues from Shane who, at 22, was much more experienced in relationships than me.

Because of the age difference, me approaching my 17th birthday, we kept our relationship secret as he and Sarah had done. Movie and restaurant dates outside of our small town and gatherings with close friends became the norm. I went to his basketball games and watched from the stands. He dined at the restaurant I worked at so we could steal gazes as I passed his table. I snuck out almost every other night to be with him, even if it meant staying awake until 2 a.m. on school nights. We continued this pattern through the entirety of my senior year.

Every encounter with Shane was a vibrant burst of color in my otherwise mundane existence. He painted my world with adoration, each "*good morning, beautiful*" text a brushstroke of affection. In his arms I felt seen, cherished, and valued like never before. I reveled in the idea that someone so captivating could see something special in me that others had failed to notice.

He wanted to talk to me all the time. On the nights we didn't spend together, we stayed on the phone for hours. He started to open up and tell me things about himself, and he showed a genuine interest in learning the same things about me.

The days turned to weeks, weeks turned to months, and before I knew it our infatuation turned to love. I discovered a version of myself I hadn't known before, basking in a warm happiness that felt like an ethereal dream.

We escaped for a weekend away together and drove a few hours northeast to a beautiful home nestled in the foothills of the Sierras. On the road we jammed to pop and country hits, Shane turning the volume up for "Our Song" by Taylor Swift and singing every word. I laughed as he serenaded me from the driver's seat. His joy and humor were infectious, and it was impossible to not feel exuberant in his presence.

We settled into our home away from home, feasting on tacos before donning our bathing suits and soaking up the last golden hour of sunshine in our private idyllic pool. Tall oak trees surrounded the backyard, separating us from the outside world. I wore my hair in a top knot, trying to maintain the curls I'd placed that morning before Shane picked me up, wanting to look my prettiest for him.

Shane, with his boyish charm and a mischievous glint in his eye, playfully splashed water in my direction.

I shot him a mockingly stern look. "Do not get my hair wet."

He chuckled. "What? Me? Never!" But his smirk betrayed his innocence.

"I'm serious," I warned, the playfulness in my tone contradicting me.

"Me too." He nodded. "So serious." He made his way toward the steps to exit the pool. "Just going to grab myself a drink." He walked in the direction of the house, then quickly pivoted and sprinted toward the pool, orchestrating a spectacular cannonball that sent water cascading in all directions.

I tried to shield my hair, but there was no escaping the splash. I gasped at Shane in mock horror as he emerged from under the surface, water dripping from my hair.

He grinned, unabashed. "Oops, my bad." He laughed.

I rolled my eyes but couldn't stifle my laughter. "You're impossible."

He swam over and placed his wet hands around my face and into my hair, gently removing the tie and allowing it to flow loosely over my shoulders. "You know, I think wet hair suits you," he joked.

I splashed him in the face. "So much for me looking nice this weekend."

He laughed, wiping water from his eyes. "You always look nice. You're the most beautiful girl I've ever known."

I shot him a disbelieving look. "Liar."

"I'm serious! I think you truly don't know how stunning you are, and it baffles me."

He reached for my hand and pulled me in for a kiss. I felt walls of insecurity crumble.

"I don't know how you do it…" I pressed my forehead to his. "But I've never felt this comfortable with anybody."

"And I've never had so much fun with someone." He pulled his head back so I could see his blue eyes gleaming in the setting sun. A smile formed across his face. "I love you, Emily."

Happiness overflowed inside my chest. Unlike Carter's hollow declaration which had left me full of disbelief, Shane's words validated a feeling of which I was certain. For the first time in my life, I dared to believe in the authenticity of love, and I trusted it wouldn't be snatched away without warning.

"I love you, too." I wrapped my arms and legs around Shane's body.

He pulled me closer and kissed my neck. "You make me so happy," he whispered.

The coziness of our bodies pressed against one another was as warm as the summer air. I wouldn't have been able to dream up a more perfect ending to an already perfect day. Our relationship was blossoming into everything I'd ever wanted, but I knew soon enough we'd have to face the conversation we'd been avoiding since I received my college acceptance letters two months ago.

I closed my eyes and breathed him in. It was a conversation for another day.

chapter three

I smiled as I read the text. We had been reluctantly counting down the days until I left in September for my first year of college at the University of California, Los Angeles, but to my surprise it was Shane who left our hometown before I did. He accepted a job an hour away and moved in July, just weeks after I graduated high school.

Despite the distance, our relationship thrived. I regularly drove to spend the weekend with him, and in this separate world our love grew tenfold. We indulged in ordinary pleasures like going for walks, dining at restaurants, and catching movies at the local theater. These seemingly mundane activities held significance for us, as they were the markers of normalcy we'd been denied due to the secret nature of our relationship.

Emily: I'm excited to see you too! I'm missing you fiercely this week.
Shane: Not as much as I've been missing you, babe.
Emily: Probably more, actually...
Shane: Impossible. You're the only thing I think about these days. Get here ASAP.

Emily: *As soon as I get off work Friday, I'm yours.*
Shane: *You are mine. Always. I love you.*

I bit my lip to stop a silly grin from taking over my face.

Shane was my sanctuary, an intoxicating blend of love and secrecy. Our time together, free of outside interference, was sacred and guarded, a treasure we shared exclusively.

Aside from Gina and a few other close friends, the world remained oblivious to the growth of our relationship. I was now four months shy of 18, and I often thought about how many people would be surprised to find out we'd been together for a year when we finally updated our relationship status on Facebook.

The best summer of my life was filled with the simplest of days. Shane and I embarked on humble adventures, strolling hand-in-hand through his suburban neighborhood to the nearby grocery store to pick out sushi and snacks, then spending the afternoon watching movies in his living room – always missing at least half of the movie distracted by the inability to keep our hands off one another.

He rarely drank alcohol, so our nights together were marked by a different kind of intoxication. Long after midnight, we found ourselves immersed in sober dialogue, exploring the intricacies of our dreams, aspirations, and the path we envisioned for our future. It was so much more mature than my high school friendships.

The more I got to know Shane on a deeper level, the more I began to understand what made him who he was. His mother and father had never wed, and his father didn't want to be part of his life. In Shane's early teen years, he sought his father out believing they could form a relationship, but his father returned no interest.

He had daddy issues, just like me.

"I get it," I told him. "I know it's different because my dad is physically in the picture, but sometimes I wonder if it'd be easier if he weren't. Then I wouldn't have to spend time in the presence of someone who acts like they don't want me. I can count on one hand the number of times he's told me he loves me."

"Hey, you still have me beat," he joked.

I laughed, even though it wasn't funny. He laughed too, but I could see a flicker of pain in his eyes. I reached for his hand as we sat together on his couch. "I'm sorry about your dad." He laced his fingers into mine and squeezed, returning my love in a single gesture. "You turned out amazing. It's his loss."

He raised my hand to his mouth to kiss my fingers. "Thanks, babe."

I felt the pain in his heart mirrored in my own. In the depths of our shared vulnerability, I understood the unfulfilled longing to be cherished by the parent who should have provided unwavering love. I saw through the 'player' facade and recognized the wounded soul beneath. He wasn't jumping from one girl to the next on a quest to break hearts; he was acting on the accord of his own fractured ego.

I could feel his reluctance to tell me these truths and I wondered how many other women had made it this far. If his emotional walls could be seen, I would be watching them crumble as he let me in.

With each passing day, the intensity of my affection deepened. I fell hard and fast, believing Shane would be the love story I had always dreamed of. But as summer went on, our focus on my approaching departure grew.

"It's only a six-hour drive," I reassured Shane as I faced him in his bed one early September night. Our weekends together were dwindling down to the final few. "I'll come visit you every month."

"It's not going to be the same, Em. You'll be in a new world. You're not going to want to come back here for me."

As he spoke, I studied the pained expression on his face and recognized the emotion behind it: Abandonment. He believed I was going to abandon him like others had.

I ran my hand through his dark brown hair and took his cheek in my hand. I placed my forehead to his. "You're my favorite person in the entire world. Nothing is going to change that."

He placed his hand atop mine. "I've never loved anybody the way I love you."

I could feel the sincerity in his words. Part of me wished I didn't have to leave, but the other part of me was excited for my new adventure. I'd always wanted to leave our sleepy little hometown. Half Moon Bay was a beautiful place to live but left little opportunity for explorative souls like mine. I hadn't even bothered applying to colleges in the Bay Area because I wanted to experience life elsewhere.

The only thing holding me back now was Shane.

This summer had been everything to us. All the simple days we enjoyed nothing but each other's company, the nights we spent wrapped in each other's arms, the hours-long phone calls on the nights we were apart. I knew, despite the boys who had failed to love me before, that Shane was sincere. Me leaving for college wouldn't change that.

THREE DAYS LATER, I was scrolling on social media when I stopped to read a post by Marissa, a girl in my hometown who was a couple years older than me.

It was a copy-and-pasted survey with her responses to questions – the type of thing I'd normally scroll past – except a name in the first response caught my attention:

Who was your last kiss? Shane :)

chapter four

My heart dropped as panic set in. There was no way it could be my Shane. He lived an hour away and had been spending all his weekends with me. But I couldn't think of any other guys in our hometown named Shane, and I knew he and Marissa had been friends before he moved.

My trembling finger clicked on her profile and, in an instant, my world crumbled before my eyes. There, in merciless clarity, was a picture of Shane with his arms around her waist, lips pressed to hers, and a smile on her face.

My Shane.

Hot tears welled in my eyes.

In a desperate act of defiance, I slammed my laptop shut – as if by shutting out the image, I could pretend it didn't exist and that my world hadn't been shattered into a million irreparable fragments. But deep within the pit of my stomach, I knew it had.

Shane loves me. Shane is with me. None of this makes sense.

Desperate for an explanation – something to undo what I had seen – I called him.

"Hey, babe," he greeted me casually as he answered the phone.

Babe. How could he call me that?

"How could you do this to me?" My voice cracked.

"Do what?" he asked, feigning innocence.

"Shane…" I paused to catch my breath. "I just saw a picture of you kissing Marissa on Facebook."

He was silent for a moment. "God damnit, Emily… I'm sorry."

"What the fuck is going on?"

"You're leaving." His tone shifted to despair. "I'm more in love with you than you could ever understand and you're leaving. What am I supposed to do?! It's fucking killing me."

"This is what you do?!" I shouted. "You start seeing someone else?!"

"I had to do something to try to get my mind off of you!"

"Do you love her?" The words tasted bitter as they left my mouth.

"Of course I don't love her," he scoffed.

"How long has it been going on?"

He paused. "About a week."

The realization hit me like a brick. *A week?* "Shane… I was with you three days ago."

The last time I lay in his arms, he let me think I was still the center of his world. He had looked me in the eyes and told me loved me, allowing me to believe it.

"I can't continue to love you knowing there's an end date –"

"There was never a fucking end date!" Fury coursed through me.

"You say that now, but in a month, you'll be in LA and you'll forget all about me. I can't just sit around here waiting for that to happen. I can't do it, Em… I can't handle it."

"You're wrong," I choked through tears. He couldn't be more wrong. In a last-ditch effort to defend myself and what little pride I had left, I said, "I never want to hear from you again, Shane. You are dead to me."

I hung up the phone. He called back three times. I let each call go to voicemail. Then, he stopped calling.

And just like that, everything between us faded into nothing.

"THIS ISN'T YOUR fault," Gina told me. After hanging up with Shane, I had gone straight to her house so that I didn't have to face the agonizing waves of pain that crashed down on me alone.

I cuddled up beside her, my tears falling onto her bed sheets. "How can he be with someone else? It's one thing to break up with me, but how can he *be with* someone else and not even tell me?" Guilt over my decision to leave for college bore down on me. Had I hurt him so deeply that he needed to seek comfort in the arms of another girl?

"Because he's an idiot and a coward," she muttered. "He didn't know how to break your heart, so he tried to take the easy way out by finding himself a distraction. You didn't deserve that."

"I love him so much," I sobbed.

"I know you do." She hugged me tighter. "But you are too much of a catch to be this distraught over a loser like Shane. We always knew he was capable of something like this."

"I really thought it was different." I let my guard down with Shane. I believed he was changing. I believed every moment between us meant just as much to him as it did to me.

"We all did," she said. "You're going to find someone amazing in LA. I promise."

I hoped she was right, because I couldn't bear the thought of hurting much longer.

I WAS DISTRAUGHT for the next two weeks as I prepared to start my new chapter in Los Angeles. It was hard to deal with the breakup of a relationship that very few people knew I was in. In the solitude of my sorrow, I yearned for Shane. The pain he had inflicted upon me seemed inconsequential compared to my longing to bask in the warmth of his love again.

I saw Shane one final time before I moved at a funeral for a classmate in our hometown. He came with Marissa, and although seeing them together struck a dagger through my heart, a small part of me lit up seeing him for the first time in weeks. I could sense a glimmer of the connection we shared, a spark refusing to be extinguished.

I approached him after the funeral and he leaned in to hug me. His familiar grip around my body and the scent of his skin was too much. He embraced me tightly as I cried – and because we were at a funeral, nobody found that to be odd. But I knew the reason for my tears was my selfish yearning to stay in his arms as long as I could.

As I began to pull away, he tightened his grip, buying us one more moment together. "I miss you so much," he whispered softly.

I winced.

His bittersweet confession hung in the coastal breeze for a moment before I walked away, knowing I had just said goodbye to the person who still held my heart.

chapter five

When I arrived at UCLA in late September, I walked into my dorm – my new home – and found a handwritten note on my empty bed.

Hey Emily!

In case you arrive while I'm gone, I'm out grabbing lunch and will be back soon. I'm SO excited to meet you!

- Nikki

I smiled and set the note back down on the twin-sized mattress. I looked around the room. My bed was opposite Nikki's, and we each had a small desk, dresser and wardrobe. Nikki, who had arrived the day prior, had already decorated her side of the room with pictures of her family and friends.

Nikki and I added each other as friends on Facebook as soon as we got our roommate assignments a few weeks prior. We'd chatted enough for me to know that she was also leaving behind an ex-boyfriend in her hometown. *But did he dump her for another girl? Probably not.*

I shook the heavy thoughts out of my mind as I began to unpack.

I had just finished placing all my shirts into my drawers when I heard the door unlock.

"Hello?!" Nikki said excitedly as she opened the door.

"Hi!" I moved toward her and she threw her arms open for a friendly hug.

"How was your drive down?"

"Six hours of highway with nothing to look at but cows," I joked.

"Welcome to inland California," she joked in return. Nikki had come from Bakersfield – not as far of a drive, but a totally different vibe from our near-coastal dwelling in Westwood.

I unpacked the rest of my clothes as we talked about our high school lives, the things we were most excited to do in college, and the highs and lows of the boys who had broken our hearts. We vowed to move forward, convincing ourselves the breakups had been for the best. We couldn't spend our college years tied to guys back home.

I could tell, as we got to know each other better, that Nikki could quickly become a close friend.

OVER THE NEXT two months, Nikki and I immersed ourselves in what our new home had to offer. We lived each day with the intention of making friends, meeting guys, and enjoying what everyone promised would be the best years of our lives.

Within our first month, Nikki found herself a new boyfriend. I was happy for her, but it cut our time together in half and I wasn't having as much luck finding someone of my own. Coming here, I had believed that a new city would be full of romantic possibilities, but even in a fresh sea of intelligent, handsome, driven guys, none of them were interested in me.

I knew my college experience held more significance than finding a boyfriend – I was also here to find myself. I'd come to UCLA with an 'undecided' stamp on my major. What did I want to do with my life? What classes interested me? I felt embarrassed to admit that most of my adolescence had been spent chasing love, and I'd failed to give thought to my future and who I wanted to become.

Ultimately, I just wanted to be happy. But I felt a deep sense of loneliness in my bones that made me worry I could never be happy alone.

I threw myself into the social scene, attended parties and put myself out there, but I felt invisible. There were some drunken makeouts and a couple one-night stands here and there, but nothing amounted to anyone wanting more of me.

With each rejection my loneliness intensified, and I found myself longing for the comfort of Shane's presence. Alone in my dorm every night, I felt the urge to dial his number and seek refuge in the familiarity of his voice. He was still the only person who ever made me feel seen. But I resisted, each time reminding myself he was no longer mine.

Before I knew it, December was upon us – fall quarter coming to a close and Christmas break inching closer. I spent most of my time outside of class completing papers and projects, and studying for my upcoming final exams. It was the most I'd seen of Nikki in weeks, as she spent most of these December nights studying in our dorm instead of crashing with her boyfriend, Nate.

I liked Nate. He was good to Nikki and had become a friend of mine, too. Nate's friend and fraternity brother Jack had also become a close friend, and the four of us frequently joined up for dinners, movies and nights of drinking. There was no romantic connection between Jack and me, but I appreciated him as a companion, and his friendship – along with Nikki and Nate – helped aid my bitter loneliness.

Nikki and I were studying in our dorm one night when a familiar name showed up on my phone. It gave me a fluttering feeling in my stomach I hadn't felt since the last time I saw… him.

"Oh my god," I said out loud.

Nikki looked up from her laptop. "What?"

I mouthed "*Shane*" to her while I answered the call. "Hello?"

"Hey, Em."

The sound of his voice made me weak. Nikki swiveled her desk chair to study my face as I began my conversation with Shane. "What's up?"

"Not too much," he responded casually. "How's UCLA?"

"Great." I kept my tone guarded. I was unsure how to speak to him. It had been so long since we last spoke – three months since we'd said our final goodbye at the funeral.

"I'm glad to hear that. What have you been up to there?"

"Class, hanging out with friends, going to parties…"

"Cool." An awkward silence followed. *What the hell was the point of this call?*

"Shane… Why are you calling me?"

"Because… I miss you."

"Aren't you in a relationship?" I made no attempt to hide my bitterness.

"No," he said quickly. "We broke up not long after you left. It was never serious."

I widened my eyes at Nikki, who was watching intently from across the room. She raised her hands as if to ask, "*What?*" I shook my head. She raised an eyebrow.

I attempted to seem unbothered by the information. "Oh. That sucks."

"Not really. It means I get to talk to you."

I could sense his smirk, and I hated that those words sent warmth through me. I didn't want him to think I was sitting around waiting for him to come back. He left me for another girl. I had every right to be pissed off. Hell, I had every right to hate him.

"Em?" I realized I hadn't responded.

"Yeah. I'm just… I'm not sure we should talk," I stammered.

"Why not?"

"Because we ended things for a reason. I'm here… you're there."

"Yeah, I mean… we don't have to get back together or anything. I just miss you. I wanted to say hi."

I let out a long sigh. "I miss you, too."

Nikki rolled her eyes.

"Do you really?" he teased.

"Shut up," I sassed, annoyed that he was already pushing it.

"Will you be home for Christmas?"

"Yes."

"Do you want to get together and catch up?"

Every part of my body came alive at the thought of being in his arms again, but I refused to give him that satisfaction. I was still so angry at him for what he'd done. "I'll think about it."

He chuckled. "I'll take it."

"Goodbye, Shane." I was ready to end the conversation before he pressed any further.

"Goodbye, Emily," he said, and I knew him well enough to know there was a grin on his face as my name rolled out of his mouth.

"Tell me everything," Nikki said before I finished setting my phone down on my desk.

"He broke up with Marissa, he misses me, and he wants to see me when I come home for Christmas," I summarized.

"Ugh. Men… they always think we're just going to be waiting around when they finally figure their shit out."

"Yeah," I agreed, but I kept replaying his words in my head. *I miss you. It was never serious.*

"Emily," Nikki directed my attention back to her. "You've got better things to focus on now."

"Right." But I wasn't convinced, because the mere sound of Shane's voice had reignited a flicker of hope inside me.

"Meeting up with him when you visit home probably isn't a smart idea," she warned.

I nodded… but not all ideas had to be smart ideas. "We'll see. For now, I just have to focus on passing these exams." I set my gaze back on the textbook in front of me to politely signal that I was done talking about Shane for now.

Nikki groaned and went back to studying as well.

As I got into bed that night, my phone vibrated with a text.

Shane: *It was really good to hear your voice today.*

I clutched my phone to my chest, recalling the warmth that had spread through my body when I heard his voice. I closed my eyes tightly, trying to shut out the beckoning thoughts in my head, but a stupid grin formed on my face before I drifted off to sleep.

chapter six

I trembled as I pulled into his driveway two weeks later. Through texting back and forth with Shane, I learned he was staying in his mom's separate unit in our hometown for the holidays, and decided there was no harm in paying him a visit. It's not like I had any college love interests holding me back.

But I had no idea what it would feel like to see him again for the first time in three months. Would it feel the same as before? And more importantly, would he still feel the same way about me?

I walked to the front door and took a deep breath. For a moment I considered getting back in my car and driving away, but he must have seen my car pull up because before I could even muster the courage to knock, the door opened.

I drank in the sight of him. He looked the same. He was casual in his hooded sweatshirt and sweatpants. He hadn't shaved in what I guessed was a few days, because brown stubble covered his cheeks and chin and gave him a rugged look – a hot rugged look.

"Hi," I squeaked, immediately embarrassed by the timid sound of my voice.

He said nothing as he smiled and pulled me into him. He held me in a tight embrace for what felt like an eternity, the closeness of our bodies whispering our unspoken feelings. His lips hovered only inches from mine as he finally breathed, "It's good to see you, Em."

I did not protest as he kissed me next. Comfort washed over me for the first time in months. It felt more like coming home than driving into my actual hometown. He made me feel full, and I realized how empty I had been without him.

"I've missed you," he said softly as his lips left my mouth.

"I've missed you, too." My arms lingered around his neck, and his around my waist, as he took a step back from the door so that I could fully enter the space, pushing it closed with his foot.

I scanned the room, just big enough for a queen-sized bed and loveseat. Arms still holding me as if I might find a way to escape, he led me to the bed, where he sat and pulled me into his lap so that my legs straddled either side of his body. We began to kiss again.

"I'm sorry," he spoke between kisses.

"I don't forgive you," I responded, my lips barely leaving his mouth.

His hands braced my hips and pulled me even closer, positioning me atop the hardness between his legs. "How can I get you to forgive me?"

But I had lied. My traitorous body had forgiven him the moment I walked through the door. My words barely came out in between breaths. "Stop talking."

Our kisses intensified, his tongue exploring my mouth and remembering its familiarity. Within minutes, we were removing our clothes to reunite our bodies and end the yearning. I felt completely invigorated by his touch, experiencing a euphoria no amount of drugs or alcohol could achieve. I wanted to see him, to feel him, to hear him, to smell him, to taste him.

After we finished having sex, I rested my head on his chest and he draped his arm around my shoulder. "Have you done any of *that* in LA?" he joked, but I knew he was prying for details.

I chuckled, then frowned. I didn't want to think about Shane and Marissa, or any other girls he'd been with since I'd left. It's not that I hadn't been with others too, but it was meaningless compared to him – one-night stands where I never spoke to the guy again, or in some cases barely remembered the sex. I didn't want to tell Shane any of that.

Instead, I said honestly, "No one is you."

He squeezed my shoulder with his hand. "That's exactly how I've been feeling, too."

"It sucks that you're here and I'm there."

"Well, *someone* had to be smart and ambitious and get herself accepted to the country's best public university," he teased.

I laughed. "Why would I do such a thing?"

He stroked my arm, strumming it with his fingertips as he took a breath to say something, but abruptly stopped.

"What's up?" I asked.

"I need to tell you something," he said.

I shifted my position so I could see his face. "What?"

He studied me, as if unsure how to deliver the words. "I'm joining the Army."

My eyes widened. "Seriously?"

He nodded. "I leave next month."

"When did you decide this?"

"I've been thinking about it over the past few months since you left, and I need to do something with my life. You're off at school and I can't just sit around here." His eyes gleamed as he looked at me, a smile forming on his face. "I'm really excited about it. I think it's going to be badass."

I felt a tug in my heart. "How long will you be gone?"

"I'll be without a phone or computer for at least eight weeks in basic training, but you can write me letters if you want."

"Where is basic training?"

"Fort Leonard Wood, Missouri."

"And then what?"

"Then advanced individual training, and then my duty station."

"Where will your duty station be?"

"I won't know that until after basic and AIT."

My thoughts rushed. I had so many questions. The suddenness of it all threw me into a whirl of confusion since it was something we had never discussed before. So much had changed in just a few months. I couldn't help but wonder if this was going to be the last time I saw Shane.

A life in the Army would take him far away from the place we once called home. He wouldn't be six hours away, waiting for me in our hometown; he'd be starting a new life somewhere. The uncertainty of our future left me grappling with a mix of sadness, confusion, worry, happiness and pride – all at once.

"I'll write you letters," I assured. "I'm really proud of you." I meant it. This was good for Shane. He worked well-paying jobs in the service industry at luxury hotels, but I knew those roles felt devoid of a higher purpose for him. He had always wanted to do more – to be more – and the truth was, I couldn't be prouder of him for making this decision, even if it filled my own mind with uncertainty.

After Christmas break, I didn't see Shane again before he left for basic training in February. He called the night before he departed to say goodbye, and even though he wasn't going somewhere forever, it felt like a real goodbye. It was the start of his next chapter, and his next chapter didn't include me.

chapter seven

Dear Emily,

How are you? I'm doing well. Things are crazy here and I don't have a lot of time to write, but I'll try to write to you when I can. I miss you.

Can you believe I've lost 10 lb already? We're working out all the time and I don't have freedom to snack like I normally do. Just wait until you see me!

I should be able to call you soon, but it will only be for a few minutes. I hope you'll be able to answer. So far, I've only been able to call my mom once. It's weird not having a phone or computer. I feel so disconnected from the outside world.

What's new in LA? Please write back. It will make me so happy to hear from you.

Love, Shane
P.S. Here's my basic training photo.

Dear Shane,

I was so happy to receive your letter and handsome picture. I taped it to my desk so I can see you every day. I'm glad to hear you're doing well. Tell me more about what you've been up to there!

Wow, you're going to be so lean when you finish basic training! I still can't believe you're in the Army now. It's so crazy. Any word on where you'll go next?

I'm doing well here. We just finished midterms for this quarter (straight A's!) so I've been studying like crazy and now I get a nice break from that! I still need to declare a major, and I'm leaning toward psychology but I'm not sure. Any idea what I should do with my life? Just kidding, but seriously... I'm so lost.

Aside from that, I've been hanging out with my roommate Nikki and spending most of my free time in Santa Monica and Venice Beach. It's so sunny here – nothing like our cold and foggy hometown, although I do miss it. Gina came to visit for a weekend, too! And I'm going to visit her next month. I'm excited for that.

I miss hearing your voice. I hope you can call soon.

Love, Em

Em,

We just got off the phone and I'm so giddy, it's stupid. It was so good to hear your voice, even if only for two minutes. Let me try to think of all the things I didn't have time to tell you.

Things have been busy here. We had a weapons qualification course and I qualified as a sharpshooter, which is the second-best level. We've also been doing crazy obstacle courses. I had to rappel from a 50-foot tower and you know how I feel about heights. I thought I was going to shit myself!

I don't know where I'm going to be stationed yet, but after basic training I will go to AIT which is also here at Fort Leonard Wood. I'll have my phone during AIT too, so we can talk more.

I forgot to congratulate you for acing all your midterms on the phone. You're the smartest person I know, so I'm not surprised. As far as what you should do with your life, have you ever considered being a military wife? Haha… just kidding!

I miss you. Have fun with Gina. Can't wait to hear from you when you get back.

Love, Shane
P.S. Send me some pictures of you so I can hang them in my locker.

Dear Shane,

I was so happy you called, even though those two minutes felt like two seconds. I had so many things I wanted to say that I didn't even know where to begin!

Congratulations, sharpshooter! That's really awesome. The obstacle courses sound fun (and hard!).

Haha! No, I can't say I've considered the option of being a military wife. I would have to fall madly in love with some Army guy first. Do you know anyone? Maybe you can introduce me ;-)

Visiting Gina at Sonoma State was so much fun! We went to a couple parties and hung out at the Russian River. It's weird being so far away from her, but thankfully I get to text her every day. I'm excited you'll have your phone soon, too!

After these classes end in a couple weeks, I only have one more quarter to go until I'm done with my freshman year! Can you believe it? This year has gone by so fast. I have to start thinking about where to live next year. I think Nikki and I are going to move out of the dorms and get an apartment together, which will be awesome!

I'm including some recent pictures. As you can see, I dyed my hair brown!

Love, Em

Em,

WOW. Your brown hair is beautiful. I love you as a blonde, but you're stunning as a brunette. It's so good to see your face in these pictures.

I can't stop thinking about you. I definitely dreamed about you naked last night. I know you just rolled your eyes reading that but it's true. I dream about you all the time.

And yeah, you jerk – I do have someone in mind for you to fall in love with. It's the person writing you this letter. I'm sorry I didn't realize it sooner, but you're the only person in this world I want to be with. I know I've fucked up in the past and I've hurt you, but I will spend every day for the rest of our lives trying to make it up to you.

I can't live without you, and I don't want to do it anymore. The distance doesn't matter. Let's give this a real chance – no more secrets, no more hiding. Let's be together for real. I love you more than you'll ever understand.

Love, Shane

Shane,

Sorry it took me a little while to write back. I've been trying to figure out what to say.

You mean the world to me, but I'm scared. You hurt me worse than anybody ever has and I'm not sure I can trust you to not do it again. Let's see how things go when you finish training. You might change your mind by then. You were afraid of a six-hour drive between us... now we don't even know what state you're going to be living in and I have three more years of college here.

I love you but I need to take it one step at a time. We have a lot to consider before jumping back into this.

I miss you. Good luck with your final week of basic training. Talk to you soon.

Love, Em

SHANE FINISHED BASIC training in April and moved on to his advanced individual training where he got his phone back. I headed into my final two months of classes for the year, still completely undecided about my future and now distracted by the possibility of entering a long-distance relationship.

I was scared. Could I let my guard down and trust him? Part of me wanted to refuse him a second chance at love, but I remembered the last time I saw him and how he blanketed me in a comfort I failed to feel anywhere else.

We texted and called each other regularly throughout those months, and he told me he'd be home for a visit after he graduated in June. As the date got closer, excitement surged through my veins. It was only a matter of weeks before I'd see him for the first time in six months. I found myself daydreaming about it in class, indulging in scenes of our reunion like movie moments played out in grand gestures.

I leaned into it. I allowed myself the comfort these fantasies brought me and the way my heart warmed when I envisioned myself back in Shane's arms. I talked about it with my friends, Nate and Jack teasing me for marking each day of my desk calendar with a big X as we got closer to Shane's homecoming. I even let my excitement spill into public spaces, posting a vague Facebook update about my heart feeling complete because "*someone*" was finally coming home to me on June 22.

Shortly after posting, I received a message.

Rose: *Hey Emily! What's happening on June 22?*

Rose and I worked together during my senior year of high school. She was two years older than me, and although we hadn't been friends in school we developed a bond as coworkers, sometimes getting together for ice cream or shopping outside of our shifts at the restaurant. We mostly stopped talking after I left for college, and I'd heard through the grapevine that she and Shane hooked up after he ended things with Marissa… though I'd never brought it up with either of them.

Seeing her name on my computer screen filled me with bitterness now, even though I had no right to be angry. I never told Rose I was dating Shane back then, so I couldn't hold it against her if she explored a fling with him when they were both single and I was out of the picture. Still, the idea of them together filled me with jealousy and I felt the need to defend my territory.

Emily: Hey. It's the day Shane comes home to visit. This isn't public yet, but he and I have been talking for a while and I'm really looking forward to seeing him!

Rose: You've been talking to him while he's away?

Emily: Yeah, we wrote letters while he was in basic training and now he has his phone again.

Rose: He wrote me letters while he was in basic training too... lol

My stomach turned. Why would he have written to Rose? I regretted telling her anything. To lessen the embarrassment building inside me, I played it cool in my response.

Emily: Oh haha really?! What did he say?

Rose: He asked if I'd be interested in giving things another shot with him, but I'm not. I have a boyfriend now. He stopped writing to me after I told him that. Haha

I sent a laughing emoji to Rose's message, but a searing blend of pain and anger resonated through my body the same as when I found out Shane was with Marissa the year before.

Fucking idiot, I berated myself. His faithless love was a hoax, and I believed it again.

I looked at his picture on my desk and my heart ached with betrayal. His blue eyes bore into mine as if he were there. "Why are you doing this to me again?" I asked, and the question hung in the air unanswered. I felt a teardrop hit my leg.

There had to be some type of explanation; I just needed to hear it from him. I clung desperately to the possibility that there might be a justification as I called him.

"Hey!" he answered.

"Did you write letters to Rose when you were in basic?" I blurted.

Shane's tone was reserved. "I… wrote to her a couple times to say what's up. Why?"

"Why am I hearing from her that you asked if she wanted to give things another shot?"

He forced a laugh. "She said that? No… it wasn't anything like that."

My frustration boiled. "What did you say in your letters to her?"

"Come on, Em, why does this matter? I've already told you how I feel about you."

"I need to know what you wrote in your letters to Rose," I demanded.

He paused and took a deep breath. When he spoke, he sounded regretful. I knew as he began that I wouldn't like hearing what he was about to say. "Look, Em… when I got here I was lonely. I just wanted to talk to people. I couldn't use the phone, I couldn't use the computer, so I wrote letters. I wrote to a lot of people, okay? It made me feel good to receive letters back from them. I said a lot of things I didn't mean because I was lonely and wanted to feel close to people."

My chest tightened. The thought of other girls receiving letters like mine made me sick. I looked at the stack of papers on my desk and, for a moment, considered ripping them to shreds. The letters once made me feel special; now, they were a reminder of how stupid and naive I was.

It's not like I was a saint – I wasn't. During the past six months since I last saw Shane, I'd explored my options. I'd gotten drunk, made out with strangers, and exchanged numbers with guys I'd never speak to again. I did this even while Shane and I were writing notes back and forth. Could I be angry that he'd also kept his options open?

But in all that time, I *never* let someone believe they were special to me. I *never* hinted at a relationship with anyone other than Shane. Because truthfully, no one else even remotely mattered. It was *only* Shane who mattered. And I thought, for Shane, it was *only* me who mattered.

As if answering my thoughts, Shane continued, "You're the only person I meant what I said to, Em. You're the only person who matters. I'm sorry if I made you doubt that again."

I remained silent as his voice became desperate.

"Emily, please say something," he pleaded.

Conflicted currents of rage and heartbreak raced between my head and my heart. My heart pulled me to Shane – even amid the pain, I longed for his comfort and reassurance. But my head argued – I couldn't continue to let myself be hurt, even if it meant losing him. I was tired of the ups and downs, the uncertainty of whether I'd be enough, the insecurity that he'd reject me again, and the fact that it cut deeper each time.

"I don't want to do this," I said. "I'm done. Don't try to see me when you come home." I hung up the phone and let his calls go to voicemail, five times in a row.

chapter eight

Despite ignoring his calls for two weeks, Shane came directly to my doorstep in June. I was conveniently home alone when he arrived, my mom out running errands.

I opened the door to a man I almost didn't recognize and held it just wide enough to survey him. He stood on my doorstep, the definition of his rounded shoulders and arms showing through his form-fitted gray t-shirt. His bicep bulged from its sleeve, displaying fresh black ink in the form of a grenade tattoo.

I moved my gaze from his body to his face and studied his features, not yet ready to form words. His buzzcut hair and cleanly shaven cheeks were an alter ego of the casual five o'clock shadow I had awoken to on so many mornings, which now seemed like a lifetime ago. I glared into eyes as blue as the summer sky behind them – the part of him that remained familiar against the rest.

"Please don't close the door," he said, those blue eyes pleading.

I kept my face devoid of emotion. "What do you want?"

"I want to talk."

"So, talk." I opened the door a few inches wider.

His eyes scanned my body as if taking it in for the first time. I suddenly felt extremely self-conscious. What was he thinking? Did I look worse than last time he saw me? As his eyes met mine again, I felt his longing. "You are even more beautiful than I remembered," he said.

Shane leaned in for a hug, and my walls of anger and resentment crumbled, no match for the overpowering love that surged within me. The embrace brought every emotion I had tried to bury to the surface. I was overwhelmed by feelings of missing him, wanting him, needing him. I hadn't seen him in six months, and I still loved him unwaveringly.

"I missed you so much." He took my face in his hands. "I love you. Will you please let me in so we can talk?"

The lies, the drama and the complications were nothing compared to the energy between our bodies. My heart made the decision that my head warned against, and I reciprocated as Shane went in for a kiss. As our lips pressed together, it felt as if nothing else mattered – like this stolen moment was enough to undo any wrong that came before it.

Lips still pressed to mine, he pushed his way inside and closed the door behind him with one hand. My yearning for him permeated every fiber of my being, and as he moved in the direction of my bedroom I allowed my feet to follow in step.

We made it to my bed, and I stopped kissing him abruptly. "I thought we were going to *talk*."

"Right now, I just want to *be* with you." There was desperation in his voice. He needed this. He needed me.

I nodded, because I understood.

As we stripped our clothing and made love, I remembered the fire in my soul that burned only for him, and I knew his soul burned the same for me.

HE LACED HIS fingers into mine as we lay in the aftermath of our primal reunion. "Be with me, Emily. We've waited so long to be together.

I don't want to wait any longer."

"What are you asking?"

"I want you to be my girlfriend." His lips curved into a smile. "Officially."

I grinned as my heart swelled. His girlfriend. His over-18-and-able-to-be-seen-in-public girlfriend. His Facebook-status-official girlfriend. I wanted nothing more than to say yes. But I thought about Marissa, Rose, the letters… and I hesitated. "How do I know you're not going to hurt me again?"

Shane's smile shifted to a frown and his eyes dimmed. Still holding my hand, he pulled it to his mouth and pressed his lips against my knuckles. "I promise you. I've made stupid mistakes, and I'm sorry." He shook his head. "I'm so sorry. I've lost you enough times now to know that I never want to lose you again. I swear, babe – you're it for me."

His eyes bore into mine and conflicting thoughts waged a battle in my head. I longed to be his girlfriend, but the fresh heartbreak urged me to tread carefully.

"Please?" he asked, a grin spreading across his face.

"I don't know, Shane," I said, but I couldn't stop my own smile from growing.

"Pretty please?" He pressed himself up so that he was kneeling before me on the bed. He reached for me with both arms, groping my waistline as if about to tickle it, and I squirmed in anticipation. "Pleeeeease, Emily?" he asked again, now moving his fingers and making me giggle uncontrollably.

"Fine!" I shouted, my compromise to end the tickling. "I'll be your girlfriend."

He leaned down to plant a kiss on my forehead. "You won't regret it. I promise."

THAT SAME MONTH was the first time I met Shane's mom, along with his stepdad and grandparents. All at once I was welcomed into a family that went from not knowing I existed to loving me the moment I walked through their door. I wasn't the first girl Shane had brought home but maybe, like me, they recognized something real between us.

We went out for lunch together in our hometown, Shane holding my hand for everyone to see. The magnitude of the moment wasn't lost on me – it was the first time I'd ever been out in public in my hometown with my boyfriend and his family. I knew it was silly to think anyone was watching, but to me it felt like a red-carpet reveal.

I introduced Shane to my mom as the first boyfriend I'd ever brought home. I decided not to tell her about our volatile history, because I didn't want to taint her first impression. Instead, she met a handsome young man who was selflessly serving his country and making her daughter glow with happiness.

After two weeks at home, Shane left for his first military assignment at Joint Base Lewis-McChord, and before he even left I was booking a flight to see him the following month.

I went to Washington for 10 days in August before my sophomore year of college began. I couldn't stay overnight in the barracks with him, so I stayed with a friend nearby, and Shane and I got a hotel on the weekends. He spent time with me in the evenings after work, introducing me to his friends and showing me around his new home.

While hanging out with him at the barracks one day, I went to use the shared women's bathroom on the co-ed floor. When I came out of the stall, there was a girl using one of the mirrors to style her hair. We made eye contact in the mirror, and I gave her a polite smile which she returned.

As I washed my hands, she asked, "Who are you here visiting?"

"Shane," I answered, then remembered the military culture of calling everyone by their last names and quickly added, "Foster."

"Foster?" she repeated with a laugh and continued straightening her hair. "Hmm. Enjoy." I sensed sarcasm in her tone.

I didn't know what the laugh meant, so I gave her tight-lipped smile, dried my hands and left the bathroom with an uneasy feeling in my stomach. I walked down the hallway to Shane's room replaying the interaction in my head. *Why did she laugh at me like that?*

I entered Shane's room. He sat in a relaxed position on his bunk bed, exactly as I'd left him minutes before. He looked up from the TV and gave me a smile as I walked over and took my seat beside him. For a moment, I debated bringing up the interaction, but it lingered in my head and bothered me too much to let go.

"I saw a girl in the bathroom." Shane looked at me, waiting for me to continue. "She asked who I was here to see and I said your name… and she laughed."

His dark brows furrowed. "She laughed?"

"Yeah, like… it felt like she was laughing at me." I picked at the skin around my thumb to distract myself from the discomfort I felt recounting this to him.

"What did she look like?"

"Shorter than me, red hair…"

A hint of recognition flickered in Shane's eyes, followed by irritation. He frowned for a moment before shifting back to a casual demeanor. "Don't worry about it. People act immature here. She wasn't laughing at you. She's just laughing that I have a girl here."

"Does she know I'm your… girlfriend?" I was still getting comfortable with the label.

"It's probably not someone I even talk to, Em. Don't worry about it." He stopped me from picking at my thumb, held my hand and gave me a reassuring smile. "You've got nothing to worry about. There is not a single person here who compares to you. I would be an idiot to even consider it." He chuckled. "You think I'd bring you here and parade you in front of everyone if I was hiding something?"

I shook my head, forcing a smile. He had a point, but I hated the way she made me feel. Shane's past indiscretions haunted my thoughts, gnawing at the trust we were still rebuilding. I couldn't help fearing that he would discard me again for another girl. But my insecurities were swept aside as we went to dinner with his friends and he showered me in affection.

WHEN IT CAME time for me to head back to Los Angeles, Shane took me to the airport. "When will I see you again?" he asked, his arms wrapped around my waist.

"You free next month?" I joked.

He laughed. "Can you come every month?"

"Anything less would be unbearable." I kissed him goodbye, then began to walk away, turning back to look at him.

"I LOVE YOU!" he hollered embarrassingly loudly, causing other people on the departures curb to stare.

"I love you, too," I mouthed back, laughing, and I smiled the entire way to my gate.

chapter nine

"I don't understand why you have to make a big deal out of this," I said into the phone.

"Because it is a big deal. I'm uncomfortable with something and you're acting like you don't care."

Shane was upset about my outfit for the second time that month. The first time, my skirt was too short. This time, I had too much cleavage showing. He had asked me to send him a picture of what I was wearing before I went out, which I was now regretting.

"You have no reason to be uncomfortable with the shirt I'm wearing."

"I'd feel a lot better about this if you changed," he insisted.

I rolled my eyes, as if he could see them through the phone. It wasn't worth the fight. Things were already tense with me going out that night. Changing my shirt was a small sacrifice.

"Fine," I conceded before ending the call and picking out a different shirt.

THINGS BETWEEN US had started wonderfully as I returned to college. But as the last four months wore on, Shane had become controlling.

It started small. He wanted to keep tabs on me.

Call me when you're leaving. Call me when you get there. Call me when you're home. Call me before you go to bed. Call me when you wake up.

And he did the same – all day long he called to let me know what he was up to, when he was leaving work, when he was heading to the gym, and where he was grabbing a bite to eat. I loved how frequently we interacted – it made the distance feel smaller.

Lately, he'd been asking to see what I was wearing every time I went out. The request began innocently enough – a sweet curiosity and an excuse for him to get a picture of me – but then his opinions became assertive, demanding changes when he didn't like what I was wearing.

I prided myself on being a loyal and trustworthy girlfriend, and his attempts to assert dominance over my choices felt like a betrayal of that trust. But I tried to understand his reasoning – if something makes him uncomfortable, shouldn't I care? If something made *me* uncomfortable, wouldn't I want *him* to care?

He had also started exhibiting cold behavior toward me when I attended parties or social gatherings. On those nights, he felt distant – his short texts stripped of their usual warmth. I hated bringing out this side in him – my world was so much brighter when Shane was happy and affectionate – so I started to confine myself to the walls of my apartment.

"You never come out anymore, Em," Nikki complained one night while getting ready for a party. In our second year of college, Nikki and I had moved out of our shared dorm into an off-campus apartment together. "Why don't you want to come?"

"I'm just tired," I lied. "I think I'm going to watch a movie with Shane on the phone." I was embarrassed to explain to Nikki that Shane would get upset if I went out.

"Okay, will you come out tomorrow night?"

"Maybe! Have fun tonight."

"I will." She applied her lip gloss in the mirror. "We'll miss you."

I felt frustrated that Shane was holding me captive from making memories with my friends, but I recalled him saying, *"If you love me, you'll respect my boundaries and the things that make me uncomfortable."* He told me the choice was mine to determine what was more important: drinking and partying, or respecting my relationship and staying home.

Nothing was more important to me than him, but I struggled to grasp why I couldn't have both. I wanted to have fun. I wanted to go to parties with my friends and experience all that UCLA had to offer. After all, these were supposed to be the best years of my life.

I tried to pick and choose my battles, but it was hard when Shane was always on the warpath. If I wasn't tucked away in my apartment by myself, there was cause for an argument. I tried to understand as he explained, *"You're a beautiful girl and people can do horrible things to take advantage of you when you put yourself in compromising positions with alcohol."* He reassured me he was looking out for my safety, because he *"wouldn't be able to live with himself if he allowed anything bad to happen to me."*

Although I sacrificed a lot of nights with my friends to keep the peace, I maintained a level of stubbornness. I wasn't willing to give up everything I wanted. I was forced to make decisions I knew would upset Shane in order to not abandon all of my own happiness.

ON THE NIGHT of my 19th birthday, I celebrated by throwing a party at my apartment. Gina flew in for the weekend, and I was so excited to have her there with Nikki and a few other girlfriends.

Shane wanted to be the first one to wish me a happy birthday at midnight and asked me via text to leave the room to take his phone call alone. Stubborn and drunk, I refused.

Emily: *I'm not leaving the room. I want to be with my friends on my birthday. Call me at midnight and I'll put you on speakerphone. You'll still be wishing me a happy birthday at the same time as everybody else.*

Shane: *Em, you're being selfish. Just leave the room and talk to me for a minute. Please.*

At midnight, Shane called and I answered the phone in the room of my friends shouting "*Happy birthday!*" in the background.

"Hi!" I shouted into the phone over the sea of voices.

"Hi," he said, frustration in his tone. "Can you go somewhere quiet?"

"Not right now!" I laughed as I watched Gina spill a tequila shot down her front.

Shane hung up.

I pulled the phone away from my face, confused by the abrupt end to our conversation. But I was too embarrassed to tell my friends about his attitude, so I pretended he was still on the phone, thanked him and hung up.

A minute later, he texted me.

Shane: *I can't do this anymore.*

I stared at my phone, caught off guard by his words. My cheeks were hot as I typed out my response.

Emily: *Do what?*

Shane: *This relationship. You do whatever you want all the time. I'm done. We're done.*

I rolled my eyes, feeling pissed. He wanted me to beg him to reconsider, and tonight I wasn't having it. It was my *birthday*. If anything, this was the one day of the year where I was allowed to do whatever I wanted. The party was going strong, and I didn't want to let Shane ruin it with an argument.

I tucked my phone back into my pocket without responding, but a few minutes later it vibrated again.

Shane: *Check your Facebook.*

I opened my Facebook app to see *Shane Foster changed his relationship status to single.*

A wave of humiliation crashed over me. He was giving the world front-row seats to the dismantling of our relationship.

My body tingling with shame, I looked up from my phone. Nikki was pouring herself a shot. Gina was belting the words to the song playing on the speakers. A few other girls were taking turns hitting a bong on my living room couch. Aside from me, nobody knew what Shane had done or said yet. I wanted to keep it that way.

"Hey!" I shouted in Gina's direction. She glanced over. "I'll be right back."

She nodded, still singing.

I stepped outside into the hallway of my apartment building where I called Shane. The phone rang twice before he sent it to voicemail. I called back four times, and he declined my call each time.

"Shane," I pleaded in a voicemail. "Please call me back. This is ridiculous." I took shallow breaths as my hands began to shake. I was angry, but I was also beginning to panic.

What if he was serious?

Was my selfishness really going to be the end of our relationship?

As tears hit my cheeks, I knew I needed to get out of my apartment building. I was terrified of how my friends might react to Shane's behavior, especially with tequila coursing through their bloodstream.

I walked out of the building and into the fresh air where I texted Jack. He lived one street over, only three minutes on foot from my apartment.

Emily: *Hey, can you come outside for a minute?*

I arrived in tears at his apartment where he was already waiting on the front porch.

He met me with concern. "What's going on? Are you okay?"

My eyes moved past Jack into the living room through his open door. The creased leather couch and soft knit blanket looked more appealing than ever. I wished I were there for another one of our movie nights. We could pass a bowl of popcorn between us and shift the focus from my ever-crumbling relationship to something on his flatscreen. As much as I knew I needed to share my heartbreak with someone, I longed for a casual hangout with a friend and an end to the drama.

Shane hated my friendship with Jack, even though it had always been comfortably platonic. This lingered in the back of my mind and made my being there feel like a betrayal, despite everything going on.

I shook off the guilt as I shook my head. "Shane broke up with me," I choked.

"Why?"

"Because I wouldn't leave my party to take his phone call so that he could be the first one to wish me a happy birthday."

Jack blinked, followed by a laugh. An honest, not cruel, reaction. "Are you serious?"

I nodded. "It's so fucking stupid."

"Fuck Shane." He waved a dismissive hand in the air. "That might be the dumbest thing I've ever heard."

He wrapped me in a tight hug and patted my back, allowing me to soak the front of his UCLA sweatshirt. When I was out of tears, I collected myself and stepped back. "Where's Nikki?" he asked.

"Back at my apartment with the other girls." I wiped my eyes. "I didn't want to explain what happened to them. It's so embarrassing."

Jack was no stranger to the highs and lows of my time with Shane. I had spilled my guts to him on more than one occasion while the movie credits rolled. His investment in my relationship was so minimal that I could vent about Shane one day and go back to loving him the next, no explanation needed. But my other friends? They would turn against Shane the minute they heard anything negative – still holding a grudge from the ways he'd hurt me before.

"Then don't. Hang out until you're done crying," he said.

I sat down on the porch and pulled my knees up to my chest. Jack sat beside me in silence until the second wave of tears and sniffles subsided. For a fleeting moment I wondered what it would be like to be loved by someone like Jack – someone who respected my feelings and would never break up with me on my birthday, putting it on display for the world to see.

Why was my love different? Why didn't Shane feel bad for hurting me?

"Thank you," I mumbled.

He nodded with a half-smile. "Go enjoy your birthday. Seriously, put this shit out of your head and keep getting drunk with your friends."

I hugged Jack goodbye and walked back to my apartment.

I walked through the door, and Gina spun around from the kitchen counter to greet me. "Em! Where did you go?! We were worried about you," she exclaimed.

"Have you been crying?" Nikki asked as she walked over. My puffy cheeks and smudged mascara were a dead giveaway.

I surveyed the room, noting that the rest of my party guests had departed. I must've been outside longer than I realized. "It's nothing,"

I lied. "Shane's mad at me because I'm drunk."

Gina and Nikki shot each other looks, and I knew exactly what they meant.

"It's fine, guys, I'm fine." I reached for the bottle of tequila and poured some into an empty shot glass on the counter.

"He has no right to be mad at you for drinking with your friends on your birthday," Nikki said.

Gina agreed.

"Cheers to that." I held the shot glass up in the air before pouring it straight down my throat. I gagged at the taste – no lime or salt to mask it – but it was the change of direction the conversation needed, and they did not press the matter further.

chapter ten

I awoke the following morning with a stiff sadness I'd hoped to sleep off. Picking my phone up from my nightstand, I began to scroll through notifications from friends and family members wishing me a happy birthday. I scanned the texts, Facebook comments and DMs but there was nothing – *nothing* – from Shane… the only person I wanted to hear from.

I felt crushed.

What should have been a day of celebration felt grim and unbearable. I wanted to rewind the clock 12 hours and do everything differently. Would it really have been such a big deal for me to step outside of my apartment at midnight to take his call? I could have avoided this entire blowup. *Why did I have to make a simple request so fucking difficult?*

I groaned and closed my eyes, my hangover pounding in my head. Maybe I was more stubborn and rude than I realized last night. There had been alcohol involved. Did I say or do more to warrant this coldness from him?

My phone vibrated and my eyes widened as I saw Shane's name.

I shot up in bed, cleared my throat – attempting to sound more awake and less hungover – and answered the phone. "Hello?"

"Happy birthday." It felt like he delivered the words out of obligation, devoid of any genuine cheer. When I remained silent on the other end, he continued. He spoke cautiously, as if the delicate apology might shatter if it came out of his mouth too quickly. "I'm… sorry things got out of hand last night. I was really struggling with not being present for you on your birthday… and I thought if I could… just have one special moment with you… it would feel like I showed up for you… instead of feeling like I… failed you."

My heart fell. I hadn't realized the moment meant so much to him. "I'm sorry, Shane, but what you did on Facebook –"

"I shouldn't have done that," he interrupted, his words picking up pace. "I regret acting that way and I wish I could take it back. It was coming from a place of hurt… and I'm sorry."

I hated that I cared so much about a label, but Shane and I had kept our relationship secret for so long – I didn't want to be hidden now. He was a thousand miles away and it felt like a security blanket to have my name front and center on his social media presence. I never considered he'd use it against me, and how humiliating it would feel for him to strip it away without my consent.

"I didn't realize the phone call was such a big deal," I admitted.

"It's not just that," he contended. "You don't know what it's like for me to be here and watch you living this life from afar. People make assumptions and it really gets under my skin."

I frowned. "What kind of assumptions?"

"Just the shit people say when they see what you post online."

"Like what?"

"You post pictures partying with your friends and drinking around guys, and I hear it all the time from my friends – '*Wow, looks like Emily is having a lot of fun, aren't you worried?*' or '*You must really trust your girl if she's out getting drunk with a bunch of college guys every weekend.*' It's not fun to hear these things, Em. It fucks with me."

I swallowed. I hadn't known my actions were perceived that way – that his friends even bothered to remark about me. I barely went out compared to my freshman year, and it was never to intentionally disrespect Shane or make him worry. "You always know where I am, what I'm doing, and who I'm with. I don't hide any of these things from you," I reasoned.

"It's the fact that you feel the need to do it in the first place."

"I don't know what you expect from me, Shane. To sit at home all the time? To only speak to you?"

"Is that not enough? I mean, what do *I* do, Emily?" he countered. "Besides going to work and to the gym, my entire day revolves around talking to you. You are the most important thing in my world from the moment I wake up to the moment I go to sleep. I just want you to feel the same way and it is fucking *killing* me that you don't."

"I do feel the same way," I argued. "You know I do."

"You don't." He sounded hurt. "Because you need so much more than me to make you happy. You want to go out and party with your friends all the time because you're 19. I should've known our age gap would be an issue. I thought it would be fine since you're so mature for your age, but I'm beginning to think I was wrong. Maybe… I'm not what you need right now."

My chest tightened as I thought about the night before, the twinge of guilt over going to Jack for comfort resurfacing and blending with fresh regret. If I had left the party to take Shane's call for two minutes, this entire fight would've been avoided. It would have been a small concession to make him happy, and I didn't do it. I chose partying with my friends over him. I let my own stubbornness refuse a loving gesture.

I went silent for a moment, sitting in my regret; not only for my actions the night before, but for every time I'd made him feel like he wasn't enough. His heart was scarred by abandonment, and the last thing

I ever wanted was for him to feel abandoned by me. I didn't want to argue anymore. I just wanted the fight to be over.

"You are what I need, Shane," I reassured. "Please don't say that. I want this to work."

He sighed. "I want this to work, too. But you need to meet me halfway."

"Okay," I agreed, willing to say what he needed to hear to get us to a better place.

"Can I take back what I said last night?"

"You want to be my boyfriend again?" I teased, attempting to lighten the conversation.

He chuckled. "If you'll have me."

I heard Nikki and Gina talking down the hall, so I wrapped up the conversation with Shane, agreeing to be his girlfriend again and letting him know I'd call him later.

I stayed in bed for a minute after hanging up to collect my thoughts. The hurt from the night before lingered even though things were on the mend. I'd experienced how quickly I could lose him, and it left a sense of dread I hoped would dissipate as my hangover wore off.

When I came out of my room, I found Nikki and Gina in the kitchen making breakfast.

"Happy birthday!" they shouted in unison.

I smiled and took a seat at the table.

Nikki poured a glass of coffee and brought it to me. "Need this?" she teased.

"Badly," I groaned, my fingers caressing my throbbing temples.

"Em, what was up with Shane on Facebook last night?" Gina asked curiously.

I sipped the coffee to delay my response, then shrugged. "He overreacted. Everything is fine. He'll change his relationship status back today."

She froze and looked up at me from the eggs she was scrambling on the stove. "He broke up with you on your birthday?"

From where she was now sitting at the table, Nikki raised a brow.

"We didn't really break up. He was just being dramatic." I didn't want to explain further.

"Nikki said you guys are always fighting," Gina said.

I shot a look at Nikki.

"It's true," Nikki shrugged. "You're always in your room and half the time you're either arguing with Shane or crying. I can't even remember the last time you came out with me."

"I just went to a party with you, like –"

"A month ago?" she interrupted. I frowned. I hadn't realized so much time had passed. "We had so much fun together last year when Shane wasn't in the picture," she continued.

"You guys don't get it." My throat tightened. Why were they ganging up on me? "Shane is stubborn and so am I. The distance makes things hard, but we love each other a lot and we're working on it."

"It doesn't seem healthy," Gina replied. Nikki shook her head in agreement and offered me a sympathetic look.

"Gina, you haven't even seen Shane and I together in more than a year!" I snapped. "Please, stop judging my relationship when you don't even know what it's like." She threw her hands up in the air and I immediately felt ashamed of my defensiveness. I looked down at the table and fumbled with the fork she had set out for me. "I'm sorry," I mumbled.

"It's fine." She handed me a plate of eggs. "You know how I feel. I hope he treats you well."

I nodded and thanked her as I took the plate. The three of us began to eat and as Nikki shifted the subject to ask Gina a question about Sonoma, I made silent plans in my head:

Going forward, I would be more discreet about my arguments with Shane.

If Nikki was home, I would go to my car or the shower to cry.

And with Gina, I'd send happy updates and leave out the bad.

I needed my friends on my side.

chapter eleven

Despite our sometimes-turbulent arguments, an undeniable resilience wove its way into our love, growing stronger with each visit to Washington. The more precious moments we spent together, the harder the farewells. We blamed the distance for making us fight and clung to the belief that all would be resolved when we were no longer separated by state lines.

Four months after the birthday breakup, a March weekend unfolded with tender sweetness in the form of fresh flowers when Shane picked me up from the airport. We'd managed to navigate several weeks without a fight, largely due to me self-isolating and declining plans involving alcohol. The sacrifices I made for our relationship became the fuel for his happiness, and when he was happy he poured that love and affection back into me.

Shane made plans for us to have a double-date weekend with his friends Brandon and Christine, both soldiers who worked at the same facility as him. We met them at the mall and Christine – to my surprise – was the red-haired girl I spoke to in the barracks bathroom the year before. I wondered if she recalled our interaction in the bathroom but decided not to bring it up.

We shopped from store to store together, Shane and Brandon

eventually leaving Christine and me at Victoria's Secret while they branched off to run a quick errand.

The boys had only been gone for a moment when Christine blurted, "Do you think Shane's going to propose to you this weekend?"

I dropped the underwear I was holding. "What? No…"

She smirked. "What makes you so sure?"

"I mean we've talked about getting married in the future… but not anytime soon," I said, my hands sifting through the underwear drawer. It was impossible. Shane and I had never talked about what kind of ring I wanted, and as far as I knew he didn't have the money to purchase one.

"Hmm. I guess we'll see," she said, and dropped it as quickly as she'd brought it up.

But her question lingered. What did she know that I didn't? Although Christine and Shane likely shared daily conversations as coworkers, she was a stranger to me and I felt uneasy about the idea of her being close enough with him to make such personal assumptions about our relationship. Shane must've said something to Brandon, and Brandon to Christine… and probably about a future weekend, not this one.

The curiosity ate away at me for the rest of the afternoon until our dinner at the Space Needle. We arrived at the iconic landmark that evening, me in a short black dress and Shane in a blue dress shirt with gray slacks. I'd been hinting for months that I wanted to have a fancy dinner here so I could check it off my Seattle bucket list, and the time had finally come. I looked up at the 600-foot extraterrestrial-looking observation tower in awe. It filled me with excitement.

We stepped inside the elevator with Brandon and Christine, who had also morphed into their evening attire – a stark contrast from our casual afternoon at the mall. As the elevator began to move, Shane laced his fingers into mine.

"You know, I read online that wind causes this tower to sway –"

"Em…" Shane warned.

I giggled. He was afraid of heights, and I couldn't help but tease a bit. He put on such a tough guy persona – especially since joining the Army – but with a change in altitude that toughness was nowhere to be found. "Sorry," I whispered.

He smiled as he shook his head.

The hostess led the four of us across the rotating restaurant floor to our table beside a window that overlooked the city and the Puget Sound. On a clear day, we would have been able to see all the way to Mount Rainier. I sighed happily as I took it all in. It's not that I was sheltered from city sights – I spent most of my youthful weekends in San Francisco, and the past year exploring Los Angeles – but new places always fascinated me to my core.

We made our way through dinner, conversation flowing along with the wine in our glasses – even my own, thanks to my fake ID. After the waiter took our dessert order, Brandon excused himself to the restroom. Christine followed suit, and they scooted out of the booth and made their way to the other side of the restaurant.

I looked over at Shane, who was smiling back at me, eyes sparkling with curious wonderment. "I love you," he said with a nervous laugh.

"What's up with you?" I asked, chuckling at his demeanor. Shane typically overflowed with confidence to the point of cockiness and catching him in a moment where he was uncomfortable was rare. "Did you look out the window and remember we're 600 feet in the air?" I teased.

He laughed and shook his head. "You love me too, right?"

"Of course I love you."

He took a deep breath and nodded.

Then, my breath caught in my throat as I watched him turn to retrieve a small box from the breast pocket of the jacket he'd placed on the bench seat, opening it to present a breathtaking diamond ring.

My jaw dropped.

The room was – literally – spinning as I took in every word.

"Emily, I love you more than anything in this world." His voice brimmed with sincerity. "There is nothing I want more than to make you my wife, and to make you smile and laugh every day for the rest of your life. Will you marry me?"

I clasped my hand over my open mouth.

Holy.

Shit.

This was actually happening.

The rush of adrenaline made my skin hot.

For a moment, the restaurant faded and all I saw was Shane. The intensity of his gaze. The unwavering commitment reflected in his blue eyes. I felt a profound sense of forever in my heart.

I could love this man for the rest of my life.

This man could love *me* for the rest of his life.

"Yes," I breathed, the words barely leaving my mouth.

He beamed.

My hand trembled as he slid the ring onto my finger.

Yes – there had been moments of uncertainty. Yes – there had been times he made me question my worth to him. Yes – I was terrified. But this? This was *love*. This was pure, unbridled love.

And Shane chose *me* to share it with.

I came back to reality as I heard Brandon and Christine cheering.

"Congratulations!" Christine shouted, and I turned around to find her just a few feet behind me with her camera out.

I realized their excuse to get up was a ruse. "You knew!" I exclaimed.

She and Brandon both laughed while nodding their heads. "Really happy for you guys," Brandon said as he and Christine took their seats back at the table.

Right on cue, the waiter arrived with our cheesecake dessert and four glasses of celebratory champagne. Shane held his glass of champagne in the air, his eyes locked with mine. "To us."

"To us," I repeated as I clinked my glass to his.

THAT EVENING, AS we lay in our hotel room bed, I texted the news of our engagement to my friends and posted an update on Facebook. Congratulatory comments and messages poured in – most people as shocked as I was.

"Everyone is surprised," I said, my head on Shane's shoulder and my gaze on the laptop that rested on his stomach.

Being engaged at 19 was crazy, I had to admit. But I'd loved Shane since I was 16 years old – and I reminded myself, for him being 24, this was a fairly normal timeline.

"Were you surprised?" he asked coyly.

I looked at him, wide-eyed. "Um, yeah! When did you buy a ring?"

"I bought it a few weeks ago but I had to go to the mall today to pick it up, and that's where Brandon and I ran off to."

The errand they had to run. It was all making sense now, even the weird questioning from Christine. "Did Christine know that's what you were doing?" I inquired.

"Yeah, why?"

"She hinted at it when we were alone together. She asked if I thought you were going to propose this weekend and was acting like she knew something I didn't."

Shane studied me, a crease forming between his eyebrows. "She said that to you? You're kidding."

"Yeah, but I didn't believe her," I quickly said.

"She put the idea in your head though. This was supposed to be a surprise. I can't believe she would ruin it like that." He shook his head, the corners of his mouth curved in a frown.

"It was a surprise," I reassured. I hadn't intended to upset him with that information. I gently grabbed his face and angled it toward mine so I could kiss him. "I was so surprised. I am so happy. Nobody, and nothing could ruin this day."

He smiled at me. Crisis averted.

Before falling asleep that night, I stared at the ring on my finger. It was beautiful. Three larger diamonds sat atop a band of smaller diamonds set in a white gold band. A symbol of our love – our commitment.

I knew with this step we were entering a new chapter together, free from the constant threat of breaking up. The blanket of security comforted me as I drifted off to sleep in the arms of the man I loved.

My fiancé.

chapter twelve

After finishing my sophomore year of college, I went to live with Shane for a month in Washington. We sublet a small place for the summer – a place we could call our own, and a trial run at living together.

After the high of our engagement wore off, we had fallen back into old habits of fighting and blaming distance as the culprit again. We desperately needed time together to reset our dopamine levels, which numbed the negative emotions and reminded us of the love we were fighting for.

But the arguments continued after I arrived.

One night while getting ready to go out to dinner, my phone buzzed with a text.

Jack: Hey, when are you coming back to LA?

"Why is he asking you that?"

I jumped and turned to see Shane standing just behind me, reading the text over my shoulder. "Because he's my friend. He probably wants to know when I'll be available to hang out or help him move into his new apartment."

"Why would he be asking an engaged woman to hang out?"

"How many times do we have to go over this, Shane?" I fired back. "There's nothing between Jack and me. He has a girlfriend. Even if he didn't, we don't see each other that way."

"Bullshit," he spat.

"We never have and we never will. He is my *friend*."

"Every guy you think is your friend secretly wants to fuck you."

I rolled my eyes. "That's not true, and especially not Jack."

"I don't want you hanging out with him," he said, stepping forward to close the gap between us, his face only inches from mine as we stood at the foot of our bed.

"Jack has been one of my best friends since the beginning of freshman year. He's friends with my friends, I'm friends with his girlfriend, and if you could meet him you'd realize you have nothing to worry about," I snapped.

Shane's nostrils flared. "You are not hanging out with some guy who wants to fuck you, Emily."

My blood boiled. "I will hang out with whoever the fuck I want."

Rage flickered in his eyes. He gripped me firmly by the shoulders as he shouted in my face, "As my fiancée, you will not!"

I pushed against the wall of his chest to loosen his grip on my shoulders. "Are you kidding?!" I turned my back to him, fuming. *How dare he put his hands on me?*

As I took a step toward the door to leave the room, forceful hands gripped my shoulders again, this time pushing my body sideways onto the bed. As I hit the mattress, I realized it was not only my body slamming into the bed but Shane's, directly on top of mine. I absorbed the force of his heavy aggression.

His arm pressed down on the back of my neck as I caught a mouthful of sheet. Then teeth sank into my right shoulder, and a sharp pain shot through me as I yelled into the bed.

Everything stilled and I heard nothing but my thoughts.

He bit me. Like an animal. He intentionally, physically harmed me.

No. Biting is playful, harmless.

No. This wasn't playful. He was trying to punish me.

But it's not like he hit me. He could have hit me if he wanted to.

As my opposing thoughts battled, I began to cry.

Shane pressed himself off me. He rubbed the spot where he bit me with soft fingers, then rested his face on it. He let out a big, defeated sigh. I felt his tension loosen, and his warm breath on my neck. For a moment, neither of us said a word.

Tears fell from my cheeks and soaked into the bed. "What the fuck…" I finally choked out.

Shane wiped my hair from my face with the same tender touch that he ran over the still-throbbing bite mark. Every trace of the rage in his eyes just a moment ago was gone. He looked somehow serene. "Emily…"

I shook my head. I had no words. Confusion wracked my brain.

"You are the most incredible girl I've ever known. Stop acting like you're not a hot commodity that every guy around you would love the chance to be with. I can't help feeling insecure knowing that you're out of my league."

"We're on the same team," I whimpered. "Stop acting like we're not."

I LOOKED AT my shoulder in the bathroom mirror as I got ready for bed that evening and traced my finger across purple teeth marks, the bruise a painful reminder of just how far he was willing to take his possessiveness. It felt wrong. But how could I make sense of it? It's not like he hit me. It really didn't even hurt, except for the brief moment when it happened. And even that was more shock than pain. It was like… a warning. And I could tell he felt sorry for taking it that far after it happened.

It was a misunderstanding. He was jealous about another guy wanting to hang out with me, and I was defensive. I could've communicated my feelings more calmly instead of immediately firing back at him.

That's what this was – a misunderstanding.

But three weeks later, it happened again.

"WHAT IS SLUTTY about my outfit?" I asked. "I'm literally wearing jeans and a shirt."

We had just walked into our apartment when Shane told me he was embarrassed that I looked like a slut in front of his friends.

"Your cleavage was out for the entire bar to see," he snapped, his eyes tracing the length of my body in disgust.

I stared down at my chest, failing to see what he saw. "You saw my outfit before we left the house. Why didn't you say something earlier?"

"I didn't realize how bad it was until I noticed every single guy staring at your tits."

"What are you talking about?!" Beyond Shane and his friends at our table, I hadn't even spoken to another guy.

He scowled. "Are you oblivious to the world around you, Emily? Every guy in that bar was staring at your boobs."

I threw my hands in the air as I walked across the living room. "How is that my fault?!"

"Because you chose to dress that way to attract attention to yourself," he scolded, following me to where I stood beside the couch.

Was he serious? I *chose* to attract attention to myself with a shirt that was barely low-cut? "You have no right to get upset about what I wear," I argued. "This is toxic, Shane. This is toxic behavior and I will not allow it."

He shook his head. "You're the one who is toxic! Do you have to be this stubborn about everything?"

Rage coursed through me. "Me?! Everything was fine until you randomly got pissed off about my outfit for no reason!"

"Because I don't need my fiancée looking like a fucking slut in public trying to draw attention to herself!" he spat.

"Fuck you," I retorted.

Shane's lip curled. His eyes narrowed as he reached for my arm, his fingers digging into my bicep. I yanked my arm, but his grip tightened.

"Let go," I demanded. "You're hurting me." Instead, he pushed me backward, the couch catching my fall and his body pressing down onto mine. The weight of his legs pinned mine down, and he continued to grip my arm. "Let go!" I shouted.

I felt Shane's tongue at the base of my neck. He licked the skin above my collarbone before sinking his teeth into me. I yelped as the tender skin at the base of my neck twisted between sharp teeth.

It was sadistic.

It was humiliating.

A surge of anger erupted within me.

"What the fuck is wrong with you?!" I shouted in his ear.

His grip loosened and he pulled back, giving me the opportunity to roll out from under him. I backed away from the couch slowly, his eyes locked on mine like a predator in pursuit of a meal, before making a run for the bedroom.

With shaking hands, I pulled open the closet door and unzipped my suitcase, then began grabbing at clothes, shoving them inside. *How is this happening again?*

Shane walked into the room. "What are you doing?" His tone was so casual that the lack of emotion sent chills through me. The monster from the other room had come to taunt his prey.

"I'm going to the airport. I'm fucking done." He stepped toward me and I shouted, "Get away from me!"

Shane rolled his eyes. "You're kidding. You're so fucking dramatic."

"I'm not kidding." Hot tears fell from my eyes. I hated that I couldn't be angry without crying. Fury coursed through my veins and came to land on my cheeks, amplifying my vulnerability and weakness.

I slid the engagement ring off my finger and threw it at him. He caught it against his chest.

"I will not stand for abuse," I said firmly.

He scoffed. "Get the fuck over yourself, Emily. You're not abused. I didn't hurt you. There are women who literally get beat, do you know how insensitive you sound playing victim when you have it better than 90% of women out there?"

A seething rage consumed me, fueled by the audacity of his dismissive response. I glared at him as I picked up my bag and headed for the door.

"You're going to regret this," he warned.

I said nothing as I walked out of the apartment.

My fingers trembled as I looked up the number for a taxi on my phone. Afraid Shane would follow me outside, I lugged my suitcase down the street and continued walking until I'd passed several streets and changed directions twice. In a spot I deemed safe enough, I put on my calmest tone as I requested the soonest possible taxi to pick me up at the address of the house in front of me.

INSIDE THE AIRPORT, reality crashed down on me when I realized I had no plan. It was after midnight and there were no flights to California until morning. I didn't even have enough money in my bank account to buy a last-minute ticket. And if I did, what would I tell my mom when she had to come pick me up at the airport a week early?

I replayed Shane's words in my head. *"There are women who literally get beat, do you know how insensitive you sound?"* It was true. He hadn't punched me. He hadn't slapped me. Everyone would think I was a fool if I cried wolf over a bite. *Playing the victim, being dramatic, asking for attention…* I hung my head in shame. I couldn't tell anyone.

I felt a profound sense of defeat as I sat down in front of the vacant check-in counters and a fresh wave of tears streamed down my face. The airport was mostly empty, save the few stragglers passing by and security roaming the lobby. They gave me looks of confusion and pity. I ignored them, my head in my hands, and let the sobs shake my body without restraint. My ragged breathing was the only sound aside from intercom reminders to report unattended baggage.

Part of me wanted to call Shane and beg him to come get me. I knew going back to him was not the answer, but the thought of being without him felt equally daunting.

Caught in an agonizing limbo, I put my headphones on and attempted to drown out my pain with episodes of *The Office* as a distraction. But even as the lighthearted scenes played on my laptop screen, my tears continued to fall. I set my laptop beside me, folded into myself and wept.

What was I going to do? Where was I going to go? Shane's voice sounded in my head. *"You're going to regret this."*

I cried for a long time, until my computer assumed I was no longer watching and the screen turned black.

After a while, I felt a soft tap on my shoulder and jolted upright, startled. An older woman in an airline uniform stood before me, looking down at me with concern. "Are you alright?"

I nodded, but a sob escaped me and I shook my head instead.

"What's wrong?"

"I'm fine, I just…" I searched for the words to say. "I just ended my engagement." Hearing it out loud shook me. My engagement. *Ended.*

"Oh, honey. I'm so sorry to hear that." She took a seat beside me. Her kind, gray eyes crinkled in compassion, and I felt embarrassment flush my cheeks. "My name is Anna," she said.

"Emily," I barely choked out.

"Well, Emily, I've seen my fair share of failed relationships and I know the endings are never easy. This man of yours, was he a good one?"

"Yeah." I wondered as the word came out whether or not I was telling the truth.

"Well, he surely won't be the last good one you meet. Are you waiting for a flight?"

I nodded. Another lie.

She checked her watch. "Check-in should open soon. Do you need anything?"

I shook my head. "Thank you."

"Hang in there, okay? Things will get better. They always do." She gave my shoulder a reassuring rub, her hand caressing the now faded mark of Shane's first bite. I shuddered as I recalled his teeth pulling on my skin. *Better?* She walked away and I scowled.

How could things possibly get *better*? The fresher bite mark above my collarbone was concealed by the sweatshirt I'd thrown on after leaving the apartment. What would she say if she saw that one? Would she still tell me things would get *better*?

I sat alone in the row of seats, replaying the interaction in my head amidst repeated announcements for TSA advisories, trying to pinpoint where it all went wrong – what I had done wrong.

Maybe Shane was right, and I was stubborn. Ever since I was a little kid, I hated being told what to do. I would push back against my parents' rules and find myself facing the consequences time and again.

I looked at my phone. No texts or calls. I stared at my background, a picture of us after he'd proposed at the Space Needle. I was beaming. He was smiling through the kiss he planted on my cheek. My outstretched hand showed off the ring on my finger.

I stared down at my finger now.

Empty.

I crumbled.

There was so much good in our relationship. Love, laughter, comfort… I ached to feel those things again. How could he be pain and also comfort?

It was nearing 4 a.m. and I was so exhausted; I just wanted to get in bed. I wanted to sleep all of this off. I let out a big sigh. Maybe it was time to swallow my pride. Maybe there was a way we could salvage this. What did I have to lose by trying?

I called Shane. To my surprise, he sounded wide awake. I wondered if the last few hours had been as hard for him as they had been for me.

"What," he said flatly when he answered, skipping pleasantries.

"Ca-can you come get me?" I stuttered, my voice ridden with defeat.

"I'll be there in 45 minutes," he grumbled and hung up the phone.

He pulled up to the curb and stared straight ahead as I got into the car. His hands gripped the steering wheel so tightly that his knuckles went white. He stayed silent the entire ride home, and I watched him from the corner of my eye. He never once turned to look at me, but shook his head as if to say, *"I'm disappointed in you."*

I felt like I was five years old again, sitting in a tense and silent car after a tantrum in the grocery store when my dad wouldn't buy me the candy in the checkout line. This was the awkward drive home after he'd slapped me in the face for misbehaving and told me I'd be sent straight to my room. I remembered the way my cheek burned after the slap, and although Shane hadn't slapped me, I felt the same burning sensation on my cheeks.

Shame.

Embarrassment.

Stupidity.

When we pulled into the driveway, he finally spoke. "Are you done acting crazy?"

Numbly, I nodded, unable to find my voice. Daylight was creeping into the dark sky, and I was so tired.

My body ached from the weight of my sadness. After crying alone for so many hours, I felt drained and depleted, hollow and empty. My head was pounding and my throat was raw. I yearned for comfort and reassurance that everything would be okay. There was nothing I wanted more than to fall into Shane's arms and sleep. It was so much easier than trying to confront the harsh reality.

Lying in bed, Shane wrapped an arm around my waist. I felt his unspoken apology in the comfort of his embrace, and some of the tension in my body loosened. I gently leaned into him, my silent agreement to wake up on better terms the next day.

THE FOLLOWING WEEK, it was time for me to return to California. Shane kept the engagement ring since the night of our big fight. Too worried to reopen a fresh wound, I waited until my final day in Washington to ask about it.

"May I have my ring back?" I asked nonchalantly while packing the last of my things.

Shane stared blankly as he shook his head. "I don't think I can do that, Emily."

My heart sank. "What do you mean?"

"You proved that you're not ready for marriage. You won't compromise, and you were ready to call it quits and leave me on a whim over one argument."

"It wasn't just an argument, Shane… you know that." I chose my words carefully, unsure of which might strike a nerve.

"It turned into something that almost ended our relationship because of the way you reacted. Instead of staying here and working things out with me, you left. I can't trust you with this ring until you show me that you're ready to be with me even when things are hard."

I bit my tongue as he patronized me, feeling my resolve waver under the burden of his blame. I wanted to demand he take accountability, but fear stole my voice. If I started a fight now and left without time to clean up the mess, we risked any chance at reconciliation.

I had been so confident the night of the argument when I packed my bags and headed to the airport that Shane was wrong, and I was right. But during those hours at the airport I experienced true defeat. I realized what my heart would go through to lose this — to lose *him*.

"Are we still engaged?" I studied his face, hoping to catch any confirmation of love.

His eyes softened. "I don't know. You're the one who said you were done."

"But I came back. Things are better." Ever since returning from the airport, Shane had shown me kindness, allowing me to cast aside the lingering pain of those traumatic arguments. He'd made love to me, fueling the passion in my blood for him. He'd reminded me of his comforting affection, calming my fears and doubts.

He moved closer until we stood face to face. His finger brushed against mine, then he took my hand and held it. "Things have been fine for a week, but what's next? Are you going to start acting like you actually want to be in this relationship?"

I nodded, my lips wobbling.

"I guess we'll see." He paused. "I love you so much, Emily, but I can't keep doing this with you if it doesn't get better." He released my hand.

I tried to grip his fingers, but they fell out of reach.

My heart throbbed. *Don't give up on me*, I pleaded silently. I couldn't bear the thought of it, so with a heavy heart I uttered the words he desired.

"I promise to be better."

chapter thirteen

Nikki and I met for coffee shortly after my return to Los Angeles. By the end of sophomore year, we'd been living different lives – she was a social butterfly, and I was confined to my bedroom talking to Shane. So, this year I moved in with some girls I knew through class – distant acquaintances who knew little of my relationship and would see it without tainted opinions.

As we sat down to chat with iced lattes in hand, Nikki pointed toward my hand with a puzzled look on her face. "Where's your engagement ring?"

My face heated, but I smiled to shake off any negative implications around the ring's absence. "Shane and I decided to slow down a little bit," I lied. "The engagement was really fast and there's a lot of things we need to work on before marriage."

She raised her eyebrows. "So… are you still engaged? Dating?"

"Um… We definitely still plan to get married; we're just not stressing the label right now." I listened to the words fall out of my mouth so casually, and I wondered when I got to be so good at lying to my friends.

"Did something happen in Washington?"

I sipped my coffee to stall. "No, it was good. It's just stressful with the distance, you know?"

"I *don't* know," Nikki laughed. She and Nate had been inseparable since freshman year. Even living with her for the past two years, there were weeks where I barely saw her because she frequently stayed at his apartment. I couldn't deny that it bothered me sometimes to see how easy things were between them, because it made me wonder why my own relationship couldn't be the same.

"Right. You're lucky. Things are much easier when you live in the same place."

She nodded.

I got the sense she was waiting for me to spill the truth. I wanted to. I wanted to tell her about the fights in Washington, to talk through them with someone… but I couldn't. If I told Nikki or Gina, they'd warn me to break things off with Shane. They wouldn't understand the intricacies of our relationship – how Shane was love, and light, and everything I needed to feel alive… but he was also jealous, and fearful, and damaged.

I needed my friends to remain supportive. I needed them to be happy for us on the day of our wedding.

Our wedding. Would our wedding even happen? How long could I live in this lie?

My heart felt heavy, but I forced a smile as Nikki and I moved into lighter conversation around our course schedules and upcoming events before hugging each other goodbye.

IT WAS MY third, and final, year of college. After Shane and I got engaged, we began to discuss how I could live with him sooner. I realized that by increasing my course load every quarter until graduation, I could meet the bare minimum requirements to earn my degree by June and move to Washington.

For two years I'd struggled to narrow down my career path. I was a booksmart, dedicated, straight-A student in all my courses, yet I couldn't pull myself together enough to pick a focus with the constant distraction of my turbulent relationship. My entry-level sociology courses interested me enough to take more, and when graduating early became a discussion, I learned I'd taken enough sociology and psychology courses to fulfill half the requirements for a degree – and thus, the decision was made for me. I didn't know if I wanted a career in that field; all I knew was that I wanted to be closer to Shane – or at least, I'd known that before this summer.

Now, my brightest memories of Shane were tainted by the dark feeling of his grip on my shoulders, his teeth on my skin, and his harsh words cutting through me like a knife. It was a side of Shane I hadn't seen before, and one I never wanted to see again.

But as the weeks went on, we remembered why we loved each other.

In between my heavy course load and his demanding work schedule, we carved out hours to talk on the phone. Late night conversations kept us giggling, talking about our future together, and I fell back under the same teenage love spell that had taken over me when I was only 16 years old. It was enough to block out the bad.

I went to visit him in late October, and while he didn't give me the engagement ring back, his actions and loving demeanor gave me the confirmation I needed that he and I were back on the right track.

Before I left Washington, he slipped a note into my bag and told me not to read it until I got back to Los Angeles. Knowing I couldn't wait that long, I opened the letter once I found my seat on the flight home.

Dear Em,

I know that I have been the reason for your pain, and for that I am so sorry.

The truth is, you're too good for me. I know how lucky I am to have you and it scares the hell out of me. You're my whole world and I would be lost without you. When the fear of losing you becomes too much to bear, I drown it with anger, and I take that anger out on you.

I now realize that this is how I will lose you – not because you don't love me, not because you realize you can do better – but because my anger pushes you away.

I need to be better at explaining my feelings to you without getting angry or yelling. You don't deserve to be on the receiving end of my rage and insecurity. You don't deserve that from anyone. I promise to treat you better. I promise to respect you. I promise to be a better communicator. I promise I will never hurt you again.

Love, Shane
P.S. I miss you already.

I folded the note and tucked it back into my bag, tears forming in my eyes. What more could I ask of him than to acknowledge the wrongs and try to make them right? Nobody was perfect; I was far from it. I loved him, despite his flaws and his broken pieces. I loved him enough to be the glue that could hold those pieces together. Because together we were so much stronger than either of us were apart.

THE DAYS CREPT into November, and the longer we went without a blowup argument, the more I convinced myself those incidents were anomalies and not the norm. As we leaned further into love and away from hurt, we began to discuss marriage again.

"Let's elope when you come up here in December," Shane said one night into the phone.

I laughed. "Babe, that's in like… a month. No way."

"Why not?"

My skin tingled as I realized he wasn't joking. I'd always loved Shane's passion to go after what he wanted – especially when what he wanted was me – but this felt impulsive. I glanced down at my hand, noting the absence of the ring. "It's too soon."

"Do you love me?"

"Of course."

"Do you still want to marry me?"

"I do," I said, meaning it.

"So, why wait? What difference will it make if we do it now versus next year?"

His question lingered in the air. I had only turned 20 a week ago. We needed time. We needed to prove this peaceful streak could be maintained for six months or a year. Why was he rushing?

"Emily?" he checked for me as I remained silent on the other end.

The smart answer was no. The logical thing to do was wait. But the fear of disappointing Shane and igniting a negative response held me captive. I tiptoed around his proposition with a fair excuse. "I want a real wedding."

"We can have a real wedding. We can have whatever you want, wherever you want." He spoke quickly, excitement spilling into his words. "This is us solidifying our commitment to one another. We can go to the courthouse, sign the papers and legalize our marriage before we start planning the big ceremony. Please, babe."

"I think my mom would be upset if I got married without telling her…" I reasoned.

"Invite her!"

"Would you invite yours?"

"Yes! Let's invite our parents and plan something simple but special. Multnomah Falls is only a couple hours away from here. We could have a judge marry us in front of the waterfall, Em. It'd be so beautiful. Please, will you marry me in December?"

There was so much eagerness in his voice that it began to wear off on me. I smiled. He was so sure – *so completely certain* – of his commitment to me that he didn't want to wait to make it official. My heart swelled. It was a battle of logic versus love, and his love was strong enough to overpower all. I succumbed to the part of me that wanted to dive in headfirst and feel that wave of love and certainty wash over me, too.

"Fuck it," I conceded. "Let's do it. Let's get married."

"YES!" he shouted.

I laughed, allowing that once broken wall of trust to stand tall again.

OVER THE NEXT few weeks, I booked a date with an officiant to marry us at the waterfall. I learned we'd need to apply for our marriage license three days in advance, so I reserved a five-night stay at a beautiful lodge in the woods. I booked my flights to arrive a few days into my Christmas break and stay through the new year.

I invited my mom, fearful she would scold us for rushing, or convey her doubts about me being too young to get married – but to my surprise she responded with support and booked her plane tickets.

As the date got closer, anxiousness and excitement coursed through me. Apart from my mom and his, no one knew of our secret elopement. I longed to share the news with my closest friends, but the fear of their judgment and disapproval held me back. I envisioned Nikki and Gina questioning me if I informed them of our hasty plans.

"Are you sure this is the right decision? Aren't you rushing into this?"

"I thought you guys were slowing down. You're not even wearing your ring."

I couldn't risk having their doubt spill over onto me. I had pushed mine deep down and feared it would resurface if given a window of opportunity. Once again, Shane and I had a fiercely guarded secret, its exclusivity strengthening our bond. He was my person, and nobody else would understand.

We rolled into December and the countdown went from 45 days, to 30, to two weeks. It was really happening.

Then, about a week before my trip, Shane got cold feet.

chapter fourteen

"Something about the timing just isn't right," Shane told me over the phone. "I'm so sorry, Em, but I think we should wait. Please don't be upset."

My throat tightened, confused by his sudden change of heart. "But this was your idea…"

"I know it was my idea, and I still love you and I still want to marry you." He paused. "I just feel like this isn't the right time."

Part of me felt relieved, acknowledging that I wasn't fully prepared to marry him either. But the other part of me was devastated. Was he doubting the timing, or was he doubting us?

Insecurity pulsed through me. Had I unknowingly done something to push him away?

Frustration also surfaced, fueled by the embarrassment of involving my mom and now having to explain to her what I couldn't comprehend myself.

Conflicting emotions ravaged my brain such that I barely paid attention to my entire six-hour drive home to begin my holiday break. When I arrived home at 11 p.m., I realized I'd been on autopilot the whole time, my head occupied by thoughts of Shane and his indecision to marry me.

I emerged from my bedroom the following morning to find my mom in the kitchen preparing breakfast.

"Emily!" She pulled me in for a hug, her bright cheerfulness a contrast to the depression which weighed her down throughout my childhood. She was now married to the man she'd dated during my high school years, and she'd found her vibrance again. I noted how she glowed in ways she hadn't before. I hoped my news wouldn't dim that.

I sat down at the kitchen table and we eased into conversation about my drive before I regretfully informed her of the change in plans. "We've decided to… postpone the elopement," I said delicately.

Concern filled her eyes. "Is everything okay?"

"Yes," I said quickly. "We got excited about the idea of marrying each other and moved too quickly. It all started feeling too real and we agreed there's no need to rush." I paused. "It's better this way, right?"

She nodded, validating my feelings. "Yes, if you're meant to be together there's no need to rush into an elopement. Are you still going to Washington this week?"

"Yeah, I'm still going to spend a couple weeks there… I'm sorry you have to cancel your flight." I winced.

She brushed me off. "Don't worry about that. I can get airline credit. I'm glad you're waiting, Emily."

I nodded and looked down, picking the skin around my thumb nail. *It's a good thing we're waiting*, I repeated in my head. In a few days, I'd be in Washington. I'd understand.

But that afternoon, my world flipped upside down.

"LISTEN, I KNOW this is going to upset you… and I hate to say it, but… I think you should cancel your flight here," Shane said calmly into the phone.

Shock reverberated through me as I tried to process what he said. "Why don't you want to see me?"

"It's just not a good time right now." He paused. "I think we need a little space."

Space? It had been nearly two months since the last time we saw each other. My heart pounded. "What is going on?"

"I'm busy at work right now and it wouldn't be a good trip for you anyway."

The excuse made zero sense. The holidays were approaching, and he had scheduled time off. I desperately struggled to make sense of the growing distance between us. "Tell me what's going on, Shane," I repeated firmly.

"Nothing's going on, Em… it's just not a good time. Please accept that." His dismissive tone pierced me in the gut. I searched for kindness or affirmation, but they were nowhere to be found.

"No!" The tightness of my throat gave way that my tears were forming. "What does that mean? Why don't you want me to come?!"

"I'm not continuing this conversation with you until you calm down," he warned.

"Calm down?! What the fuck is happening?!" I shouted.

Shane abruptly ended the call.

I called him back; no answer.

I called, over and over, as he repeatedly sent my calls to voicemail.

I began to spiral.

I couldn't grasp how I was meant to accept this, as if we hadn't been counting down the last six weeks to be together again. Two weeks ago we had been discussing forever; now he wouldn't take my calls.

My imagination ran wild with worst-case scenarios. The fear of losing him intensified, magnifying every minor flaw and insecurity within myself. The uncertainty was suffocating, and I longed for his reassurance that everything would be alright.

My fingers fired rapidly across my phone screen.

Emily: *I'm driving to Washington.*

I walked out of my room and straight to my car, frantically plugging his address into Google Maps. It would take me 15 hours to drive there. I had nothing but the clothes on my back, but I didn't care. Getting to Shane was all that mattered. I'd be there by morning, and I'd be able to throw my arms around him and remind him that he loves me.

I began to drive and had just reached the coastal highway when he called. Pulling off into an empty beach parking lot, I answered the phone.

"Stop. Don't come," he ordered. My text had struck a nerve.

"Why?!" I begged through panicked sobs.

"Stop making this difficult!" he shouted. "Listen to me when I tell you not to come."

I stared, dumbfounded, at my phone. *What the fuck is happening?* I took a deep breath, attempting to calm my demeanor as much as possible before I continued. "Unless you explain to me right now what is going on, I am coming."

"This isn't how I wanted to tell you…" he said.

"Tell me what?"

He breathed a long sigh. "I'm seeing someone."

I'm seeing someone.

The words came out of Shane's mouth and into my throat, where they choked me.

They sliced through my chest and stabbed relentlessly at my heart.

I tried to speak, but incoherent words were all I could manage. "You… what… who…" I sputtered through inconsolable sobs. "No… no…," I repeated, hoping to undo the last words he spoke.

"Emily… you know I can't speak to you when you're like this. I need to go. *Don't* drive here." And without a hint of sorrow or regret, he hung up the phone.

I called him back. The phone rang three times before going to voicemail. I hit the call button again, and again, and again, until my call log showed 87 outgoing calls to his number and he shut his phone off.

"No!" I wailed at his voicemail recording. "No, no, no!"

I pounded my phone against the steering wheel. Tears streamed down my face, blurring my vision. I was helpless. The world as I knew it was collapsing, and I could do nothing to hold it together.

Heaving and hyperventilating, I went into a complete breakdown.

How could I be so fucking stupid? How could he do this to me? What have I done to deserve this? Who is she? How long has he been seeing her? Is this why he canceled the elopement? Why won't he talk to me?

I can't do this. I can't handle this. I need him to fucking talk to me. Please answer the phone. Please talk to me.

"Why don't I matter?!" I wept aloud to no one. The question lingered, unanswered. "Why don't I fucking matter?!"

It tormented me. The ache in my chest pummeled me as emptiness consumed me, gripping my heart and blocking my lungs. In a desperate attempt for air, I rolled my car windows down to let the cold salt air hit me in the face and bawled until my tears ran dry.

He's leaving me. Like my father, like Carter, like every guy I met in Los Angeles… Shane is leaving me for someone better.

I sat in a dissociative state for an hour, hollow and detached from my own emotions. I stared blankly at the ocean before me, my breath rising and falling with each swell of the tide. The ocean was furious, its roaring waves coming to collide with the rock jetty, their briny foam splashing the ground at the foot of the parking lot. I wanted to throw myself into it. I wanted to disappear into its unforgiving deepness.

Upon realizing it was dark outside, I reluctantly returned to my mom's house.

"Emily! What's wrong?" she asked as I walked through the door.

There was nothing I could do to hide the fact that I was shattered. The weight of my heartbreak was unbearable. Too full of hurt and embarrassment to admit what had happened, I simply said, "It's over. We're over."

As she reached to hug me, I pulled away and retreated to the privacy of my room, locking the door and throwing myself into bed.

I BARELY SLEPT, the torturous thought of Shane with someone else gnawing at my heart throughout the night. I held myself tightly as I sobbed, on and off, until morning light came. The hurt remained.

It was an abrupt shift in the universe. I had awoken the day before with plans to marry the love of my life; today, I awoke with nothing.

Today, my fiancé had another girlfriend.

And I didn't know how to be something he missed.

Aching for answers, I opened the Facebook app on my phone. *Shane Foster changed his relationship status from engaged to single.* Three messages in my inbox asking me what happened. I ignored them as the knife in my heart twisted.

He hadn't unfriended me, so I stalked his behavior from the last few days. I looked at the profiles of all the women who had engaged with his posts – checking to see if they were in his local area, if they were in a relationship, and if they had any activity featuring Shane.

I tapped on the profile of brown-haired Megan and saw her posts with her husband – one of Shane's coworkers – and son. Couldn't be her. I tapped next on blonde-haired Brittney. She was in another state and engaged to be married. Couldn't be her either.

Then I came across red-haired Christine. Though we'd spent the engagement weekend together in person, we never became Facebook friends. She and Brandon had stopped dating shortly after that weekend, so we hadn't spent any time with her since then – outside of whatever interactions she and Shane had at work.

I tapped on her profile, which to my benefit was not set to private. I had noticed the frequency of her liking Shane's posts, but it was now that I saw the frequency of him liking hers. As I looked deeper, the pieces of the puzzle began to come together.

She had checked in at a restaurant where Shane was three nights ago with his friends, and at a sports bar he'd visited the weekend prior. She checked in at the fitness center at the same time of day he worked out. She didn't tag him in any of these activities, but I knew enough about his whereabouts to recognize this couldn't be a benign coincidence.

I tapped open her profile picture and sealed my fate. Right there was a comment from Shane left only one day ago – the day he shattered my heart.

Shane: *So beautiful.*
Christine: *Thanks baby!*

My heart swelled with rage. Pain and fury collided, creating an inferno within me. The girl I met in the bathroom, the girl who was present the day we got engaged, how the fuck could this be possible?

Although all my attempts to call Shane the night before had been ignored, I decided to try sending a text.

Emily: *Christine? Are you fucking serious?*
Emily: *How could you do this to me?*
Emily: *Have you been cheating on me this whole time?*

His silence confirmed my fears.

I threw my phone onto my bed and began to cry again. How could he throw away our our future for someone else? How could it be *her*? The heartbreak enveloped me as I tried to analyze where I went wrong.

I wasn't enough.

A soft knock sounded on my bedroom door, and my mom opened it slowly. She frowned when she took me in, sobbing into my pillow which was now a canvas of black mascara. She took a seat on the foot of my bed. "What is happening?"

I didn't want to tell her. I didn't want it to be real. But it *was* real. And it was too much. "He's seeing someone else," I choked.

"Oh, Emily." She placed a hand atop my leg. "I'm so sorry."

Panicked sobs once again took over my body. "Why doesn't he want me?"

She studied me sadly, as if I were a reflection of her pain a decade prior. "You need to be done," she said. "Block him on social media. Change your phone number. Do not allow him to do this to you again. He has shown you his true colors… you *must* believe him."

"I'm not ready," I sobbed. I felt like a child again, throwing a tantrum because I couldn't have my way. I allowed her to hug and console me, promising I'd be okay.

She left my room, called the phone company, and within an hour I had a new phone number. My mother's strength to take control of the situation while I helplessly drowned was superhuman. I ached at the thought of her suffering through years of this with nobody to pull her out. How had she survived?

She handed me my new phone number on a sticky note. "Do not give it to him," she instructed. This time, she wasn't fooling around.

I nodded.

Reluctantly, it was time to start a new chapter without Shane.

chapter fifteen

"I hate that asshole," Gina huffed as we sat on a bench overlooking the coast.

Losing Shane meant I no longer needed to cover up for his indiscretions. That morning, Gina met me for a long walk along the foggy beach, staying silent as I spilled all the details to her about how abruptly he'd ended our engagement for another girl.

"He's a piece of shit and I'm so glad you guys are done. I'm so sorry that you're hurt… but you are dodging a bullet. Imagine if you got married and then he did this?"

I stared at the gray ocean, unable to meet her eyes. "We almost got married in December."

"What?!"

"Yeah," I admitted. "We had plans to elope. That's why this is all such a shock to me."

"Why didn't you tell me?"

I faced her, shrugging my shoulders. "I didn't want anyone to talk me out of it."

"Emily," she sighed. She studied the waves for a moment, then looked back at me. "Do you *really* think it's healthy if you feel the need to keep your wedding a secret from your best friend?"

I shook my head. "I'm sorry."

"Don't be sorry." She hugged me. "Be done. He's manipulative. He's toxic. You're safe now."

I appreciated her willingness to love and support me, my guilt tugging at me from all the things I kept hidden from her. I leaned into her embrace and tried to find solace in her friendship.

THE FOLLOWING DAYS were hard, but eventually the days turned into weeks.

My mom had told me, "*A sign of getting over him is when you wake up and missing him isn't your first thought. Eventually, you'll go until noon without thinking of him. And finally, you'll go an entire day without him crossing your mind.*"

I wasn't there yet, but I promised myself that time would heal all wounds. As I stood in front of my bathroom mirror, it was her eyes from my childhood that stared back at me. I saw the dark shadows beneath them, the dry, red skin around my nose from boxes of cheap tissues. She had gotten through this, and so would I.

But the days of making it until noon without Shane crossing my mind felt farther away than ever when I returned to Los Angeles. Framed pictures of him smiled at me from the wall above my bed. I took each one down, staring blankly at the once-happy couple shining back at me. Tears streamed down my face as I tucked the frames away in the drawer of my nightstand. I would deal with those another day.

In an effort to distract myself, I pulled out my phone to text Nikki.

Emily: *Hey, I just got back to LA. What are you up to tonight?*
Nikki: *Nate and I are at Jack's apartment. Come by!*
Emily: *Alright, I'll be over in 30.*

Nikki greeted me with a hug as soon as I walked through the door of Jack's apartment. "I'm so sorry." She'd heard the news about Shane via text weeks before.

I thanked her, then turned to hug Nate, then Jack.

"Does this mean we get to hang out with you again? You're seriously behind on *Dexter*," Jack joked.

I laughed. "I guess so."

"You were too good for him," Nikki said. "He knew that, and that's why he fucked it up."

"It just doesn't make any sense," I replied. "I loved him so much."

"Do you remember how much fun we had freshman year? You loved him then, too, and you were able to get past it," she said.

I nodded, but so much had changed since then. Shane felt imprinted in my DNA. Parts of my identity had merged with his and I felt a hollowness without him.

"Do you want to come to Palm Springs at the end of this month?" Jack asked. "The whole fraternity is heading there for the weekend. We rented out a resort. It's going to be wild."

"What about Chelsea?" The weekend getaway was something they did every year. The guys were each allowed to bring one guest, and Jack's guest spot should be filled by his girlfriend.

"She can't come because she has a swim meet," he said. "I'll have to talk to her about it, but I'm pretty sure she'd be fine with you coming as my friend. It would be good for you."

"Yes!" Nikki squealed. "You must come! That would be so fun!"

"Palm Springs – let's go!" Nate shouted, high-fiving me.

A FEW WEEKS later, we were off to Palm Springs.

Going as Jack's guest meant we had to share a room and a bed, but this didn't faze us. Not that I'd ever admit it to Shane, but I'd innocently fallen asleep next to Jack on a couple occasions after partying too hard and not wanting to walk back to my apartment after midnight. He snored, but that was far from a deal breaker if it meant I got to get away for a little while. I thought about how angry Shane would be to know about this trip and the sleeping arrangements. I half-smiled at the thought of it, but my smile wore off when I remembered he was also sleeping next to someone else – someone who wasn't a platonic friend.

Thankfully, the trip was just what I needed. My heartbreak tugged at me a bit, but it was nice to have fun without someone angry at me over it. It felt wild and rebellious to do what I wanted to do without needing to check in with someone about my whereabouts.

We checked into the resort, and I felt the weight of guilt rise off my shoulders like the steam from the hot tub that was waiting just through the main lobby. I never once worried about the cut of my shirt or the length of my skirt. I relished the feeling of wearing a bikini and not needing to wrap a towel around myself any time I passed another person. We headed down to the pool for drinks and I imagined how sweet they would taste, untinged by Shane's judgment.

I looked over at Nikki from across the poolside bar and smiled as she raised her glass with a wink. I lifted mine in return and felt a heaviness in my chest when I thought of all the memories we didn't get to make because of my relationship. But I was here now. And, like Gina said, I was safe.

We partied late into the night, and when I crawled into bed next to Jack later, no tears spilled out onto the bed sheets. Maybe my ending with Shane was a blessing in disguise.

I resented him for holding me captive. But as hard as I tried to hate him, and as much as his betrayal wounded me, I still found moments where I missed his love.

I missed the way it comforted me on nights when I was alone.

I missed the way his jokes made me laugh harder than anyone else's.

I missed the way he looked at me like nobody else ever had.

After the weekend in Palm Springs, I numbed missing him with alcohol and hook-ups. I flung myself into the social scene just as I had done at the beginning of my freshman year. I found myself entangled in a couple one-night stands, desperately hoping the distraction of being with someone else would ease my heartache.

But each one left me feeling hollower than before.

Then, I met Max.

WHILE DRUNK AT a party with Nikki at Nate and Jack's fraternity, I reached for an unopened can of beer on a table just as another hand swiped it away.

"Hey," I shouted at the tall, blonde man who stood before me. "That was mine."

He laughed. "This is *my* beer. I just set it down for a minute."

"Who sets their beer down at a party?"

"Who grabs random beers they find at a party?"

I laughed. "It was unopened."

"Fair enough." He shrugged.

I narrowed my eyes. "You're not in this frat." I hadn't seen him in Palm Springs, nor ever before.

He shook his head. "My friend is. I'm visiting from Georgia. Well, I'm not *from* Georgia. I'm from the Bay Area."

"Wait, me too!"

We moved in closer to one another, excitedly sharing stories about our hometowns. He grew up only an hour away from me, and we were the same age and year in college.

"So, what brought you to Georgia?" I asked.

"I'm attending the University of Georgia ROTC program to become an Army officer."

"Ugh!" I groaned. "You're kidding."

"What?"

I scowled. "My ex-fiancé is in the Army. I'm not a fan of Army guys right now."

"Ex-fiancé?" He looked surprised. "Aren't you… a little young to be engaged?"

"I'm not engaged anymore," I retorted, rolling my eyes.

"And I'm not an Army guy – yet," he smirked.

"Max!" A guy shouted from across the room, stealing his attention from our banter. "We're heading to a different frat!"

Max looked back at me. "Gotta go. I'm here for the next three days if you want to hang out." He pulled out his phone and handed it to me. "Put your number in."

I took his phone, doing my best to type my name and number correctly while the room spun around me.

"Emily," he read from the phone screen when I handed it back to him. I nodded. "See you later, Emily." He smiled, then left with his friend.

I shook my head in disbelief. *A fucking Army guy. Go figure.*

I AWOKE TO the sound of my phone vibrating the following day. Groggy and hungover, I reached for it to read the message.

Max: *Emily! What's up?*
Emily: *Sleeping… Why are you up so early?*
Max: *Haha. Stuck on east coast time. Want to hang out?*

I considered his question. My roommates happened to be out of town this weekend.

Emily: *Give me an hour, then my place? Bring coffee :)*

I sent him my address and, an hour later, Max arrived with lattes in hand. And that was the beginning of the best weekend I'd had in over a month.

The morning passed in a blur of shy smiles and touches. Our time together flowed seamlessly from introductory conversation to a shift in body language that let me know he was feeling exactly what I was. Max turned to me from his place on the couch, his eyes moving down from mine and stopping to rest on my lips. He leaned into me and took my chin in his hand. It was rough against my skin, and I felt my desire burning beneath his touch. We moved from slow, passionate kisses to desperately tearing our clothes off.

Max and I hooked up three times that day. We went from having sex on the couch, to the shower, to my bed. It was exhilarating. He was a stranger, someone I'd probably never see again after this weekend – yet he filled me with a comfort I hadn't felt in weeks. It was as if we'd known each other for years. And I made it well past noon without thought to spare for Shane.

That night, we went back to the fraternity for another round of drinking. We hung out with Nikki, Nate, Jack, and Chelsea, and rotated matches of beer pong and flip cup. By the end of the night, Max was kissing me in public, garnering nods of approval from my friends. I knew they were happy to see me moving on.

He stayed the night with me, and we spent the next day repeating what we'd done the day before. Each room in my apartment took on a new meaning as we found ways to wrap our bodies around one another.

At the end of our second afternoon together, I'd gone 48 hours without thinking of Shane.

"I better spend tonight with my friend," Max laughed. "I've accidentally spent the entire weekend with you."

"Sorry," I shrugged.

"Don't you dare apologize for this amazing time." He kissed me. "I'm going to call you when I get back to Georgia. Maybe we do this again next time I come out?"

"Yeah." I smiled, but my heart sank slightly. He was meant to be a fling, and I now found myself sad that he was leaving. It was unlike anything I'd experienced before – developing that kind of closeness immediately with someone and diving in with zero inhibitions.

But Max didn't call.

I waited a week before I texted him. He read my message but did not reply. And I felt stupid for once again believing I meant something to someone, when really, I meant nothing.

chapter sixteen

The rejection from Max combined with the heartbreak of losing Shane made my body ache all over. As Valentine's Day loomed closer, I cringed at the thought of hiding in my room binging TV shows on Netflix while everyone around me celebrated love.

I was wrapping up a homework assignment before bed when my email notification went off. I glanced at my inbox, expecting to see spam, and what I saw instead made my jaw fall open.

Shane: *Em, please call me as soon as you get this. I've been trying to get a hold of you but you blocked me on social media and I'm getting a message that your phone number is no longer in service. Are you there? We need to talk.*

I stared at Shane's email, every muscle in my body stiffening. I had spent the last six weeks trying to pick up the shattered pieces of my self-worth and rebuild my life without him. And there it was, a tempting invitation to revisit the pain.

I couldn't do it. I owed myself more than this. He deserved to be met with nothing but silence. I shut my laptop and went to sleep, tossing and turning as the nerves riddled my body.

Over the next 72 hours, Shane sent three more emails.

Shane: *Emily, are you getting this? Call me please. It's urgent.*
Shane: *I know you are hurt and angry. You have every right to be. Please just hear what I have to say.*
Shane: *Em, I'm worried about you. Please say something.*

I felt a sense of satisfaction ignoring him and protecting myself from further hurt, but curiosity tugged at my heartstrings.

Should I risk it? What if he can undo all the pain I'm holding onto? What if – somehow – there's a way to fix this? What if I respond just enough to see what he wants and then shut him out again?

For some masochistic reason, I decided to tempt fate.

Em: *Why?*
Shane: *I made a terrible mistake. I need to hear your voice.*

I wasn't ready to give him access to my life again, but I wanted to hear more.

I stood delicately on a tightrope, teetering between holding onto my sobriety and plunging back into the addiction which ravaged me. There, was the obvious opportunity to block his email address and cut him off while I still had the power. But the small flame in my heart for him was begging to stay lit.

I spent two more days thinking about the emails. They were the first thing in my head when I woke up, and they distracted me during my lectures. On the evening of the second day, I opened the drawer of my nightstand to search for a book when the framed pictures of Shane hit me in the face.

I picked up a frame and studied a picture of us at the Army ball in

Washington one year ago. I beamed in the photo, and I wondered if I'd smiled that big since losing him. Beside me he was laughing, his eyes alive with happiness, one arm wrapped tightly around my waist pulling me close to him. I remembered how happy I felt that night, dressed like a queen on the arm of my king.

Would it be so wrong to hear him out?

I had nothing without Shane. My bitter loneliness ate at me each day and I feared that one day there would be nothing left. My rendezvous with Max reminded me how little anyone else cared to see me – to love me – the way Shane had.

My fingers typed and erased multiple responses to his email, unsure what to say. Finally, I sent a message saying we could talk on Skype so that I could keep my phone number private.

I opened Skype on my laptop and the green bubble beside his name indicated he was online. Within seconds, the ring tone sounded. I took a steadying breath before I accepted the call.

When it connected, my heart skipped a beat. Gray hoodie. Five o'clock shadow. Pain in his eyes. A frown on his face. He looked… horrible. Yet, I drank in his features as if seeing him for the first time.

"My god, Em, I've missed you so much. Please don't hang up," he pleaded.

The sound of his voice sent nonconsensual warmth through my body. I gritted my teeth.

"I made the biggest mistake of my life letting you go," he continued. "When we started planning our elopement, I panicked. I don't know why. I got so close to marrying you and then I was so afraid of losing you that I pulled out –"

"You didn't pull out. You cheated on me."

"What I did with Christine was stupid. She knew she meant nothing to me, and I was just self-sabotaging my relationship with you… and

Emily, I need you to know I did *not* sleep with her until I ended things with you."

"But you *did* sleep with her."

He looked down. "I did sleep with her," he confirmed.

My stomach churned. I looked away from the computer as tears formed in my eyes. "That hurts," I whimpered, my words barely audible.

"Em…"

"Do you have *any fucking idea* how much I wanted to die when you told me you were seeing someone else?" My voice quaked with anger.

His face sank. "Yes, and I'm so sorry. It's the worst mistake I've ever made in my life. I would do anything to take it all back."

I shook my head. "But you can't."

"I know. So, I will spend every day of the rest of my life showing you how sorry I am."

"It's too late, Shane. My mom and my friends hate you."

He shook off my words. "I don't care what they think about me. The only thing that matters to me is *you*. You and I are the only people who know what the past four years have been like. We hid our relationship from the world for over a year. We stayed in love with each other for a year after breaking up. We dated long distance for over a year. There is no one – *no one* – I could ever love as much as I love you."

I wiped my eyes, his words bringing another rush of tears. "I can't…"

"You don't have to forgive me right now. I will earn it."

"You can't…"

"Give me a chance," he pleaded.

"I've given you chances." *How many chances does one person deserve?*

"I know. And I have fucked up beyond repair. But I will never stop loving you. I don't know why I keep sabotaging this, Emily." Shane looked down and his shoulders began to shake. As I watched his body convulse, I realized what was happening. He was crying. It was the first time I'd ever seen him cry. My throat tightened, and he continued to speak through his tears. "I can't fucking live without you, Em. I love you so much it physically hurts me."

He was desperate.

I recalled the times where I had begged for his love, and how powerless it made me feel. Now, I held the power. I held the decision that would determine his perception of his worth. I had the opportunity to crush him the way he had crushed me.

He deserved it.

But I couldn't do it.

From the beginning of our relationship, all I ever wanted was to see Shane happy. He was damaged, and like me he deserved to be loved. I wanted to be the one to love him, to fix him – I wanted to be the thing that made him happy.

I wanted it so badly that my own self-preservation came second.

I nodded. I wanted his crying to stop. "I know. I love you, too."

"Please don't stop loving me," he begged.

"I don't know what I'm supposed to do, Shane."

"Come here for Valentine's Day weekend and give me an opportunity to show you how sorry I am. If you haven't forgiven me by the end of the weekend, you can choose never to talk to me again. But please, give me one more chance."

He stared at me, blue eyes pleading. I rubbed my fingers along my brow bones, closing my eyes to think. *Run,* my intuition said. The conflict within me waged, torn between love and the fear of being hurt again. With my eyes still closed, I heard him softly repeat, "Please."

A montage of memories played in my head. The moment he asked me to be his girlfriend. The first time he told me he loved me. The look in his eyes when he asked me to marry him. The feeling I felt in those moments; I wanted – no, *needed* – to feel it again. I was empty without it.

"I'll come for Valentine's Day weekend," I conceded. As Shane's eyes lit up, I added, "You're paying for my plane tickets, and this doesn't mean we're getting back together."

"I will take anything I can get," he said.

As a smile formed across his face, I couldn't stop one from forming on my own.

NIKKI STOPPED BY my apartment the next day on her walk home from class. Sitting in my living room, I let her know Shane had found his way back in.

Her eyes narrowed. "After what he did to you, why are you even considering this?"

"Because I need some type of understanding, or some type of closure." I knew my reasoning didn't make sense.

"You're not going to get closure. You're going to wind up in a toxic situation again if you let him back in." She shook her head. "Why would you put yourself through this? It's not only stupid, Emily, it's insane!"

I fired back in self-defense. "I don't need you to judge me for decisions you could never understand. You barely know Shane. You've only seen the bad. You don't know the good."

"Seriously? I've seen enough to know that there's not a lot of good."

Anger made my skin hot. I didn't know if I was angry at Nikki because she was wrong, or because she was right. She was a voice of reason, telling me I was making the wrong choice. "There is good," I insisted. "You don't know him like I do."

"I know I can't talk you out of this, but I really hope he treats you better this time." She checked her phone. "I gotta go. See you later."

She stood up from my couch and walked toward my door.

I let her leave without saying goodbye.

She didn't understand – no one could possibly understand – the bond between Shane and me. I decided not to tell anyone else that I was letting Shane back into my life yet. They'd react the same way Nikki had, and I couldn't handle disappointment from anyone else.

I needed to see first for myself what he had in store for us that weekend.

chapter seventeen

I stepped off the plane at Seattle-Tacoma Airport, my heart pounding with a mix of anticipation and trepidation. After four months of separation, I was about to face the man who shattered my heart.

Was I making a mistake?

He stood on the arrivals curb holding a bouquet of yellow daffodils. My heart raced as the sight of him brought forth a flood of memories, both joyful and painful. As I approached, he smiled, extending his arm for a friendly embrace. "Hi," he said as he offered me the bouquet.

I couldn't help but smile breathing in his cologne along with the scent of the fresh flowers. "Hi."

He opened the passenger door and waited for me to settle in before taking my bag to the trunk. As we began our drive to the house he was now renting, our silence was deafening – avoiding conversation like one wrong word might make the other disappear into thin air. Twenty minutes in, he placed a hand atop my thigh. I stared at it, my icy facade slowly melting under its warmth.

As we walked through the front door of his house, I caught a glimpse of red. Rose petals lined the entryway to the stairs and up to the second floor. I motioned toward them. "What's this?"

He smiled coyly. "Hopefully the beginning of a good weekend."

Neither of us spoke as I followed the petals up to his bedroom. The awkward anticipation had every nerve in my body at attention.

As I opened the door, pictures greeted my eyes. Photos documenting our years together covered every wall of his bedroom. I took in our smiling faces, the memories flooding me again.

My gaze moved to the bed where an array of Valentine's Day gifts lay out for me, including a stuffed animal wearing an Army uniform, a framed photo of us, and a diamond heart-shaped necklace. I picked up the necklace and held it in between my fingers.

"Beautiful," I remarked.

"Do you want me to put it on you?"

I nodded, then turned around so he could clasp the necklace around my neck. My former lover approached with caution, as if I were fragile enough to shatter under his touch. He secured the necklace, then placed his lips gently on the base of my neck. He held them there for a moment, and my eyes closed as a chill traveled down my spine.

I opened my eyes, and looking at his dresser I spotted my engagement ring tucked in its box. He hadn't thrown it away or pawned it off during our time apart. During all that time apart, he hadn't given up on us.

He noticed my focus on the ring. "I want you to wear it again." I turned to face him. "I know it's going to take time to earn your trust back. I'm sorry for everything. I don't ever want to lose you again."

I wasn't sure what to think, but I saw sincerity in his eyes. An overwhelming longing surged through me that made me almost forget the pain and heartache of the last two months. Why subject myself to another minute of it?

Without hesitation, I wrapped my arms around his neck and pressed my lips to his, savoring the sweet taste of familiarity.

Shane was my drug. I was addicted to the pain and withdrawal he put me through, because the high was so intense every time it returned.

There was no person or substance in my life that could have the impact he had on me. With one hit of his love, I found myself able to feel and see clearly again. And ten minutes later, I lay next to him in bed, breathless.

OVER THE WEEKEND, in between bouts of making love, we worked to rebuild our foundation. Unsurprisingly, it came easily. Though we'd been apart for months, we fell back into each other like puzzle pieces into place.

We sat hand-in-hand on his couch enjoying Netflix and popcorn on our final night together. As our movie came to an end, he reached for the remote to turn the TV off and faced me. "I need to tell you something."

"What?" My interest piqued.

"I need to apologize, fully." I gave a nod, encouraging him to continue. "I take full accountability for this relationship being so unstable. I'm sorry for every time I blamed you as a way to deflect my own insecurities. I'm sorry for making you believe you were anything less than the most amazing girlfriend and fiancée I could have ever asked for."

The hand that was holding mine squeezed softly as his other hand came to meet it, cradling mine from both sides. He pulled my fingertips to his mouth where he pressed them against his lips. I breathed but remained quiet.

"I'm sorry for picking fights with you. I'm sorry for every time I've made you feel unwanted. And I am so, *so* sorry for the way I ended our engagement."

Thoughts of him and Christine together made my throat tighten. I pulled my hand away from him, gulping in an effort to suppress the intrusive thoughts. He was saying the right things, but I didn't know if I could move past... that. "I don't think you'll ever understand how badly you hurt me," I whispered.

"I'm so sorry." He reached for my shoulders to pull me into him. My face met his chest and pressed against the warmth. I could feel his heartbeat as he continued. "This was the worst mistake I've ever made in my life. I know I don't deserve you, but I will spend the rest of our lives trying to earn your love and trust again. You are the love of my life."

"How can I expect things to be any different this time around?"

"Because I thought I lost you forever, Em." I looked up at him. Tears formed in his eyes and he quickly wiped them away. "I called your number and it was disconnected. I had no way to get through to you. I really thought I lost you. It killed me."

"You did lose me." I held his stare as I said the words, wanting them to sink in. My mind and heart waged war with one another. The thought of surrendering to him again was both terrifying and exhilarating.

He cradled my face in his hands. "I can't lose you." And then he pressed his mouth to mine. I felt it in the way he kissed me – the desperation, the sorrow, the longing.

I wondered if anyone else could awaken the same depth of emotion within me. If my choice was between a dull life, or a life full of indescribable highs and colors – with the tallest peaks and the lowest valleys – how could I choose anything but him?

If I didn't give this one more chance, my thoughts would be haunted by what could have been. I needed to see if our love was strong enough to conquer all, because the thought of never knowing scared me more than the fear of what might happen if I embraced it.

"I want to make a commitment to you, and this time I know I'm ready." He knelt before me, pulling the ring box out of his sweatpants pocket. "There's no one else in this world for me, Emily; and there's nothing I want more than to marry you if you'll still have me. Will you be my wife?"

I balanced on the precipice of uncertainty as I stared at Shane.

This weekend, he'd shown me glimpses of the person I longed for him to be. I took in his blue eyes, his smile, waiting for my response. My heart pulled strongly in his direction.

But is it the right choice?

Amidst my doubt, one truth shone through: I loved him and I trusted that our journey would lead us to where we were meant to be. I embraced my uncertainty with a calming breath, then nodded enthusiastically.

His lips curved into a wider smile. He slipped the ring back on my finger as he arose from the ground to meet my mouth with his again.

As I savored his sweet kiss, I felt reassured for the first time in a while that everything was going to be okay. I released a breath I'd been holding since December.

"Now can I please have your phone number?" Shane joked.

I RETURNED TO Los Angeles riding the high of my heart set afire again, but with the daunting task of telling my friends I'd decided to give Shane another chance. After unpacking my suitcase, I hopped into my bed for comfort as I called Gina.

"Hi! I have news," I said with nervous excitement as our call began.

"Tell me!"

I recounted everything from the moment Shane emailed me to his proposal the night before. She was mostly silent while I talked, with the occasional gasp and "*oh my gosh*!" When I finished, she asked, "Are you sure this is the right decision?"

"I am," I spoke with confidence. "He's changed. He wants to make this right."

"I know you want to believe that, but he's still the same person he was before. Men don't change that quickly. Don't forget he broke off your engagement to date another girl…"

I winced. I hated her words. "He was confused and insecure. He apologized for everything. I really don't think he would ever make a mistake like that again."

"He knows how to manipulate you into thinking he's changed, but what if he goes back to his old ways as soon as he gets comfortable?"

I frowned as my chest tightened. I pushed myself through these same reservations with Shane, and now my patience wavered trying to push Gina to believe the same. "I know you're looking out for me, but I love him," I said defiantly, not leaving room for argument. "I want to give him another chance. I believe he can change."

Gina breathed a long sigh. "I don't want to see you get hurt again, Emily. Promise me you'll be careful."

"I promise. Thank you for being there for me."

My heart felt heavy as we ended our call. Gina was being protective of me, as a good friend should, but I hated feeling like I disappointed her. My thumb hovered over Nikki's name on my phone screen. I knew she'd be unsupportive given the interaction we had before I went to Washington, but I called her anyway.

"Hey," she answered.

"Hey, what are you up to tonight?"

"Nate and I are about to head over to the frat house. You?"

"I just got back from Washington."

"Oh, cool." Silence followed.

I felt uncomfortable as I formed my next words. "Shane asked me to marry him again."

"What did you say?"

"I said yes." I waited for her to process the information.

When she spoke, her tone was flat. "I don't know what to say, Emily… I think you're making a mistake."

My heart fell. "Can't you just be happy for me?"

"You deserve better. You deserve someone who treats you with respect and love, not someone who manipulates and –"

"He's not manipulating me. I want this. And I want you to support my choice," I pleaded.

"I've watched you cry alone in your room for the better part of two years." She paused. "You're not the same person I met at the beginning of freshman year. You used to want to hang out, have fun, enjoy life… now you do nothing but sit at home and argue with Shane."

I clenched my teeth. "That's not true. I'm just not into partying –"

"I just watched you come back here two months ago utterly heartbroken over him," she interrupted. "And then I watched you come alive again in Palm Springs. I was so happy, thinking I got my best friend back. I can't pretend to support something that I know is going to hurt you again."

A lump formed in my throat as I fought back tears. "Then I guess we don't need to continue this conversation."

"I guess we don't," she snapped. "Goodbye, then."

Nikki hung up and I threw my phone down on the bed. I pulled my comforter over my head, cocooning myself in darkness while I sifted through my thoughts.

This is my engagement. People are supposed to be happy for me. People are supposed to be excited. Why is everyone so hurtful? Why don't they understand?

A dark heaviness enveloped me. I had hoped my friends would set aside their opinions and support me, but instead I felt judged and alone.

I began to cry.

And the only person I could reach out to for comfort was Shane.

chapter eighteen

"Shane?" the barista called, and he arose from our table to retrieve two hot lattes from the cafe counter.

A month after getting back together, I had returned to Washington during my midterm break in classes. Dreary weather had us holed up in a local coffee shop for its cozy warmth and I relished the time together.

Shane smiled over his shoulder as he walked to the counter, and I felt the same rush of attraction that drew me to him so many years ago. I was in a city I loved with the man I loved. Our time apart felt like a distant memory as I sat waiting for him. I spun my engagement ring with my thumb and smiled. Things were finally good.

Shane returned with the drinks in hand and a mischievous grin on his face. He extended one coffee to me. "You know what we should do this weekend, babe?"

I accepted the cup with both hands. "What?"

"Get married."

I laughed. Things had been smooth sailing since Valentine's Day, Shane holding true to his word and treating me better than he ever had. Every day of his kindness was validation for the decision I made to accept his proposal a second time.

He sat down and locked eyes with me. "I mean it."

I stared, waiting for his face to break into a grin and tell me he was joking; but it remained deadpan. "You can't be serious…"

"I've never been more serious about anything in my life."

"Shane, I'm giving you a second chance… but I'm not confident about us yet. You were just dating someone else –"

"I was never dating her." He shook his head. "It was a stupid, meaningless fling."

I sipped my coffee, the clarification making no difference. "I feel like we need more time to figure this out."

"What more do we need to figure out?" he asked. "I made a horrible mistake. I thought I wasn't ready, but I am. Almost losing you made me realize I'm more ready to marry you than I'll ever be." He studied me intently. "Why are you holding back?"

I recalled the pain of him blindsiding me only three months ago. "Because I was heartbroken when you left. I'm not over it, and it doesn't feel right jumping into this."

"We're not jumping into anything – we've loved each other for four years." I sensed impatience in his tone. "Why would you accept the ring back if you don't want to marry me?"

I took my eyes off Shane and glanced around the coffee shop, feeling anxious about eavesdroppers. We sat on armchairs with a small round table in between us. Another couple sat no more than 10 feet away. Lowering my voice, I calmly explained, "I *do* want to marry you. I just don't want to marry you *this weekend.*"

But he made no attempt to lower his. "What difference does it make?"

"I'll feel more comfortable if we wait." I looked down and began to pick at the skin around my thumb.

Noting my discomfort, he reached across the table for my hand. I obliged. "Babe, I know you're scared. I'm scared, too. But I *know* we're meant to be together. Prove it to me that you feel the same way I do."

I pointed to the ring on my finger. "Wearing this ring is proof that I feel the same way. I don't want to rush this. I want a real wedding. I want my friends and family around. I want a dress, pictures –"

"We can still do all those things later."

I shook my head. "This isn't the wedding I want."

"Right now, this is just you and me, making a decision to spend the rest of our lives together." He squeezed my hand. "Em… this is the decision you already made when you said yes to marrying me. Stop thinking so much about the timeline."

I bit my lip. "I just feel uncomfortable rushing this." Uncomfortable was an understatement. It was getting harder to find the words to defend my position and I was almost certain other people were listening now. My heart raced.

Yes – I agreed to marry him; the ring was my commitment to that promise. No – I hadn't agreed to marry him this weekend. But I didn't want to upset him. The past month of pure, unbridled happiness had breathed new life into me. Maintaining that harmony was crucial to my wellbeing. Did it really make a difference whether we got married now or later?

Shane sipped his coffee and studied the ring on my finger. There was a moment of silence as he thought about his next words. "If you don't want to marry me, maybe we made a mistake getting back together."

Again, I scanned his face for signs of a joke but was met with adamance. My chest tightened. "Why would you say that?"

He ignored the question. "Do you love me?"

"Of course."

"Then prove it. Marry me. If you can't, then you're not really in this. You don't really mean *that*." He pointed at the ring.

"I DO mean *this*," I argued, placing my fingers around it.

He shook his head. "I don't want to spend another minute with you if I don't know whether it's going to end in heartbreak or not. I can't do it." He looked at the ring, then at me. Specks of hurt clouded his blue eyes. "If you love me, marry me. If you can't marry me this weekend, you don't love me… and I'm done."

I absorbed his words as panic boiled beneath the surface of my skin. Lose him, or trust him. Flashbacks of the hurt from losing him in December rippled through my body and cornered me into the only decision that made sense.

The only choice… was to trust him.

THREE DAYS LATER, a judge married us.

The morning of our elopement, I stood at the mirror in Shane's bathroom, pinning my hair back and trying in vain to get the thin swoops of black eyeliner on my top lids to take something resembling the same shape. *Gina always made this look so easy*, I thought. *If only she were here. Or Nikki. Or anyone.*

I wore a strapless, baby pink dress – something cute enough for a special occasion, but not what I envisioned wearing on my wedding day. I stared at my reflection, unsatisfied.

Shane leaned into the bathroom fixing his tie. He wore a black shirt and pants, his pink tie a nod to my dress. "Almost ready?"

I nodded. *Was I?* I'd spent the morning attempting to disconnect my mind from my body with every turn of the curling iron and nervous coat of lipstick, burying whatever negative emotions stirred within me.

He smiled at me in the mirror, then walked over to place his arms around my waist. "In just a couple hours, you'll be my wife." He squeezed me as he planted an enthusiastic kiss on my cheek. "I love you. You look beautiful."

I felt warm in his embrace, and his compliment made me smile.

I gazed at the reflection of our happiness in the mirror and felt my dissatisfaction fade in the face of our future together. "I love you, too."

We walked downstairs and got in the car, then drove a short distance to the courthouse. The Washington weather taunted us and Shane covered me with his jacket as we walked in from the parking lot, carefully keeping my curls dry from the rain that felt like anything but good luck on my wedding day.

As we stood before the judge and the official ceremony began, time seemed to move at least three times faster than normal. The judge prompted Shane with his vow to me, to which Shane replied, "I do."

Then the judge faced me, and a battle began to wage inside my head.

"Emily, do you take this man to be your husband, to live together in matrimony…"

Can I trust him? Will he stay committed to me this time?

"… to love him, to honor him…"

My brain ping-ponged between emotions. Pain. Abandonment. Fear. He was heartless when he discarded me. The wound of the breakup still felt raw. *What if it happens again?*

"… to comfort him, and to keep him in sickness and in health, forsaking all others…"

I thought about the reactions of our friends and family. What would my mom think? Surely she would be hurt by my hasty decision to marry Shane without telling her. I had barely broken the news to her that we were back together a few weeks ago. And my friends? I was keeping secrets, excluding them from major moments in my life, choosing Shane over them… things I had vowed to never do again.

"… for as long as you both shall live?"

I looked at Shane, then at the judge, then back to Shane. They stared, each awaiting my response. Shane squeezed my hand three times and raised his eyebrows in anticipation.

I scanned his eager face. The smattering of freckles that lingered despite constant cloud cover; the soft stubble that he rubbed against my face in the morning while I lingered in that sweet spot between sleep and waking; and the full lips that could lift to form the most charming smile I'd ever seen. His love for me was palpable. It brought sunshine to a dim life. It brought color to a black and white world. Sure, there was fear; there was uncertainty; and there would be naysayers… but I couldn't bear the thought of a life without Shane.

"I do," I vowed, and I was rewarded when that smile I loved so much spread across his face.

We repeated our promises to one another after the judge. Shane slipped the wedding band onto my finger, joining it with the engagement ring, and my heart pounded as the diamonds glistened. We would leave the mistakes of the past behind. We would move forward, united and stronger together. We locked eyes.

"I love you," he mouthed.

I nodded in return. *I'm making the right decision*, I told myself.

After our small ceremony, we called our families to break the news. We told Shane's mom first. She had always loved me, and because she wasn't privy to his indiscretions, she had nothing but joy for us. I could hear the elation in her voice, and I started to feel like maybe the elopement wasn't such a bad idea after all.

Next, we called my mom, who had been so headstrong about me getting over Shane that she had changed my phone number and bought me a stack of self-help books to mend my broken heart. I remembered how hard she had worked to heal her own wounds and the pride she exuded when I agreed to walk away. I hesitated with my finger over her name. Part of me wanted to stay in this bubble forever – just Shane and me without the outside opinions of others. Fingers trembling, I pressed it.

When I heard her answer on the other end, I summoned the strength to spit it out. "Shane and I got married today."

"You what?" she asked, bewilderment in her voice.

"We went to a judge here in Washington and signed the paperwork. It was very small and simple. We plan to have a real wedding later this year." The words spilled out of my mouth in a stream so fast that she didn't have a chance to ask anything else.

"Wow! Emily – I… I don't know what to say. Congratulations! I love you." Her tone relayed more confusion than excitement, but her words comforted me, whether sincere or faked.

My dad wasn't one for sugarcoating, though. I called him after hanging up with my mom. Although our relationship was strained, he was my father, and this was a big life announcement he needed to be looped in on.

"I have good news!" I said through the phone after he picked up.

"What is it?"

"Shane and I just got married."

A long silence followed on the other end.

"So, what is the good news?" he asked, and again I felt the heavy blow of disappointment punch me square in the gut.

Shane saw the hurt on my face and reached for my hand, stroking it while I wrapped up the conversation with my dad. "We can be our own family now, Em," he said after I hung up the phone. As he held my fingers with his own, I hoped with all my heart that was true.

chapter nineteen

I flew back to Los Angeles two days after our elopement, ready to settle into my last three months until graduation. A knock on my door told me Jack had arrived to pick up the books I had borrowed from him.

I answered the door. "Hey!"

"Welcome back, and congratulations!"

We hugged and I thanked him. I knew Jack harbored his own opinions of Shane, but unlike my female friends he didn't argue with me over my decisions.

We walked over to my living room couch to sit down and catch up about everything that had happened over the past month, concluding with the elopement.

"What did Nikki say?"

My heart sank. I hadn't yet spoken to Nikki. I knew she must've seen my social media announcement – a smiling picture of Shane and I at the courthouse pointing to our rings – but she hadn't said a word about it. "I haven't talked to her."

Jack raised his eyebrows. "At all?"

"Not since the elopement." I pulled my phone out of my pocket and opened the Facebook app, curious to see what Nikki had been up to for the past few days. Maybe she'd been too busy to see my announcement.

I typed her name into the search bar and tapped on her profile. A preview of her profile appeared on my phone screen with an "Add Friend" button. "What the fuck…" I said out loud.

"What?" Jack asked.

I turned my phone screen to him. "She removed me as a friend."

He studied the phone. "When?"

"I don't know. She must have done it when she saw my update about marrying Shane." A sinking heaviness tugged at my heartstrings.

"Huh…" He rubbed his chin. "I'm sure she'll come around. She cares about you."

I shook my head. The sting hurt almost as bad as when I'd lost Shane. I swallowed to maintain my composure. "This is not how you show that you care about someone."

"We all want you to be happy, Emily… and we've seen Shane do the opposite," he reasoned.

"It's different now," I snapped. "She won't even give that a chance."

He shrugged. "Okay. Prove her wrong then."

I nodded. My eyes began to burn, but I didn't want to cry in front of Jack about this. Instead, I stood up and walked over to the dining table where his books were and carried them back to the couch. "Thank you for letting me borrow these."

Noting my silent request for him to leave, Jack nodded, stood up and accepted the books. "Anytime," he said, and we said our goodbyes at the door.

I sat back down on the couch and looked at my phone again. As much as I wanted to reach out to Nikki, I felt too overcome by shame and anger to find the right words to say. I couldn't force her to be happy for me, but for her to stop being my friend all together? It didn't make sense.

I felt the sting from other relationships, too. While Gina said she was happy for me, I assumed she was hiding her true feelings to be polite.

I knew she felt hurt by our elopement. When I had called to give her the news, she told me she couldn't believe I'd gotten married without inviting my best friend to be there.

"I would've been there for you," she had told me through the phone. *"No matter how much I despise what Shane has done to you, you didn't have to do this alone."*

Some of my other friends had not sent congratulatory texts or even reacted to my Facebook post. I wasn't blind to noticing these things. I felt alienated from my family as well. My parents had no choice but to accept my decision, but I knew this wasn't the wedding nor the partner they envisioned for their only daughter.

It was hard to pretend all the disappointment didn't hurt me. I longed for people to validate my happiness. Getting married was my biggest life decision to date, and there I was – a newly married woman without the support of anybody around me. I thought about the women whose friends threw them engagement parties, bridal showers and bachelorette parties. I felt a deep sense of regret for doing this the wrong way, and hurt as I mourned what I felt I had lost.

But there was one person who was happy: Shane.

Since the day of our wedding, Shane had taken every opportunity to remind me how happy he was to be my husband, and to have me as his wife. He thanked me for marrying him, and trusting him, and he no longer picked arguments over insecurities.

It was us against the world.

He provided the love, support and happiness I needed and wanted from my family and friends. The more I felt it lacking from them, the more I sought it from him. I truly felt as if we had turned a new page.

Until our first argument, one month after the elopement.

A LAZY MORNING in Washington began curled up in his bedsheets. I basked in the comfort of my head on his chest, his fingers twirling lazy circles on my shoulder.

"You know… You never told me if you hooked up with any other guys when we broke up earlier this year."

My breath caught in my throat as my smile faltered. *Why would he bring this up now?* I attempted to dodge the question. "I don't really think that matters now."

His fingers stopped twirling. "So… you did?"

Goosebumps formed underneath his now still fingers. I thought about Max. My mind searched for the right words. Fear crept in as I recalled Shane's jealousy manifesting as fiery outbursts of rage.

I considered telling him there was no one, but I didn't want our marriage to begin on a foundation of deception. There was no way I could tell him about the entire weekend I'd spent with Max, not when I'd seen how he reacted to the mere idea of me with Jack last summer. Desperate to bring us back to the sweet moment we'd been enjoying only seconds before, I balanced delicately between protecting myself and preserving the integrity of our relationship.

"Like, really meaningless hookups. None of them meant anything to me," I said. An almost-truth.

"Multiple guys?" he asked, his tone growing impatient.

Fuck. I was saying all the wrong things. "One-night stands. It doesn't matter now."

"How many?" From underneath my head, I felt his chest stiffen.

"Shane, stop." Suddenly feeling too close, I lifted my head to create distance between us. As I attempted to do so, his hand gripped my shoulder in place as his other hand grabbed my throat. Fear enveloped me as he held me in a chokehold. As I struggled, his grip tightened, his hand pressing harder against my neck.

"How many?" he repeated.

"Three," I choked, gasping for air.

With sudden force he pushed me away from him toward the edge of the bed. I regained my bearings as shock bounced through me.

He stood to face me, an inferno in his eyes. "*Three?*"

"Please, stop!" I pleaded. We were getting too far to bring him back. "I told you it meant *nothing*. I was lonely and heartbroken. You were sleeping with someone else, too!"

"One person, Emily," he spat, shaking a finger at me. "*One* person! Not three, you filthy fucking lying whore!"

His words shattered the illusion of my fairy tale. I began to cry. "I didn't lie. You never asked. This all happened before you reached back out to me!"

"Shut the fuck up!" he ordered. He clenched his hands, paced back and forth angrily across the room, then took a swing, his fist leaving a hole in the drywall.

I flinched as if my body absorbed the blow.

He reached for his sweatpants and sneakers.

"Where are you going?"

"The fuck away from you," he retorted. And with that, he stormed out of the bedroom. I listened to his footsteps pound down the stairs and out the front door.

I got out of bed and walked to the window, where I watched him get into his car and drive away.

I sat back down on the bed and looked at the hole in the wall as silent tears streamed down my face.

What have I done? What have I done... was all I could think as my body began to convulse from my sobs.

SHANE RETURNED TO the house two hours later. He found me drinking tea at the kitchen table and slid a pizza box in my direction as he took a seat.

I eyed him cautiously, waiting for him to say the first word.

"This is not off to a good start," he said coldly.

I looked down at my lap.

"How do you think it feels for me to find that out from you *after* marrying you, Emily?"

I winced. I wished I could take back all of it. I looked at him. "I should've told you sooner. Honestly, it all felt so insignificant to me. None of those people mattered."

He took a deep breath to steady himself. "Anything else to tell me?"

I picked at the skin around my thumb as I thought about Max. "No. That's everything."

He plated two slices of pizza from the box and handed one to me. I accepted, but let the pizza sit untouched before me. We sat in silence while he ate his slice.

"I guess there's one way you can make it up to me," he finally said.

I studied him. "How?"

"Do the thing I've been asking for."

My stomach sank. I knew what he meant. Shane had wanted to try anal sex for the past year, and I always denied him. There was nothing desirable about it to me, and each time he brought it up I felt annoyed that he wouldn't accept no for an answer. I shook my head. "I've already told you I'm not interested in trying that…"

"How can you judge it when you haven't even tried it?"

"I know I'm not going to like it. I don't need to try it to know that. You shouldn't be asking me to do things I'm not comfortable doing."

"What if I forgive you for fucking three guys, lying to me about it, and promise to never bring it up again?"

I glared at him. He held my gaze, the coldness in his eyes unwavering. He was dealing me an unfair hand; but my wounds from the morning argument were fresh, and desperately I longed to feel the happiness I felt before he reminded me of the monster lurking under the surface.

I bit my thumb. I had two choices: Refuse and ignite another argument, potentially worse than the one we'd had only hours before – I cringed at the thought of the hole in the bedroom wall – or compromise. Use my selflessness to show my love… to gain my forgiveness.

Blood pooled in the nail bed of my thumb from the chunk of skin I bit off. I pressed my index finger to it to curb the bleeding.

"If I try it once and hate it, will you stop asking me to do it?" I asked.

He nodded. "That's all I'm asking for. One try. And all will be forgiven and forgotten."

I wanted to make him happy. I couldn't bear another person being disappointed in me – especially not Shane – because up until today it had felt like he was the only person who wasn't lately. If one sacrifice could bring harmony back into our relationship after I'd destroyed it this morning, it was one worth making. "One time," I reluctantly agreed. "But I'm telling you, I'm going to hate it."

For the first time since that morning, he smiled at me. "You're going to make me the happiest person on earth, Emily."

LATER THAT AFTERNOON, I lay on my stomach, anxiety coursing through my veins. Sex was meant to be an act of love, desire, trust and commitment.

This felt like a sacrificial ritual.

"Relax," he cooed.

But as much as I tried to relax, and as much lubricant as he used, my body refused. I tensed with immediate discomfort on his first unsuccessful attempt at entry, and with his next attempt my discomfort became excruciating.

"Stop – please, I can't do this," I pleaded.

Shane was so casual, so calm as he responded, "Come on, babe. It's not that bad."

But it was.

With every thrusting motion I felt my insides ripping as he forced something to fit where it didn't. Pain paralyzed my body as my narrow cavity tried to accommodate him.

"God, you are so tight," he marveled, and my heart sank at the enjoyment in his voice.

"Stop… Stop doing this," I whimpered.

He did not stop.

"You *owe* me this, Emily."

The words were as cruel as the actions that followed. He pounded into me as I wept, and even as my cries became louder, he continued.

I gripped the floral bedspread underneath me and closed my eyes, trying to disassociate from the relentless throbbing. I concentrated hard on the bedspread. Shane purchased it from the mall because it was on sale, and I had poked fun at him for buying something so girly. It was ugly. I hated the red and orange colors. I pressed my forehead into it, feeling the wetness of the tears that had fallen from my eyes. I sank my teeth into my thumb.

It will be over soon. He will love you more for this. He will forgive you. Everything will go back to the way it was yesterday. God, I hate this ugly bedspread.

chapter twenty

It felt like Shane had won a battle I didn't know we were fighting. Whatever victory was his, the loss was mine. I mourned that loss deeply but couldn't seem to make sense of it.

I returned to Los Angeles feeling incomplete – as if some part of myself remained in Washington with him, and the part that returned with me was not my own.

I agreed to do something I didn't end up liking. That didn't make him a villain. I made the wrong choice, let myself down, and there was no one to be angry with other than me. And in return, he forgave me for my transgressions. He loved me again.

I ached to confide in someone, but what would I say? "*I agreed to have sex with my husband, and I didn't like it. Now I'm upset and want it to be someone else's fault.*" It seemed foolish when spoken aloud. The words didn't add up to the feeling inside of me. "*Overdramatic. Attention seeking. Playing the victim.*" That's what they'd say.

I told myself to stop making a big deal out of it. The painful part was over, so why couldn't I stop thinking about it? Was it because Shane didn't stop when I asked him to? Was it because I hadn't tried hard enough to stop him? Was I angry with him for putting me in that situation or was I angry with myself for agreeing to it?

I hopped in the shower to distract myself. After what felt like an eternity of letting hot water pour over me to cleanse every inch of my body, I stepped out and wrapped myself in a towel.

Checking my phone, I noticed a text from Shane.

Shane: *I have a surprise for you. Can you hop on Skype?*

Feeling intrigued, I pulled a shirt over my head and grabbed a pair of sweatpants. I wrapped my wet hair in a towel and opened my laptop to connect to Skype.

"You are not going to believe what I did," Shane said as our video call connected, nervous laughter following.

"What?"

A huge grin spread across his face. "Are you ready?"

"I… think so?" I felt anxious, knowing Shane could be impulsive, but excited for the reveal.

To my surprise, Shane removed his shirt. Immediately, I saw it. On the left side of his chest was a fresh tattoo of a red heart with my name written across it.

I gasped. "Is that real?"

He chuckled. "Do you like it?"

"You got my name tattooed on your body?!"

"Right over my heart!"

"What… when?"

"Right after I dropped you off at the airport." He laughed and repeated, "Do you like it?"

"That's crazy…" Speechless, I stared at the tattoo. It took up his entire left pec. *Emily*, in bold, black script, filled the space from his chest cavity to his armpit.

"What's crazy about it?"

"What if you… change your mind? That's… permanent."

His face contorted, as if what I said was ridiculous. "Emily, seriously? So is our marriage. You're my wife. Forever. You showed me how much you love me this weekend, and I wanted to prove to you how much I love you, too. I want you to feel reassured."

He smiled a huge, cheeky grin. Any anger or violence he had shown this past weekend was annihilated. He looked at me now, his eyes swimming with love and happiness.

Despite my shock, it really was a sweet gesture. It was the most permanent gesture of love he could come up with. How could he leave me for another girl with my name written across his heart?

I looked at my sweet, impulsive husband with adoration. My hurt from the past few days began to melt away. "I love it," I said, meaning it.

"Yeah?"

"I do. I love it, and I love you. Thank you for making me feel special."

I SPENT THE next five months planning our wedding reception. Due to military obligations Shane was unable to attend most appointments with me, like checking out the venue in California and visiting with the planner. Gina, my maid of honor, came with me instead. We went cake tasting together, picked out floral arrangements, and she watched me try on wedding dresses until I found my perfect match.

I stood before Gina in a beautiful, strapless white gown adorned with floral details that flowed from my waist to the floor. It was stunning. "I think this is the one." I smiled.

She grinned. "It is so beautiful, Emily." She circled around me, taking in every detail of the dress. "I can't believe you're getting married so young." She shook her head as she corrected herself. "I mean, sorry, you ARE married."

"Yeah," I laughed. I had turned 20 just a few months before Shane and I eloped, and I was the first of my friends to be married. "But Shane and I have been together for four years, so it doesn't feel like it's too soon, you know?"

She shrugged. "I guess. I just want you to be happy." She placed a hand on my arm. "I mean that."

I nodded. "Thank you. Your support means the world to me."

I looked at my reflection and felt a tug in my heart as I noted the empty room around us. I should've been surrounded by friends helping me say yes to the dress.

I faced Gina. "I wish Nikki were here."

Gina nodded. "Have you heard from her?"

"No. I don't even know if I should send her a wedding invite."

"Do you want her there?"

I pondered for a moment. "Of course, she's one of my closest friends. Or at least, she was…"

"She *is*," Gina countered. She paced across the dressing floor and took a seat on the couch. "I'm sure she will show up for you if you ask her to."

I looked away from Gina and back to the mirror, speaking to my reflection. "I don't know. I never thought she'd just… stop being my friend over this."

Gina sighed. "I think it's hard for her since she has seen you very hurt over the past few years. That was hard for all of us. Nobody wants to see you hurt, and that's all she knows of Shane – the hurt."

"Yeah." I could feel tears forming in my eyes, so I distracted myself with one of the intricate lace details on the dress. This was meant to be a happy moment, not a sad one.

"And just know that if he hurts you again, I'm going to kill him," Gina mockingly threatened.

I laughed, but deep down I felt guilty that I'd never told her about what happened between Shane and me last summer, or what had happened only a month ago. The anger, the bites, the sex… I desperately wanted to confide about all of it, but I couldn't.

I could never tell Gina.

If I told her about any of it, she would hate him. Shane had struck out twice with Gina already – first, when he started seeing someone before I moved to Los Angeles; and second, when he ended our engagement to date another girl. He was on thin ice, and another strike would mean he was out.

I couldn't do any of this without Gina's support, because her support was all I had.

"You won't need to," I assured. "He promised to be better."

chapter twenty-one

I felt everyone's eyes on me as I walked down the aisle at our wedding ceremony four months later. Nearly a hundred people showed up to celebrate our union and I finally felt like I wasn't alone in my decision to marry Shane.

As we spoke our vows in front of the crowd, I felt validated by the response. Happy tears, laughter, applause. My husband held my hands and my gaze, his adoring eyes beaming into mine as he was given permission to kiss his bride. He pulled me in for a kiss, dipping me and prompting cheers from our family and friends.

We parted lips and faced the rows of people. I surveyed their smiling faces. My mom, in the front row, grinned tearfully – happy to witness our ceremony after being robbed of the elopement. Even my father clapped his hands. I scanned the crowd and found Jack, Nate… and Nikki smiling back at me. My heart brimmed with joy.

A month prior, I had finally reached out to Nikki. I apologized for getting upset with her so many months ago. I told her I understood her doubts and hesitations with Shane, but that it would mean the world to me if she attended our wedding. And there she was. She should have been standing with me at the altar in a bridesmaid dress, but things had become so awkward between us. I was simply grateful to have her there.

Shane and I marched hand-in-hand down the aisle, waving at our loved ones as we made our way to the private space at the back of the venue. Once we walked through the doors, he spun me toward him and gripped me tightly in his arms.

"We did it." He smiled. "Again."

I kissed him, my heart bursting with adrenaline. His hands held my face as he kissed me in return, his warmth blanketing my body.

"I love you." He pressed his forehead to mine.

"I love you, too," I replied.

We smiled for photos and made our grand entrance to the reception hall shortly after. Again, the crowd erupted in joyful applause. We mingled briefly with guests as food came out to the tables, then made our way to our seats. Stunning arrangements of yellow and pink roses spread across the tables, the largest and most intricate of them all lining our head table.

I took a minute to scarf down a few bites of the food I had selected – an herbed chicken breast with vegetables and mashed potatoes – before I heard the clinking of a champagne flute and Gina began her maid of honor speech. The room filled with laughter and tears as she recounted our nearly 20 years of friendship leading to this moment.

"We've been through it all together, from playground adventures to heartbreaks, and it fills my heart with immense joy to witness this day." She neared the end of her speech. "We know that Emily and Shane have faced their fair share of struggles, but it's in those moments of testing that their love truly shined. Their bond has weathered storms, and they have emerged stronger than ever. As you embark on this new chapter together, may your love continue to conquer any obstacle that comes your way. Cheers to the bride and groom!"

We held up our glasses, took a sip of champagne, and I mouthed the words "*I love you*" to Gina as she finished. She hugged me, then Shane, and I beamed at the friendship that was healing between them.

Shane's best man Cody, his closest friend for more than a decade, gave his speech next, recounting the relationships Shane had been through before landing where he was today – and how our connection was undeniable from the first time he heard Shane talk about me.

"Emily, you have brought out the very best in Shane," he concluded. "Your love and unwavering support have shown him the depth of what a relationship can truly be. Let's raise our glasses to Shane and Emily. Cheers!"

I could've sworn I noted the twinkling of tears in Shane's eyes as he stood up to hug his best man. The room erupted in cheers as we all raised our glasses, and Shane and I kissed.

I clinked my champagne glass with my knife. "One more thing!"

I walked over to the DJ, the only person in the room who knew my secret plan. When I approached, he handed me a microphone and I turned around to face Shane and the rest of the wedding party. Shane looked at me curiously while Gina squealed in excitement.

My lips curved into a nervous smile. "This song is for my husband."

The DJ played a karaoke instrumental for "Marry Me" by Train and I serenaded Shane, holding his gaze until I'd finished the song. It was incredibly cheesy, but he drank in every word. His face glowed and he burst into applause at the end. The rest of the room cheered and clapped as I made my way back to the table.

Shane stood up to hug me and whispered, "That was so special. Thank you."

As the dancing and mingling began, Nikki made her way through the crowd to find me. She approached, arms wide for a hug. I returned the hug, squeezing my long-lost friend.

"I'm happy for you," she declared. "And I'm sorry."

"I'm sorry, too. But I'm so happy you're here."

"I'm happy I'm here, too."

Jack butted in. "And I'm happy I'm here, too." He and Nate had followed Nikki through the crowd. I laughed and hugged them both. My closest college friends.

I had graduated early as planned only two months ago. Shane had been present at my graduation, along with my parents. I hadn't seen any of my friends that day or in the days that followed, since I hastily left Los Angeles to live with Shane in Washington. The three of them still had one more year of classes.

"Thank you, guys." My favorite memories of our times over the past few years played in my head, from our crazy frat party nights to our quiet movie nights. "It means everything to me to have you here. I'm really going to miss you next year."

Nikki raised her drink. "Well, then we better make this a fun night!"

The rest of the evening was a blur of excitement and love as we drank, danced and hugged our way through the crowd. It felt so good, for the first time in our relationship, to have an entire room full of people supporting us and celebrating our love. I felt intoxicated by their joy, not wanting the feeling to ever fade away.

AFTER THE RECEPTION ended and we bid farewell to friends and family, Shane and I retired to our hotel room, exhausted from the eventful day. He plopped down on the bed, inviting me to do the same with a pat of his hand on the mattress. I sat beside him and began to unfasten my heels.

"This was the best day of my life," he gushed.

I smiled. It was the best day of my life, too. I knew in my heart that despite our struggles, I was madly, undeniably, head over heels in love with Shane.

He continued, "That was the most fun I've ever had, babe. We should do it again… with each other, obviously." He laughed.

"Three weddings?" I joked. Then, I rubbed my stomach. "I'm starving."

His eyes widened. "I was just thinking the same thing. Do you want to order pizza?"

I positioned myself between his legs, and lowered my body until we were face to face. "There is absolutely nothing in the world I want more right now… than to order pizza," I whispered.

"I can think of one thing I want more than pizza," he purred, wrapping his arms around my waist.

"Wait…" I sat up straight. "Let's order the pizza first."

He laughed. "Smart thinking."

We placed the order then hopped in the shower together. Shane kissed my neck as his hands moved up and down my body. We made love, warm water droplets and steam blanketing our bodies, and I felt more connected than ever riding the high of the wedding energy.

After our shower, we got into cozy shirts and sweatpants just in time for our pizza to arrive. We devoured it while sitting on our hotel bed looking through our wedding cards, taking turns to read them out loud.

When it came time to sleep, we lay our heads on the pillows facing one another. Shane leaned over to give me a kiss. "Goodnight, wife."

I grinned at him. "Goodnight, husband."

He settled into sleep after a few minutes. My heart brimmed with contentment, but something tugged. A line from Nikki's card remained in my mind.

"I think you and Shane will be happy together for a long time," is what she'd written. Not forever, not for the rest of our lives… but *for a long time*. Why did she say it like that? Would we eventually fall apart?

With my natural high wearing off, I couldn't help feeling like a bit of a fake.

Our wedding guests didn't know about the night I'd spent crying at the airport, questioning whether I was in an abusive relationship.

They didn't know about the way Shane had broken off our engagement for another woman right after telling me he was ready to elope.

They didn't know he'd given me an ultimatum to marry him in March or he'd end the relationship.

They saw our love, our smiles, our happiness – and they wished us a lifetime of it.

Except for Nikki, who wished us *a long time*.

And I lay awake thinking about it as Shane snored beside me.

part two

chapter twenty-two

Six months later, we were living a different life. Shane received military orders to Germany the summer we got married, and we packed up our lives and moved just one month after our wedding reception. We settled into our first apartment together on the military base in Heidelberg, filled it with furniture from online marketplaces, and decorated the walls with photos from our wedding.

Two weeks into living in Germany, I realized I needed a best friend. Shane worked 12-hour shifts, and the 9-hour time difference to California made phone calls with Gina inconvenient, especially with her being in her senior year of college. When I saw an online ad for a puppy named Sadie whose family couldn't care for her anymore, I knew I'd found my new best friend.

As one of our first family adventures in our new hometown, Shane and I took Sadie to explore the Heidelberg *Altstadt*, or old town. I swooned as we walked down cobblestone streets lined with bookstores, casual cafes, restaurants and buildings dating back to the 16th century. Above us, the breathtaking ruins of the Heidelberg Castle perched atop a hill overlooking the streets. Unlike many German cities and towns, Heidelberg was spared from bombing during World War II, creating a setting that felt like stepping back in time, or directly into a fairytale.

"This is incredible," I gushed to Shane.

He reached for my left hand, my right occupied by Sadie's leash. "I'm excited to be here with you," he said. I squeezed his hand in return.

We stepped into a dog-friendly cafe to order something to eat. Mouthwatering baguettes with various ingredients filled the windowed shelves of the counter. I scanned the display of item names and descriptions in German. Shane and I had practiced a few phrases – mainly "hello," "goodbye," "please" and "thank you" – but the food names were as foreign as could be.

"*Bitte*," the cashier prompted us for our order. Flustered, I pointed at the one that said *Tomate-Mozzarella* – the only one I could understand. The bewildered look on my face must've conveyed that I couldn't speak German, so she asked in English, "One?"

"Two, please," Shane responded.

She plated our baguettes and handed them to us, pointing to the total on her register.

Shane pulled out his euros to pay and said to her, "Don-key *schön*."

I stifled a laugh. *Danke schön* – meaning "thank you" – was what he intended to say.

We took seats at a table in the cafe's outdoor seating area, Sadie by our feet.

"Don-kah," I corrected Shane, sounding the word out phonetically.

"*Ach du scheiße…*" he cursed in German, evoking laughter from both of us.

"You seem to have no trouble remembering that one!" I joked. I drank in the cheerfulness of his smile before he took his first bite of the sandwich. My husband. My partner in this new life.

I studied the architecture lining the street and watched the bustling crowds of people walk along the cobblestone. I listened to the cafe-goers carrying out conversations in German around us.

I could be happy here, I thought.

Sure, there were things that tugged at my heart. I hadn't spoken to Nikki, Nate or Jack since the wedding, and I sometimes thought about how much fun they were having without me at UCLA. I wasn't heading into grad school to pursue a master's degree like my friends would following their final year of undergrad. I was unemployed, and my lack of fluency in the German language would limit my job options to whatever was available on the military base. And I was so far away from home.

But these buildings? These streets? The ability to travel through Europe and see places I'd only ever dreamed of with my husband and dog by my side? *This* I could get used to.

I could be happy here.

I smiled before taking a bite of my own sandwich.

WE SPENT THE following weeks exploring our new surroundings together. We took Sadie for walks through the fields near our house, boarded a day cruise down the Neckar River, and hiked to castle ruins in the nearby town of Neckarsteinach. We tried new foods, like *Bratwurst, Currywurst, Brötchen* and *Schnitzel*; and new drinks, like *Hefeweizen* and *Pilsner* beers.

As fall transitioned to winter, we experienced our first German Christmas market together. Walking into the Heidelberg *Altstadt* following an afternoon snowfall, a symphony of sights and smells greeted us. The old town looked as if Christmas had thrown up all over it in the best way possible.

Wooden stalls lined the cobblestone streets decked in holiday garland and lights. Local vendors sold steaming hot mugs of *Glühwein*, hand-carved ornaments, intricate arts and crafts, and a variety of souvenirs for us to keep for our own memories or send back home to family and friends. It was the most festive sight I'd ever seen, and my heart brimmed with excitement taking it all in.

Shane laced his fingers into mine. "Should we get something to eat?"

I nodded. But where to begin? A stall beside us served a heaping hot platter of *Bratwurst*, *Käsekrainer*, *Frikadellen* and *Knoblauch-Champignons* – varieties of sausages and meats, and sauteed mushrooms in a creamy garlic sauce. The enticing smell of roasted chestnuts wafted through the air. I wanted to sample everything.

Shane settled on *Bratwurst* served in a bread roll. He squirted mustard onto his sausage while I meandered a couple stalls over to where a line of people waited for *Dampfnudel*. Completely unfamiliar but noting the item's popularity, my curiosity piqued. I ordered one and received what appeared to be a steamed dumpling with a ramekin of white sauce.

I inhaled the sweet scent as I took a bite of the soft ball of dough. Warm deliciousness filled my mouth, salty and sweet at the same time. I dipped a piece of the dumpling into the white sauce and placed it in my mouth. Vanilla custard. I savored the sweet and salty contrast, my tastebuds begging for more.

"What is it?" Shane joined me at the wooden table where I stood.

"It's the best thing I've ever tasted in my life."

"Let me try!" He reached for a piece of the dough, plunging it into the vanilla custard and dropping it into his mouth. His lips closed around the bite and his eyes widened with delight as he chewed. "Wow, you weren't kidding." He reached for another piece.

"Get your own," I laughed, batting his hand.

He looked over his shoulder at the stand. "How do I say it?"

I shrugged. "Domf-noodle?" His eyes bulged. I laughed. "Just say, '*Eine, bitte.*'"

"Got it." He hurried to the stall and placed his order for "one, please" and returned to our table with another warm dumpling and vanilla sauce.

"Now, we need a drink," I suggested, wiping my lips with a napkin as we finished indulging in our delightful treat. "Want to try some *Glühwein*?"

His shoulders shrugged as he nodded in agreement, and we strolled over to the stand where a woman stirred a large pot of mulled wine, cinnamon sticks swirling with the deep red liquid.

"Eine... Glühwein... bitte." I sounded out each word with false confidence. She nodded and began to ladle *Glühwein* into a ceramic mug. Shane raised his eyebrows at me in approval. I raised mine in return.

The woman presented the mug to me and explained in English, "You return the mug for two euros back, or you keep it."

I gleamed as I handed my euros to her. "Keep it? *Danke schön*!"

I studied the mug's decoration depicting the setting of the Heidelberg Christmas Market, with artsy wooden stalls painted along cobblestone streets below the majestic castle ruins on the mountain. *Heidelberger Weihnachtsmarkt 2011*, it read. A beautiful keepsake item –definitely worth the €2 deposit.

I sipped the hot *Glühwein* cautiously, careful not to burn my mouth. It was perfect. The warmth traveled down my throat and into my belly. "Mm, this is so good." I offered the mug to Shane.

Shane sipped delicately. His face contorted but he nodded politely.

I laughed. "You don't like it?"

"I'm not a big fan of wine," he admitted. "But it's interesting. You should enjoy it." He handed the mug back to me and I happily accepted, the hot vessel spreading comfort through my cold fingertips and turning them warm.

Staring up at the castle ruins above us, I sighed. I couldn't imagine a more perfect place to be. This was a dream. I glanced at Shane, who also admired the castle. I slipped my hand into his, sharing the warmth of my fingers with his cold palms.

"What are you thinking about, babe?"

He smiled, a chuckle escaping his mouth. "I'm thinking…" he wrapped his arms around me, pulling me into his chest, "… about how badly I want…" he brushed his lips across my forehead and down my earlobe, where he whispered, "… another domp-noodle."

I erupted into laughter.

chapter twenty-three

Through fall, winter and the holidays, I painted an idyllic picture of our honeymoon life in Europe on my Instagram. And in most ways, it was a honeymoon life. I married my best friend – the man with my name tattooed across his chest. We were in a bubble, far away from the opinions of those betting against us.

But in some ways, it wasn't. Our arguments returned and increased in frequency. No matter what I did, it always seemed like there was a reason for Shane to be mad. I felt like I was walking on eggshells, tiptoeing through a minefield of unpredictable moods.

We lived in a stairwell apartment with thin walls and floors, and I was mortified by the thought of our neighbors listening to us fight. Anytime Shane raised his voice, I did whatever I could to deescalate the situation. Calming him down became priority one, while communicating my own needs took second place.

I started working part-time at a restaurant and bar down the street from our apartment to keep busy and earn a little spending money. We made friends with a few other married couples who lived in military housing and tried to build a community for ourselves.

Of all the couples we'd met, we grew closest with Jen and Tom. Jen was an avid traveler, and I could listen for hours as she told me about her adventures across Europe. She and I were close in age, and neither of us had made the move into motherhood yet. Being childfree as a military spouse made it hard to connect with the community, since most of the socials were geared toward families – playdates at the park or Mommy & Me at the base gym. Jen and I would meet for coffee, go grocery shopping together, try bottles of local wine, and attempt to cook German food. These simple activities made me feel tethered to someone so far from home.

I joined Jen and Tom for trivia night at the bar one night after my day shift ended. Shane had left for work by the time I got off, so I changed out of my uniform and joined my friends on the other side of the bar without going home first. Abiding by the no-phones rule, my friends and I tucked our phones away for the duration of trivia, relying on our existing knowledge to answer the questions. When the game ended, I pulled out my phone to check for missed notifications.

A Facebook message request from a name I didn't recognize greeted me on my lock screen. I tapped to open it, and as I read the contents, the world around me blurred.

Message request from Lauren: *Hey, I know you don't know me, but your husband has been messaging me asking me for naked pictures. I just thought you should know.*

Attached to her message was a screenshot of a conversation that had taken place earlier that day during my shift.

Shane: *You are so beautiful, Lauren*
Lauren: *Thank you!*
Shane: *I'd love to see more pictures of you*
Lauren: *Aren't you married?*

Shane: *Just looking for fun… I won't tell anyone if you don't*
Shane: *I want to see more of you*
Lauren: *There are plenty of pictures on my page*
Shane: *Do you ever take naked pictures?*
Lauren: *Only for people I'm in a relationship with*
Shane: *I promise I won't share them with anyone else*
Shane: *Come on, please*

Something in my chest cracked. I began to feel sick reading the words from my husband to this stranger. *Who is she?* I clicked her profile – private. I couldn't see anything beyond her profile picture, a face I did not recognize. I knew nothing of this person my husband seemed so intimately connected to. My heavy heart fell into my gut as I began to take frantic breaths.

Jen noted my change in behavior. "Emily? You alright?"

I faced her, swallowing hard. Bringing others into my drama with Shane was something I had sworn to avoid, but what else could I do? Shock, pain and fury coursed through me. I tilted my phone screen to show Jen the message.

She studied my phone, tapping open the screenshot from Lauren. "Oh my god," she breathed as she looked back up at me. "Who is this?"

I shook my head. "I have no idea."

Tom leaned over to see what was going on. "What's up?"

"None of your business," Jen snapped, and I appreciated her for that. It was the just the kind of thing Gina would have said, and I was grateful to have a girlfriend by my side for this. Tom shrugged it off and returned to his beer.

"What do we need to do?" she asked, and I noted pity in her expression.

"I need to go home," I whimpered, wiping tears from my cheeks. "I don't want to cry here."

"Let me take you." She stood up, gathering her phone and purse. "I'll be back," she said to Tom. He nodded.

Jen drove me to my apartment as I cried in the passenger seat. We lingered in the parking lot, Jen sitting silently while I collected myself. She passed me a tissue from her purse and stepped out of the car. She walked to the trunk, popped it, and returned with a bottle of wine we'd been saving for our next cooking date.

"I think you need this more than I do right now," she said with a soft smile. "Do you want me to stay with you?"

I attempted to return the smile but failed. "No. Thank you."

"What are you going to do?"

Drive to his work, I thought. "I don't know yet. Attempt to sleep and address it tomorrow," I lied.

"Promise me you're not going to drive to his work." *Damn.*

"Promise," I lied again.

But I needed to see Shane. I needed to see the look on his face when he explained to me that somehow, someway this was all a misunderstanding. There was an explanation, an alternate truth – *something* – that would stop this pain before it pierced me further.

I thanked Jen as I stepped out of her car, and after she drove away I got into my own.

Shane couldn't use his cell phone in the secure facility where he worked, so I called the phone number for the front desk. When an unfamiliar voice on the other end answered I asked, "Is Shane Foster there? This is his wife… it's urgent."

A minute later Shane was on the phone. "Emily? Are you okay?" he asked, panicked.

"No," I choked through my tears.

"What's wrong, babe?!"

"Why are you messaging girls on Facebook trying to get nude

pictures of them?" The words came out fiercely demanding, even though they weakened me as I spoke.

Excruciating silence followed by a painful exhale. "Emily... Fuck. I need to talk to you about this but we're on a monitored connection right now. Can you come here?"

"I'm on my way." I hung up.

Anguish consumed me the same way it had when he told me he was seeing someone else the year before. I felt worthless. Stupid. Destroyed. I wasn't ready for our marriage to be over. How humiliating would it be for everyone to find out he couldn't remain faithful to me for even one year of marriage? How could I face that type of judgment from my friends?

Thirty minutes later, I arrived at Shane's facility and stepped out of my car. I walked across the dark parking lot, empty except for the night shift workers' vehicles. A figure paced back and forth at the illuminated entrance – Shane, my eyes confirmed. Noting my presence, he walked quickly toward me. As our footsteps met, I said nothing.

He wore a tight-lipped grimace, eyes full of sadness. "There's a room we can speak privately in."

He began to lead the way into the facility. Down a short hallway to the right, we entered an office where he closed the door behind us. His voice was shaky as he began to speak. "I'm so sorry. You were at work and I had a weak moment –"

"Who is she?" I interrupted.

"Someone I barely knew in Washington." He shook his head. "She means *nothing* to me."

"Then why did you do it?"

He threw his arms up in the air. "I don't know, Em. I had a stupid, awful lapse in judgment. I didn't mean for this to happen. I promise you with all my heart it meant *nothing* to me."

My heart sank deeper into my stomach with every word. I'd clung to hope that somehow he would explain this as something other than the cruelty it was. But a confession? This was real. This would change the course of our marriage. We'd rebuilt our relationship once before, but this… this was a black stain on my white wedding gown.

I shook my head. "I can't do this." Shane reached for me, but I didn't want to feel his touch on my skin. I avoided him as I moved to the other side of the room. "I can't go through this again," I continued, hands shaking. "Why are you doing this to me?!"

I stared at him at a loss for words. His eyes were sunken, the corners of his mouth pulled down. He sat in the desk chair behind him and dropped his face into his hands. When he looked at me moments later, his cheeks shone with wet tears. "I fucked up. I fucked up so bad and I'm so sorry," he choked.

"It's not enough!" I yelled, for once not caring who heard me. Hurt and anger surged beneath my skin. The apologies, the excuses – none of it was enough. My sobs made the sound of my yelling pathetic, but I continued. "We've been married for less than a year and you can't even *pretend* to stay faithful to me!"

"I am faithful to you, Emily." He stood and moved across the floor toward me. "Not once in the last year have I done *anything* to jeopardize that. I promise you. This was *one* stupid mistake and a meaningless online chat –"

"You disrespected me, you lied to me… and we're *married*, Shane!" The word pierced me as it came out. The man I *married* wasn't supposed to do this to me.

He reached for my arm. "Please, let me fix this. Don't say this is over. Give me a chance to come home and talk to you tomorrow."

"Where the fuck else am I going to go?!" I shouted, my arms outstretched. Helplessness enveloped me. I was thousands of miles from the comfort of home, in a foreign land with no source of familiarity other than Shane – my best friend, my husband, my family, my provider, my lifeline. An ominous feeling swallowed me and I realized what it was: powerlessness. There was nowhere for me to go, and he knew that.

It was almost midnight and my body ached with exhaustion. Shane tried a second time to hug me. Too ridden with defeat to push him away, I allowed it.

His arms wrapped around my body. Warmth collided with icy fury atop my skin. I closed my eyes. For a moment, I remembered the warmth. I remembered the safety and comfort his embrace had once held.

"I'm so sorry," he repeated.

Opening my eyes again, I shook my head and pulled free of him. Then, I walked out of the office and into the hallway toward the exit.

"Emily," he pleaded, following me.

I faced him, one hand up. "No."

He did not follow me farther as I reached my car and got in.

I drove home, tears streaming, my mind empty. I made it all the way home before realizing I had been sitting in silence the entire drive. I entered our apartment and crawled into bed with Sadie, who rested her head on my leg and looked at me lovingly.

"What are we going to do, Sadie?"

She studied my sadness with curiosity and concern and wagged her tail in response. I reached out to hug her, a tear falling into her fur.

"What am I going to do?" I repeated, this time to myself.

Sadie moved closer, curling up in a ball against my side, and placed her head on my chest. I surrendered to her comforting embrace and fell asleep as texts from Shane silently filled my lock screen.

Shane: *It killed me to see you so hurt.*

Shane: *I never want to see you hurt again. I'm so sorry.*

Shane: *I hate myself for what I've done to you.*
Shane: *I promise it meant nothing.*
Shane: *You are the only person in the entire world that matters to me.*
Shane: *I love you so much.*

chapter twenty-four

I awoke the following morning before Shane arrived home from work. I checked my phone – 6:30 a.m. He would be home within the next 30 minutes. I grudgingly scrolled through the texts he had sent throughout the night and left them unanswered as I got up to let Sadie outside and feed her breakfast. As she gobbled down her food, I returned to bed.

Heart-wrenching pain consumed me as those messages came rushing back into my mind. How could I be so stupid? I had wrongfully assumed infidelity was only a risk when we were in a long-distance relationship. I never thought it would strike so close, taking place within the walls of our own home while I was only blocks away.

What was I supposed to do? If we moved forward together, how would I be able to focus on anything with this lurking threat in the back of my mind? How could I go back to work, realizing the risk of leaving Shane at home unattended? How could I trust him when he went to work behind closed doors with female coworkers?

And the question that weighed heaviest on me, that echoed through my soul – *why am I not enough?* It crushed me. I couldn't bring myself to tell my friends or family back home. Embarrassment engulfed me when I envisioned them saying, *"We warned you this would happen."*

The weight of it all was too much for me to carry.

Tears had begun to form in my eyes again when I heard the front door unlocking. Sadie, who had rejoined me in bed, hopped out and ran down the hallway to greet her dad. I remained glued to the bed.

His footsteps sounded down the hall until he appeared at the bedroom door frame. Only my eyes greeted him, the rest of my body frozen in place.

He crawled into bed. I turned onto my side, facing away from him. He snaked an arm around my waist and slid into the space behind me. I wanted to hate the feeling of his touch. I wanted to reject it. But somehow it brought comfort to the parts of me that were aching deep inside.

"Emily, I need you to know how sorry I am," he spoke softly as he nestled his face into the base of my neck. "Never in a million years did I want you to hurt like this again. I have been so horribly selfish."

"How many other girls have you talked to like that?"

"Zero."

I wanted to believe it. I ached to forget this mistake. "How am I supposed to know if you're telling the truth?"

"I'm not interested in talking to other girls." I felt the warmth of his breath on my skin. "You are the love of my life. No other girl means anything to me."

"Then why did you do it?"

His hand caressed my stomach, his finger tracing a line across my lower abdomen to my hip. "I know this isn't an excuse, but we had that fight over my uniform… and I was mad… and I guess this was my stupid way of acting out."

My mind flashed back to the morning before. We'd argued because I'd accidentally washed his uniform with a pen in the pocket, causing black ink to leave blotches all over the sleeves. As I tried with stain remover to rectify it, I blamed him, saying it was his fault for not checking his pockets before throwing his uniform into the hamper.

It was a trivial thing to argue over, but he'd gotten so heated over the situation and my own defensiveness fueled the flame. I recalled retorting that since Shane did nothing else around the house, he could at least do his own laundry; and I'd left the stained uniform atop the washer for him to deal with as I went to work.

"Us having a fight is not an excuse for you to be unfaithful to me," I countered, but a sting of regret pierced me as I grimaced at the memory. My mistake. My attitude. My unwillingness to help. Maybe I was the one who overreacted by not acknowledging the stressful situation I'd put him in only hours before he needed to don the uniform for work.

"I know that," he agreed. "I know. I will never do something so stupid again. I don't care about the uniform, Em. I don't care about anything but you. Please, give me another chance."

I weighed my options as Shane's lips traced the back of my neck – face the humiliation of my marriage ending in less than a year, and deal with the stress of trying to move me and Sadie and all my belongings back home; or stay and give love another chance.

His lips moved up my neck to my earlobe, carrying love and regret in their path. The gentle caress sent a shudder down my spine. I ached to feel his forgiveness. I longed to understand his sorrow. I was hurt, and he was the person who hurt me. But he was also the source of my comfort.

He was the cause and the cure for my pain.

His hand gripped my hip and pulled it closer to him, my backside meeting the erection between his legs.

Two options. Leave… or stay.

And because I so desperately needed that cure, I silently chose the latter and gave myself to my husband.

chapter twenty-five

In the weeks that followed, Shane and I argued about what I needed to feel secure in our marriage again. He had diminished my trust, and every day I felt the added stress of needing to know where he was, what he was doing and who he was talking to. The same desperation I felt in his phone calls in college seeped into my own voice.

I wanted access to his Facebook, which he wasn't willing to provide. And although he repeatedly told me no, I continued to demand it.

"It's an invasion of privacy and I don't want to be that type of couple." He placed his fork down at the dining table where we ate.

I set mine down as well. "We are that type of couple… because of your actions."

He shook his head, irritation forming in the lines between his brows. "I've told you already, I will never make that mistake again. You need to trust me if this is going to work."

But I insisted, "I can't trust you unless I can see what's going on."

He rolled his eyes. "Trying to keep tabs on all my conversations is crazy. Listen to yourself."

"It's not crazy when you've given me a valid reason to feel this way!"

Darkness clouded his eyes. His next words came out slowly but sharply, carefully spaced so that I'd feel the impact of each one. "It is this *exact* type of behavior that makes me want to be unfaithful to you."

I stopped breathing.

"I can't stand you when you act this way," he continued. "You accuse me of cheating on you all day, every day… so I might as well just do it, right? If I'm going to be accused either way, I might as well just fucking do it, right?!" His palm hit the table.

I flinched at the sound. Sadie retreated from her place beside the dining table and hopped on the couch.

"Don't you get it? Your behavior is the problem, Emily!" He pointed a finger across the table in my face. "There will be no problems if you stop acting like this. Do you understand?"

My heart pounded as feelings of hurt stirred in my gut. I recalled the words Shane spoke to me on the brink of our engagement crumbling: "*I can't keep doing this with you if it doesn't get better.*"

My lip quivered. *I'm doing it again*, I thought. I had promised to be better and here I was, sabotaging us – and subsequently my own happiness – because I couldn't give him the trust he asked for. My insistent nagging, my paranoid behavior – *this* was what would drive him away from me.

My chest ached, reliving the sharp stab of Shane's messages to Lauren; recalling the pain of him leaving me for Christine; remembering the hurt of him blindsiding me with Marissa so many years ago. I couldn't go through it again. He couldn't leave me for someone else.

I wouldn't survive it again.

I stopped arguing.

I nodded to Shane solemnly as I picked up my fork and resumed my meal, although I no longer felt hungry. He resumed eating as well. As we finished our meal in silence, I calculated my next steps. I would stop asking for access to his Facebook. I would stop bringing up the incident with Lauren. I would show Shane that I could stop giving him reasons to act out. I could – and I would – be better.

And in return, he would love me better for it.

A FEW WEEKS later, Shane got sent to work in another part of Germany for a month. We talked on the phone every day, but I couldn't help but feel uneasy about the distance between us. I had no way to keep tabs on his whereabouts or who he was talking to while he was away.

After two weeks, Shane asked if I wanted to come stay with him for a weekend. This felt like a chance to close the growing space between us, so I quickly texted a couple of my coworkers, got my weekend bartending shifts covered, packed an overnight bag and loaded Sadie into the car.

We drove three hours to Grafenwöhr where Shane was temporarily assigned for training and checked into a pet-friendly hotel. Shane waited at the hotel, hopping out of his truck as soon as we pulled into the parking lot. He ran toward us and greeted me with a big hug, lifting my feet from the ground and burying his face in my neck. After placing me back on the ground, he tilted my chin and kissed me. He traced the lines of my lips with his and sighed.

"Always sweeping me off my feet," I said with a giggle.

"I missed you so much," he gushed.

"We missed you, too," I replied, my body warming to his familiar touch. Sadie stood on her hind legs, excitedly greeting him with a joyful bark.

That afternoon, the three of us bundled up and went for a long walk through the forest. I loved the hush that settled over me as I walked along the trails in Germany, and Shane had researched ahead of time to find the perfect route for my first visit to this part of the country. The snow crunched under our boots and we linked our gloved hands together. With Sadie walking ahead of us on her leash, Shane asked me about my drive out to see him. He asked about work and how things were going at home, what movies I'd been watching, and if I was making time to get to the gym. These were all topics we'd covered during our talks on the phone, but I was happy to repeat myself and hear his interest in my life. Tall trees encircled us, and I felt like we were the only people on earth.

We spent the rest of my visit watching TV shows and snuggling through the cold and snowy weekend. It was good to be reunited. With him gone, I often traveled to the worst-case scenarios. My mind conjured horrible things – Shane meeting other girls, bringing them to his room, and giving them parts of him that were reserved for me. But here in his arms again, those thoughts quieted. Feeling his love and how much he missed me was the validation I needed that I was the only person he cherished, and I was silly for thinking otherwise.

On our final night together, we lay beside each other in the hotel bed binge watching old episodes of *The Office*, half-listening, half-talking between funny moments.

"Sometimes I still can't believe it." Shane eyed me, smirking.

"Believe what?" I stroked Sadie's head, who had positioned herself between us.

He tucked a strand of my hair behind my ear and ran his finger across my cheek to my lips. "I just can't believe how far we've come."

I absorbed the soothing touch of his finger on my lips. He was right. I was only 16 years old the night Gina and I went over to his house for a movie, and my entire world changed. "I know. Here we are. Five years later."

"Forever to go."

"We'll see," I joked, then playfully bit his finger.

"I really do love you more than you'll ever know, babe," he said.

"I love you too. I can't imagine this life with anyone else." And I meant it. We had issues to work out, but this was love. I knew it. I felt it in the way my heart rose to meet him and my stomach fluttered in his presence.

"I can't either." He kissed my forehead and scratched Sadie behind the ear. "My girls! I love you both. Thank you for coming to stay with me."

SHANE CAME HOME two weeks later, just in time for our first wedding anniversary. He made dinner reservations at the Fernmeldeturm Mannheim, a tower vaguely resembling the Space Needle in Seattle where he had proposed, and I was excited to have a reason to get dressed up with him. As I stood in the mirror putting the finishing touches on my makeup, he leaned in and adjusted his tie – the same pink one he'd worn at our wedding. He planted a kiss on my forehead. "Beautiful."

Just like the Space Needle, the Fernmeldeturm had a rotating restaurant with panoramic views of the surrounding city. We sat at a table beside the window and watched the sparkling city lights below us. I sighed, taking it all in.

"What's wrong?" Shane asked.

I looked at him. "Not a thing." I smiled. "I love this." I motioned toward the window, entranced by the sight.

"You really love a good view, don't you?" he teased playfully.

"It's not just the view…" I pondered for a moment, unsure how to put words to my feelings. "It's… being in new places. It's the excitement that comes from seeing things I've never seen before. There's something that calls me… to the unknown."

He nodded. "And what about the familiar?"

I met his eyes lovingly. "And something that calls me to the familiar, as well."

Shane raised his rare glass of champagne. "Cheers to our first year of marriage."

I met it with my own. "Cheers. Happy anniversary."

We both sipped.

"Emily… I'm sorry if I made you doubt my love for you this year."

I winced, not wanting the painful memory to spoil the moment.

"You mean the world to me," he continued. "Thank you for staying with me and allowing me another chance to prove that to you."

I studied his face – the soft lines that had formed on either side of his blue eyes from smiling; the smile which contained the smallest gap between his two front teeth. I could paint him in my sleep. My familiar love. I nodded.

We were far from perfect, but he was trying. And I would try as well.

chapter twenty-six

Slowly but surely, my dull days began to shimmer again. Shane and I enjoyed a honeymoon phase following our time apart, his homecoming and our wedding anniversary. Our summer months were filled with fun and adventure. We explored new cities in Germany – like Köln, Rothenburg ob der Tauber, and Berlin – visited lakes and waterparks, barbecued with our friends, and spent warm evenings by bonfires enjoying sunlight until 10 p.m. – one of my favorite parts of the German summertime.

I sometimes wondered if I'd made the right decision sharing Shane's infidelity with Jen. Memories of my friends back home urging me to leave him, never holding back their negative opinions, came to mind. But Jen was quick to forgive, and so was Tom. I didn't blame her for sharing the information with him; I was just grateful to have friends around that I could be honest with.

We all moved forward and jumped into making new memories. Jen got a job at the restaurant where I worked and we spent every Sunday breakfast shift laughing our way through customer drama, kitchen madness and what felt like endless amounts of side work. And because I got to do it all with her, it became my favorite shift of the week. I was really growing to love Jen, but I missed my old friends too.

As I neared the one-year anniversary of moving overseas, Gina made plans to visit. She had graduated from college and wanted to explore Europe before settling into a permanent job. We planned a two-week European adventure to Oktoberfest, Switzerland, Italy, Greece and Croatia. Shane, albeit reluctantly, agreed to stay home with Sadie so Gina and I could enjoy quality girls' time.

On the first day of her visit, we rode the funicular railway to the Heidelberg Castle perched above the *Altstadt*. It wasn't my first time up there, but it took my breath away just the same. The red sandstone ruins dominated the hill. The castle, dating back to the 13th century, had been destroyed in war and rebuilt, only later to burn in a fire caused by lightning. Some parts were restored while others were left in ruin – and every bit of it was fascinating to take in. It was a symbol of ruin and resilience – greatly damaged but still standing after the world had tried repeatedly to destroy it.

We stepped onto the terrace overlooking the Neckar River and the *Alte Brücke*, or old bridge, connecting both sides of the city. The Königstuhl mountain across the river rose to greet us, outlined with expansive green and yellow foliage. In the town below, orange rooftops along cobblestone streets reflected glimmers of sunlight. The 14th-century Heiliggeistkirche, the biggest church in town, loomed above them boasting its Gothic architecture and red brick steeple.

Gina let out a long sigh. "I can't believe this is your life." She motioned around her to the castle and the river below. "This is incredible."

"I think the same thing every time I come up here," I replied. Heidelberg was undoubtedly one of the most beautiful cities I had ever set foot in, and I was lucky enough to call it my home away from home.

I studied the people walking across the *Alte Brücke*, who had become tiny figures from our high vantage point. And standing there with my best friend, admiring the breathtaking surroundings, I noted the heaviness within my heart.

Over the past year, I'd watched on social media as Gina and my other hometown friends continued their college lives. They partied, went to music festivals, gathered during holiday breaks and summer, and celebrated graduations together – and although I had left, from the outside looking in, it looked as if nothing was missing from their lives. They had moved on without me.

Gina and I chatted frequently, but my other friendships fizzled. I barely even spoke to Nikki, save for a few online interactions here and there. I knew the strain of my friendships began before I moved to Germany – because I focused all my time and attention on Shane, only running to them when we were fighting or separated – but with distance, it had increased tenfold. Having Gina here brought forth a strong nostalgia and longing for the connections I once had. How had I become so isolated, allowing Shane to be my only source of love?

She turned to face me, smirking. "How's married life?"

"It's good," I said, pushing conflicting thoughts aside. "How's dating life?"

"Ha!" She rolled her eyes. "College boys will be college boys. You're not missing out."

I laughed, but inside, something faltered. "Sometimes I wish I didn't graduate early."

She turned again to face the view. "But you're here…" She extended her arms to the city below us. "This is a hundred times cooler than LA."

"I know. I wouldn't do it differently… because otherwise Shane and I wouldn't be married, and I wouldn't be here… I just wish I could have had both, somehow." I noticed the sky shifting from a welcoming blue to ominous clouds, and I also shifted from the uncomfortable topic I now regretted bringing up. "Looks like it might rain."

She studied the clouds. "Yeah. Let's head inside."

We explored inside the ruins, rode the funicular back down to the

Altstadt, found my car and made our way back to my apartment to prepare for our early morning departure to Munich.

WE ARRIVED AT Oktoberfest the following morning and it was unlike anything I'd ever seen. Giant beer tents lined the fairgrounds surrounded by amusement rides, food stalls, and blue and white Bavarian flags as far as the eye could see.

We sifted through crowds of people donning traditional *Lederhosen* and *Dirndl* attire, beautiful flower crowns adorning the heads of the women, and Alpine hats covered with souvenir pins atop the heads of the men.

To ensure we found our way into a beer tent without a reservation, Gina and I had arrived at the festival before noon. We took in our surroundings, excitedly wandering the area for a bit before deciding which "tent" to enter – if they could even be called that. The tents were large wooden structures built specifically for the festival, some designed to hold up to 10,000 people at once. They were incredible.

We entered the *Hacker-Festzelt* and our jaws dropped as we marveled at the interior. A larger-than-life mural depicting blue sky, clouds, Munich scenes, and the phrase "*Himmel der Bayern*" greeted us. Among it, thousands of people danced atop fest tables to live music coming from the round center stage. Gina and I looked at each other beaming.

"*Hallo!*" someone shouted from the table to our right. I turned to see a group of German men and women waving and motioning to the empty seats at their table. We graciously accepted their invitation, and within minutes our new friends helped us order liters of beer from the waitress, who somehow managed to carry six giant beer steins in her hand at once.

In between songs and dances, we engaged in conversation in broken English.

"Your boyfriends are here?" one of the men asked.

"I don't have a boyfriend!" Gina exclaimed.

"My husband is at home," I added. "Girls' trip!"

"Husband?" The man eyed me curiously. I nodded. "Why?"

"He has to work."

The man shook his head. "*Nein*, no… why do you have a husband?"

I laughed. The man looked older than Gina and me. I noted no ring on his hand. "I don't know why I have a husband… I just do," I shrugged.

"*Ach so*… it is a bad idea." He shook his head teasingly.

"Having a husband is a bad idea?"

"*Ja*." He raised his beer stein. "This is more better."

"*Prost* to that," Gina laughed and clinked her beer stein to his. My laughter followed.

We spent the entire day drinking liters of beer and dancing atop fest tables. Although I felt guilty admitting it, it was the most fun I'd had all year. I loved Shane with all my heart – but with Gina, I came alive.

There was a part of Shane that was stiff and unyielding, and combined with the fact that he rarely drank alcohol, it could sometimes be hard to loosen him up. We had our own fun together, but it was a different kind of fun.

This was the type of fun I hadn't yet experienced in life, finally turning 21 shortly after arriving in Germany. Of course, I'd partied in college… but now I could visit drinking establishments and enjoy libations without restrictions, or fear that my fake ID would fail me.

Unsurprisingly, neither Gina nor I could remember how we'd made it back to our hotel room when we awoke the following morning. But we knew, based on the flower crowns atop our heads and the empty *Lebkuchen* necklaces around our necks – which had once held giant gingerbread cookies – that we had a successful time at Oktoberfest.

AFTER MUNICH WE made our way to Geneva, Switzerland, where rich, Swiss men doted on us. Gina's uncle, a local, introduced us to his group of friends, who bought us €19 vodka-cranberry cocktails and told us stories about how they could fly us in private planes around the world, ignoring the fact that we were younger than their daughters.

We explored the city on foot and rode a boat across Lake Geneva, admiring the Jet d'Eau – the 460-foot fountain erupting from the water. With clear skies, the Swiss Alps provided a majestic backdrop that could only be compared to a real-life postcard. I swooned, never wanting life to be anything less than what it was in that moment.

We left Switzerland for Italy, where we stayed at a beautiful waterfront property in Bari before boarding a weeklong cruise through the Mediterranean to Greece and Croatia. With each new city we set foot in, I felt my soul awaken more.

We swam in the crystal-clear waters of Corfu, explored the ancient Acropolis in Athens, admired the blue-dome buildings of Oia in Santorini, partied our way through beach bars in Mykonos, and stepped back in time into the walled medieval city of Dubrovnik. It wasn't lost on me that I was living out my dreams, traveling through Europe with my best friend.

As much fun as we were having, our interactions with flirtatious men and copious amounts of alcohol caused guilt and anxiety to weigh heavily on me. A lingering curiosity pestered about what Shane was doing back home. I checked in as often as I could, but since my cell phone plan was limited to Germany I had to rely on places where I had access to Wi-Fi.

Aboard the ship, Wi-Fi was limited to one area and cost €5 for a 10-minute pass. I tried to contact Shane daily, but routinely missed getting a hold of him due to his shifts conflicting with the times I was able to access the Wi-Fi. A few days went by without speaking and Gina could tell I was stressing about the lack of communication.

"Emily, why are you so stressed out about it? I'm sure everything is fine!" Gina sipped her margarita as we lay on lounge chairs beside the pool on our ship.

We had only one stop left in Venice before our cruise ended and we went our separate ways. I felt so torn between wanting the trip to go on forever because of how alive it made me feel; but also longing for the security of being back with Shane.

I took a sip of my own margarita and answered casually, "I know, I just like to check in."

"Enjoy yourself. You're on vacation. He'll be waiting for you when we get back." She downed the last of her drink and pulled her hat down over her face to shield from the sun.

It was easy for her to say this since she didn't know about Shane's recent infidelity. I must have seemed crazy trying to contact him every day of our vacation, but the dark threat of him betraying me again lurked in the back of my mind. If I could check in frequently enough, I could keep myself at the forefront of his thoughts. If he went several days without hearing from me, he might experience another moment of weakness. I couldn't let that happen. This was my way of protecting myself.

I watched the other cruise-goers around us. One couple loosely embraced each other in the pool. Another applied sunscreen to her partner's back while they lounged on poolside chairs. Across the way, a man returned to his partner's table with two drinks in hand, his partner smiling while accepting one. Had any of these people experienced infidelity? Did any of them fight the way Shane and I did behind closed doors?

My stomach felt unsettled as intrusive thoughts poured in. *You're out enjoying drinks with your girlfriend while your husband cheats on you at home. If you were home, this wouldn't be happening.*

I shut my eyes and took a deep breath, pushing the thoughts out of my mind. I had to abandon this fear. I had to enjoy my final two days with Gina… who now snored lightly beside me, enjoying an afternoon nap. And, I figured, maybe that was exactly what I needed too.

WHEN OUR TRIP came to an end, I bid farewell to Gina at the airport in Italy as she flew back to the United States, and I returned to Germany. We hugged for a long time, not wanting to let go and have another year go by without seeing one another.

"Love you, Emily. Don't be a stranger. Come visit home soon."

I nodded. "Love you, too. I'll try. Thank you for visiting. I've really missed you."

"I've missed you too! I'll visit again. Keep having an amazing time out here." And with that, she squeezed me one final time before heading in the direction of her gate.

I fought a tear as I watched my best friend leave. I hadn't quite realized how lonely I'd been for the past year. Shane and Sadie meant everything to me, but I missed having my best friend – my support system.

I headed in the opposite direction toward my gate and my sadness shifted to anticipation as I began to think about what awaited me on the other end of my flight.

When I walked through the door of my apartment that afternoon, my heart brimmed with comfort to see my sweet husband and dog sitting together on the couch.

He stood up to greet me, a wide smile spreading across his face.

I threw my arms around his neck. "I missed you!"

"I missed you, too, babe." He wrapped his arms around my waist and squeezed, planted a kiss on my forehead, then one on my lips. His scent was intoxicating; I breathed him in deeply as the warmth of his body coated my skin.

"Everything go okay here?"

"Yeah, we spent a lot of quality time together; didn't we, Sadie?"

I turned my attention to Sadie who was waiting patiently to cover me in kisses, tail wagging ecstatically. I knelt and pulled her in for a giant hug. She licked my face repeatedly while I laughed.

"Okay, Sadie," Shane laughed. "My turn." He looked at me with desire in his eyes, and I knew exactly what he hungered for as he scooped me up and carried me to the bedroom, my laughter filling the hallway.

chapter twenty-seven

I went back and forth between bliss and anxiety throughout the following days, frequently checking my phone for another stranger telling me about messages my husband sent her while I was away. But the days turned into weeks, the weeks turned into months, and the messages never came. I began to let my guard down.

We sailed through my birthday and the holidays with exquisite trips to Paris and Strasbourg, France, and Prague in the Czech Republic. I was thrilled to have Shane by my side as we adventured through more soul-awakening cities together. And I found, through my adventures, that traveling was my solace. Whether I was missing home, feeling removed from my friends, overwhelmed by loneliness, or insecure in my marriage, all of it faded when I set foot into a new city – like walking into a fresh new chapter, even if only for a weekend. I found comfort in it, and I planned trip after trip to maintain that mental reset.

As the new year began, I left bartending for a full-time role as a marketing assistant on the Army base. It began to feel like things were falling into place as I put my college education to use in a new setting. My new coworkers welcomed me with open arms, and I overflowed with excitement about my new responsibilities and tasks. I felt more confident about everything – my marriage, my career, and my overall happiness.

IN MARCH, SHANE and I celebrated our second anniversary in London. We walked along the River Thames, took pictures of each other in red phone booths and in front of Big Ben, and enjoyed an evening ride on the London Eye – one that required major convincing on my part, promising Shane the views would be worth overcoming his fear of heights.

High above ground overlooking the London skyline, Shane stood behind me and wrapped his arms around my waist, nestling his chin atop my shoulder.

"You know how much I hate being up here," he whispered.

I giggled. "But you love me, right?"

He gave my earlobe a playful nibble which caused me to laugh harder. "I love you too much… so much so, that I put myself in these dangerous situations over and over again for you."

I grinned, pushing my cheek against his. "It's not dangerous; it's beautiful. And you know it's tradition now, right? You proposed at the Space Needle, we celebrated our first anniversary at the Fernmeldeturm, and now we're celebrating our second anniversary atop the London Eye. We're going to have to find somewhere even higher for our third…" I teased.

He groaned, but his hands were gentle as he stroked my lower abdomen. I felt a slight shift in his energy as he said, "Hey, I want to ask you something."

"Yeah?"

"We're going into our third year of marriage. When do you want to start a family?"

An uneasy feeling formed in my gut beneath his touch. We had discussed children before. He wanted them, but at 22 years old I was nowhere near ready. I had told him I wanted to wait until we'd been married for several years and I was at least 25 before we started thinking about it seriously. Truthfully, I wasn't sure the idea of children interested me, but I hoped that as I got older my maternal instincts would kick in.

I spoke gently. "Well, like we said before… I'd like to wait at least a few more years…"

His cheek left mine. "A few *more* years? Why?"

"Because… I'm not ready. I'm only 22."

He scoffed. "We know other people who are the same age and have children. Age doesn't matter."

"I just want to enjoy my life right now. I want to travel, and –"

"And party," he interrupted.

I frowned. "No. But I like to be able to go places and have fun…"

"That's all you've been doing for the past two years." He removed his arms from around my waist. Coldness covered my midsection in the absence of his warmth.

I looked at him, then around us. We shared the pod with one other couple who were staring out the windows on the other side. I was fairly sure they couldn't hear our conversation, but I didn't want to risk the embarrassment if Shane started getting louder. I navigated carefully. "You were okay with waiting until I'm 25, right?"

He sucked his teeth. "I don't see the point in waiting. I'm ready now. And I'm worried you're making me wait, and then once you turn 25 you'll change your mind again and say you want to wait longer. I want a family, Emily. It's important to me."

"I know." I nodded. "But don't you want our families to be closer? I'd like my mom to be closer when I have my first baby."

"So then fly her out," he said, as if it were the obvious solution to the dilemma I posed.

I felt challenged by his stubbornness. "We're only in Germany for another year and half," I reasoned. "Can we spend this next year traveling and having fun, then when we move back to the States we can start planning for a baby? I'll be 24. You'll be 30. That's the perfect age to start a family."

Shane looked away from me and shook his head. "You're so selfish. It's always just about whatever you want."

I didn't want to cause a scene, so I bit my tongue instead of telling him that another huge reason for my hesitance was that I didn't feel completely comfortable in our marriage. I didn't fully trust him. What if we had a baby and then he cheated on me? What if I had to end our marriage but we had a child together? These were questions that needed to be answered before I could confidently bring a child into the world with him; but they couldn't be answered today.

I reached for his hand, and he pulled it away.

"Stop," he snapped, and I could feel the eyes of the other couple on our backs.

Tears began to form in my eyes, and I swallowed in an effort to stop them. Crying would make him angrier, and I didn't want to cause a scene. It seemed like the only way I could make him happy right now was to agree to have a baby and I couldn't do that. One tear escaped my eye and hit my cheek, and I quickly wiped it away.

"Damnit, Em, are you crying?" The harshness in his voice made it harder for me to stop the stupid tears from forming.

"I'm fine," I whispered. "Please, just don't get angry here."

"Pull it together," he hissed. "We're about to be back on the ground."

We didn't speak for the next few minutes. I stopped my tears by refocusing on the skyline and admiring London's beauty, dissociating from the negative feelings the argument had stirred. London was wonderful, and I had a bird's eye view. I studied the lights and the bustling crowds of tiny people along the riverfront below. My thoughts silenced as I focused on Big Ben's magnificent presence, and his reflection glimmering on the River Thames.

Our pod eventually reached the ground, and we got off the London Eye. As we walked back into the vibrant city, I searched for ideas to lighten the mood, noting an illuminated ice cream parlor at the end of the block. "You want to get ice cream?"

"Sure," Shane replied.

I smiled. The small act of agreeing with my suggestion meant the argument was over.

But I knew it wouldn't be long before he pressed the matter again.

TWO MONTHS LATER, I settled into bed in our hotel room in Garmisch-Partenkirchen, exhausted from a long day on the road. To kick off the beginning of summer, Shane and I had driven down to the Bavarian Alps to spend a long weekend in the mountains.

We'd stopped along the way at the famous Neuschwanstein Castle and walked onto the *Marienbrücke*, a narrow bridge hanging across the steep gorge overlooking the castle. I had learned that Germany was home to upwards of 20,000 castles – ruined reminders of the power they once beheld, each one strikingly beautiful in its own unique way – but this one, the *Schloss Neuschwanstein*, had to be the most beautiful of all.

Perched atop a jagged ridge in the foothills of the Alps, the white limestone towers of the impeccable structure bore a stark contrast to the greens and blues of the meadows and lakes in the background. It could not possibly be more idyllic. It was a picture-perfect postcard scene – a literal fairytale that came alive before my eyes and struck me to my core with awe.

And now, we began our two-night stay in a wooden lodge in the mountains, our room overlooking the majestic peaks of the Alps. At 9:30 p.m., the sun had only just set, leaving the sky above the mountains a colorful painting of pink and orange hues.

I sighed with contentment as I reached for my water to take my nightly birth control pill... only, my pill packet wasn't where I'd left it.

I sat up, checking the area around the nightstand.

"Have you seen my birth control pills?" I asked Shane.

He barely glanced up from the TV as he responded, "Nope."

"Weird. I know I put them right here." I opened the drawer to check, though I was certain I'd placed them atop the nightstand. I went to the bathroom to double-check my toiletry bag, but they were nowhere to be found. Puzzled, I returned to the bed and looked at Shane.

"Guess you don't need it," he shrugged.

I shot him a glare. "I do need it."

"Do you really?" A mischievous glimmer in his eyes gave way to his deceit.

My face fell flat. "Did you take my birth control?"

His lips gave way to a devilish grin. "Maybe."

"Not funny. Give it to me."

"Oh, come on…" he reached for the drawer of his nightstand and pulled out my packet of pills. "Would it really be the worst thing in the world if you didn't take it?"

I snatched it. "Don't do that again."

He scowled. "Take a joke, Emily."

I scowled back. "It's not a funny joke."

"You act like getting pregnant would be the worst thing in the world," he muttered.

"It would!" The words left my mouth quicker than I could think about their impact.

His brows furrowed as my words sunk in. "I knew it… I knew you were lying about being ready to have a baby in two years." He paused. "Do you even want kids?"

My chest tightened. "I mean, in the future… probably," I stammered.

"Probably?"

"Shane, we're living in a fairytale right now. Look around you!"

I motioned at the mountain peaks now illuminated by purple twilight through our balcony doors. "Seeing that castle today took my breath away. Don't you want to have more of those moments before we're tied down?"

"Tied down?" He took noticeable offense to my question. "As if seeing some building that you can look at online is somehow more important than having a family with me?"

I frowned. Had he not felt the same sense of wonderment as me seeing that castle in person? Did his soul not awaken in new places the way mine did? I sat down on the bed and bit the skin around my thumb, overcome with worry that we were on two very different pages… and maybe we'd never be on the same page. Something deep within me hurt. The thing stopping Shane from having the family he so desperately desired… was me. And that didn't make me feel good about myself.

I looked at him. "I just need time."

In his eyes was sadness, not anger. He held my gaze long enough for me to absorb the pain before he looked back at the TV, ending our conversation.

chapter twenty-eight

Shane sat in bed on his laptop as I showered in the bathroom attached to our bedroom. I had felt a distance between us after our summer arguments around having a baby. In the weeks that followed, many things remained the same – we laughed, we kissed, we made love – but his eyes told me he was somewhere else, and I began to notice things.

He closed his laptop when I came nearby.

He added a passcode to his phone.

He took his phone with him to the bathroom when he showered.

As I felt him grow distant, I couldn't help but wonder who or what he was gravitating toward. An aching emptiness grew in my gut. I wondered if my hesitance to start a family was driving him away. I wanted to be enough for him, but I couldn't give him the one thing he truly desired… and that began to terrify me.

I stepped out of the shower, dried off, and brushed my wet hair in the mirror. I listened to Shane chuckle a few times, typing in quick bursts in between his laughs.

I stepped into the bedroom door frame and asked casually, "Who are you chatting with?"

He glanced at me. "Just coworkers."

His added levels of privacy were driving my descent into madness.

I desperately needed reassurance that he never provided. I hated myself for being so needy, but I was convinced he was falling out of love with me. While I lacked the logic to explain it, my intuition promised me something was terribly wrong.

I fumbled with the door handle. *If he's truly messaging his coworkers, he should have no problem proving that to me.* "Can I see?"

He shook his head. "We've gone over this before. I'm not giving you access to my Facebook. It's an invasion of privacy."

"I'm not invading your privacy. I'm just asking for you to show me your inbox. I don't need your password or anything. You can hold the computer while I look," I reasoned.

He frowned. "Emily, this is insane. I'm sitting here messaging my coworkers. I have done nothing to warrant this behavior from you!"

"If you have nothing to hide, why can't you just show me?"

"It's the fucking principle! I told you to stop being crazy and here you are being crazy again, acting like you have a right to invade my privacy because you don't trust me!"

His shouting increased my panic. For him to not even be willing to turn the screen in my direction, it had to mean there was something he didn't want me to see. "You're hiding something from me!"

"What am I hiding from you?"

"I don't know, because you won't show me!" My voice cracked from the tightness in my throat, and tears began to form.

He rolled his eyes. "Do you hear yourself? You're making things up in your head again and now you're crying. This behavior needs to stop. I'm not doing this."

I wasn't making things up. He had been distant; he had been increasing his privacy. *I wasn't imagining it.* I grew desperate. "If you aren't hiding something from me, then let me see what's on your screen!"

"I'm not hiding anything from you. I'm not showing you because I will not reward this type of behavior and encourage you to do it again." He began to close his laptop as my panic reached a boiling point.

I swiftly stepped toward the bed and grabbed his laptop by the screen. As he pulled it back, I tightened my grip, squeezing too hard on the screen and causing it to crack beneath my fingers.

I immediately let go and threw my hands in the air. "I'm sorry!"

"ARE YOU FUCKING KIDDING ME?!" he bellowed. Within an instant, he reached over to my nightstand, grabbed my laptop, and chucked it past me at the concrete wall of our bedroom. My jaw fell open as I watched my laptop break into two pieces as it collided with the wall and landed on the floor.

Sadie ran out of the room.

I picked up my laptop and scurried to the bathroom where I locked the door behind me. I inspected the pieces. Totally broken. As I held it up to examine all the sides, I heard shattered pieces rattling inside.

Desperately, I pressed the power button to no avail. Nothing was backed up. Everything I had – the pictures I'd saved since high school, the music I'd downloaded, all my documents – everything was gone. All because I had accidentally cracked his screen. My legs gave way as I sank to the floor and began to cry harder.

Shane's voice appeared on the other side of the door. "This is your fault. Once again, you acting like a fucking child got you into a mess. Are you happy now?"

So much hatred in his voice. His storm of anger left me voiceless.

"Well, Emily?! Are you fucking happy now? Dumb bitch."

I stood and opened the door just far enough to show my face. "You will NOT call me those names."

"What are you going to do about it?" he taunted.

I searched my mind for words that would wound him. Then, I struck. "I'm done. I don't want to be married to you anymore."

I wasn't sure how I expected him to react, but what happened next surpassed it.

Shane threw his body into the door. Carrying his force, the door collided with my face. Flashes of pain and a burning sensation hit me. I blinked away stars as red specks appeared on the floor.

Blood.

My blood.

Upon seeing the blood, his demeanor shifted. He quickly grabbed a towel from the rack behind me and held it to my face as he guided me to the sink. "Shit, fuck… are you okay?"

I didn't even know what part of my face was bleeding. The white towel filled with splotches of red in his hands. I pushed it away, needing to see my face. Red pooled in the sink below me as I caught my reflection in the mirror. Silent streams of tears joined streams of blood, which poured from my nostrils and a split in my lip, which I assumed I had bit when the door hit my face.

I watched myself… crying, panting, bleeding.

Pathetic.

Shane wet the towel and patted it softly on my face. While one arm cleaned my face, the other held the small of my back. I watched him in the mirror, fear and concern spilling from his own eyes.

He did this.

I shifted on my feet, creating space between his hand and my body.

"I'm getting you ice, hang on." He rushed out of the bathroom and returned moments later with a bag of ice wrapped in a towel. He dabbed my face with the towel again and applied the ice. "I'm sorry that happened, Em. You know I didn't mean for you to get hurt. You know that, right?"

I ignored his question, pushing his hand away from my face and taking the ice into my own. I gave my pathetic reflection one last glance

before turning to walk past my broken laptop on the bathroom floor –
now covered in specks of blood – and over to the bed where I sat down.

I leaned back onto the pillow, my head throbbing. The cold ice burned
against my lips. Everything hurt… including my heart. I couldn't stop
crying, nor could I find the words to respond to Shane.

Sadie returned to the room, nostrils flaring as my scent reached her,
concerned eyes seeking me. She quickly jumped onto the bed and began
to sniff the towel and ice I held over my face, her eyes meeting mine with
confusion. I patted her head. She licked my hand and curled up close to
my side, placing her head in my lap.

I'm sorry, I thought as I looked at Sadie's sweet face. She didn't
deserve the stress. *I'm so sorry.* I hugged her closely while Shane watched
from the door frame. He placed his own shameful face in his hand for a
moment, then walked out of the room. I listened to his footsteps in the
hall until he reached the front door and left.

chapter twenty-nine

I heard the front door unlock one hour later. Shane came down the hallway and into the bedroom where I lay with Sadie still in my lap. My face had stopped bleeding. The pounding had subsided. My tears had dried.

But my heartache persisted.

He held a large bag in his hands. "I got this for you." He placed it beside me.

I peered inside at a white box. A brand-new MacBook. Frustration filled my bloodstream, as if this could somehow replace what I had lost. Thousands of photos of me, and my friends, and all of my travels. An entire library of downloaded music. Five years of school, work and personal documents. I scowled at the empty MacBook. I didn't want it. I wanted my stuff back.

Shane looked at me eagerly, as if he had delivered a grand gesture for which I should be thanking him. "Well?"

I glared.

"It's a new computer… to replace yours," he explained.

"Does it replace all of my memories, too?" My voice dripped with sarcasm. I pushed the bag away from me.

He frowned. "Emily, I just spent $1,500 on that for you."

My knight in shining armor.

I rolled my eyes. "I don't care what you spent."

He scoffed. "Are you kidding me? I just went out of my way to immediately replace your computer without you even asking. I haven't even thought about the damage you did to mine. Can't you be grateful for once in your life?"

"I'd be grateful if you didn't break my laptop in the first place."

"Maybe next time you'll think twice before acting like a child."

I clenched my teeth. "I wouldn't have to act like that if I had a husband who treated me the way I deserve to be treated."

Shane threw his arms in the air. "What world are you living in? You get everything you want. You have nothing to complain about."

My mouth fell open in disbelief. Had he forgotten pushing a door into my face an hour ago? "I'm living in a world where I can't trust my own husband to not message girls behind my back if I'm away from home for four hours."

"That was one fucking time!" he shouted. "You've got to stop living in the past!"

"And instead of doing *anything* to comfort me or reassure me, you're just a fucking asshole!"

He eyed me angrily. "You have it better than 90% of women out there. Do you know how many of my coworkers cheat on their wives? *Every single one of them.* You have *no idea* how lucky you are to have a faithful husband."

I couldn't believe the words coming out of his mouth. "A faithful husband who pushes doors into my face for asking questions?"

"You know the door was a fucking accident, so don't put that on me, Emily." He pointed a finger at me. "I didn't get mad at you for asking questions. You were acting crazy and accusing me of things I haven't done."

"How am I supposed to know what you have or haven't done when you hide everything from me?"

"It's called *trust* – you have none of it." He paced across the floor toward me. "What's the point of being faithful to you if you're not going to believe it? I might as well go fuck whoever I want!"

My lip quivered. I tried to stop them, but felt the tears fall to my cheeks. "This is exactly the shit I'm talking about." My voice broke. "That's mean."

"Oh, and now you're crying. Poor Emily is the victim again." He rolled his eyes.

The mocking, the name calling, the complete inability to provide me with any reassurance or validation – it was too much. Fury surged through my body. I could think of only one thing to say that would provoke an emotional response from him – and right now, regardless of whether I meant it or not, I wanted to hurt him. I wanted to hit him where it hurt deepest. Abandonment.

"I don't love you anymore, Shane," I said with the coldest tone I could muster.

"No?" he sneered. "Good luck finding anyone else to put up with you." And with that, he opened the doors of my closet and began taking my clothes off the rack and throwing them onto the floor.

I jumped out of bed. "What are you doing?!"

"You don't want to be with me anymore, so get the fuck out of my apartment," he snapped.

I moved to position myself in between him and my closet. "Stop!"

He reached around me, pulling folded clothing off shelves and throwing it into a pile on the floor. "I'm just helping you, Emily." His sarcasm made my skin hot. "You don't love me anymore. So, let's pack your stuff and get you the fuck out of here."

"Stop…" I whimpered.

"Oh, boo hoo," he mocked. "Poor Emily can't figure out what she wants."

"I fucking *hate* you," I choked.

I retreated to the bathroom, locking him out again, sat on the floor and hugged my knees into my chest.

"You have no idea how lucky you are to have me! You think anyone else is going to want to be married to a fucking child?" Shane shouted through the closed door.

I put my fingers in my ears to try to drown him out.

I was four years old again, throwing a tantrum on my bedroom floor because my parents weren't giving me the attention I needed.

"You think anyone else is going to love you?!"

I was 15 years old again, weeping in my bedroom because Carter didn't want me after giving all of myself to him.

"Think again, you ungrateful bitch."

I was 17 years old again, crying in the car my dad had given me because I'd failed to maintain the oil and he was disgusted by my stupidity. *"I give you a car and this is how you treat it? Ungrateful idiot."*

I held myself tightly.

I was 22 years old, sobbing on the bathroom floor because even my own husband didn't want me.

I was a disappointment to everyone in my life.

Lost in my own cruel thoughts, I didn't notice when Shane's voice faded from the other side. My focus recentered when I heard Sadie sniffing the crack under the door. I opened it slightly – Shane nowhere to be seen – and let her in.

She sniffed my face, then licked it fiercely when she realized it was covered in salty tears. Her sandpaper tongue was rough against my tender wounds, but her kisses filled me with comfort. A broken smile formed on my face. *At least you love me, Sadie.*

Many minutes later, I stood up and walked out of the bathroom. I looked at my clothes on the bedroom floor. That would have to be dealt with later. I walked down the hallway to the living room where I found Shane on the couch with his eyes closed.

I studied him for a moment – quiet and peaceful.

What if he was right? What if nobody else could love me? What if something within me was so seriously flawed, and he was loving me the best he could?

I thought about the recent argument. It wouldn't have happened if I had just thanked him for the laptop. I thought about the door hitting my face. He couldn't have known the door would collide with my face when he pushed it open. None of it would have happened if I hadn't reached for his laptop screen in the first place.

What if I was the common denominator in all of it?

Every instance of rejection compounded within me.

I was… unlovable.

And I continued to push away the only person who stuck around.

I sat down on the couch, careful not to wake him, but Sadie's approach was less guarded as she leapt into the space in between us. Shane's eyes opened suddenly, and he looked from Sadie to me. "I didn't mean to fall asleep. I came out here to calm down."

I didn't speak.

His eyes were soft as he studied me. It was incredible, the way he could flip a switch. One minute he was a raging monster; the next, a comforting embrace. Was that also how he saw me – one moment, a calm and loving presence; the next, paranoid and accusatory?

He reached for me, and my body stiffened as he pulled me toward him. My face, swollen and tender, met his chest as his strong arm draped over my body. *Thump. Thump.* I listened to his heartbeat as he breathed.

"What is it going to take for you to be happy?" he asked.

I considered the question, and what had driven me to madness to begin with. Most of our fights stemmed from my lack of trust. Even my resistance to have children with him was rooted in my insecurity of him leaving me again. I said the word that came to mind. "Reassurance."

His voice was soft. "What kind of reassurance?"

"Reassurance… that you're not going to leave me for someone else."

He sighed. "Em, if we didn't fight, our relationship would literally be perfect. I would never want to leave. Don't you agree?"

I did. I thought about the moments when Shane was kind. I closed my eyes and felt the warm embrace of his love when it was comforting and affectionate. My lips curved slightly upward when I thought about the way he made me laugh.

He was my lowest valley and my highest peak.

"Yes," I agreed. "Things would be perfect without the fights."

We were silent while his finger traced idle circles around my shoulder.

"I have no idea who you're talking to everyday, or if those people even know you're married," I finally said.

"Everyone knows I'm married."

I frowned. "Do they? It's not like you show me off."

With his free arm, he pulled his phone out of his pocket. I watched as he opened the Facebook app and tapped the icon to update his profile photo. He scrolled through photos, selecting one of us on our wedding day. In the photo, I smiled brightly at the camera while he planted a kiss on my cheek. We had just left the altar, our photographer capturing our first private moment after leaving the crowd. He tapped the button to set it as his profile picture.

It was a small but meaningful gesture. This was Shane trying to reassure me. Throughout our relationship, he had mostly kept me out of his profile pictures. I told him before that I wished he would show me off, but he told me I was taking it too seriously due to my own insecurities.

He tilted his phone screen toward me. "Does this help?"

I nodded once. "I need more."

"Please trust me." He kissed my forehead. His lips left a warm imprint on my skin that radiated down my face. For a moment, my aching nose stopped hurting. "I love you, Emily. Now, and forever."

My heart felt slightly less heavy. I leaned closer, wanting more of that kind cure.

He kissed my mouth. The kiss blanketed me in comfort and numbed the soreness of my split lip. I felt the heaviness lifting from my body as he kissed me, so naturally, I kissed him harder. He returned my longing. His hands moved through my hair, then down my waistline, stopping to tug at the band of my shorts. I allowed them to slide off.

I wanted the heaviness gone.

I wanted the heartache to subside.

I wanted the emptiness to be filled.

I wanted him to make me whole.

chapter thirty

"Do you guys ever get into fights so bad it makes you reconsider being married?" I asked Jen. We sat on my apartment patio with drinks in hand while Shane and Tom manned the grill. The final days of summer were upon us, and we were soaking up every bit of warmth and sunlight until the days grew colder and darker.

"Doesn't everyone?" she joked. I raised my eyebrows. "No, seriously… yeah, there's been a couple."

I was surprised. I admired the easy way Jen and Tom seemed to love one another. I never felt any tension between them, and it gave me hope that Shane and I would reach the same peaceful place in our marriage.

"Really? How bad?"

She rubbed her finger along the rim of her beer bottle. "When Tom gets mad, he can be a dick. But I try not to take it personally because he's usually just stressed about work or tired."

I nodded. I wanted to ask if Tom called her a "bitch" or an "idiot," or if he ever hurt her physically, but it didn't feel like the right place to do so with the men just barely out of earshot. I sipped my beer. "Shane, too. Sometimes… I'm not convinced he loves me."

"Get out of here." She gave me a disbelieving look. "Why do you think that?"

For the past couple months, I had been delicate in my approach to Shane. I didn't want to trigger another blowup argument. I did everything I could to be the calm and trusting wife he wanted. I remembered the words he spoke to me: *"I love you, Emily. Now and forever."*

But I *swore* his distance from me was still increasing. He didn't kiss me when he got home from work. He made comments about my appearance: my "linebacker shoulders," and the small layer of fat forming around my lean waist as a result of indulging in German bread and beer. He stopped telling me I was beautiful.

I frowned. "I don't know, it just feels like there's this growing distance between us sometimes –"

"It's probably just in your head." She smiled and took my hand in hers. "I've known you guys for a couple years now, and I see the love you have for each other."

I opened my mouth to reply but was interrupted by Shane delivering a plate of hamburgers to the table. "Ladies first," he said.

"Thanks!" Jen squealed.

"Thanks," I echoed, smiling at Shane as he took a seat beside me at the patio table.

"Oh, shoot," he started, jumping back up from his seat. "I forgot to ask if you guys need another round of drinks?"

"Sure, babe," I raised my empty bottle.

"Me too, *babe*," Jen mocked as she held her bottle in Shane's direction. I laughed.

He took each of our bottles and returned moments later with fresh drinks for the table. "Now that we all have drinks in hand, I'd like to make a toast to my wife." He raised his drink, locking eyes with me. "Congratulations on your promotion!"

A grin spread across my face. Things were going so well at my new job. In less than a year, I'd been recognized twice as an outstanding performer and just this week I'd been told I was being promoted to assistant manager of our marketing team.

"Congratulations, Emily!" Jen said. "I miss Sunday breakfasts with you, but you deserve this." She raised her drink and Tom followed suit gleefully.

Shane continued speaking. "You're really kicking ass, Em. I'm proud of you. I brag to my coworkers all the time about how smart you are, and here you go proving me right like you always do."

I laughed. "Thank you, guys. It's awesome to be able to celebrate with friends."

Shane sat down again beside me, and I gave his knee an affectionate squeeze. Maybe Jen was right. Maybe it was in my head. Shane had the most charming demeanor in front of our friends. It was only behind closed doors that the rare, ugly side of him revealed itself to me. They got to love him for what they saw – charismatic, funny, agreeable, captivating Shane; the Shane I fell in love with.

The four of us enjoyed our food while conversing about work, dogs and travel. We told stories and jokes late into the evening. It felt good to have friends who supported us, and I felt less alone knowing that maybe they faced some of their own similar struggles.

A FEW WEEKS later, Shane and I sat on separate ends of the couch watching a movie with Sadie in between us.

Following my promotion, work had become increasingly busy. Between working out every morning, working overtime, and walking Sadie every afternoon, I was left with only a couple hours in the evening to catch up with Shane before he left for his overnight work shift.

Thankfully, tonight was his night off, which meant we had more time than usual to enjoy each other's company. Only… he wasn't enjoying my company. He was sucked into his phone. From the corner of my eye, I watched him respond to text after text, his fingers dancing across the screen with excitement.

It's nothing. Relax, I told myself.

But it was the way he grinned that made my heart race. I recognized it. It was the grin he gave me when he was being playful and flirtatious. My skin started to feel hot and I could no longer maintain my focus on the movie. "Who are you texting?"

"One of my coworkers," he mumbled, his eyes not leaving his phone.

"Which one?"

He shot me a warning look. "Don't start."

"All I've done is ask who you're texting."

"And I just told you it's one of my coworkers." He looked back at his phone.

"Which one?" I repeated.

He shook his head. "You don't even know him."

Drop it. Don't say another word. "Show me your phone." I winced at my own words. *Why can't I fucking drop it?*

He rolled his eyes. "Here we go again." As he looked at me again, anger filled the creases between his brows. "Do you see how fucking crazy this is?"

My own anger seeped through flared nostrils. "If there's nothing to hide then why can't you show me your phone?"

"Because you're fucking psychotic and I'm not going to reward your behavior," he snapped.

I took a deep breath and attempted to be calm. "Please… show me your phone and I'll stop."

"No." His tone was stern. "You need to stop now. You're inventing things in your fucking head again." His focus returned to his phone.

My blood boiled.

If there was nothing to hide from me, then why couldn't I ever see his phone?

Why was it password protected?

Why were his notification previews hidden?

Why did he turn the screen away from me whenever a text came in?

I rubbed my brows. *Maybe I am crazy. Maybe I'm losing my mind.*

But my intuition argued otherwise and begged me to listen.

The persistent, nagging truth was that Shane could calm me in seconds if he just showed me the phone – if he just reassured me that I had nothing to worry about. *Reassurance.* It's what I had asked for, and here I was being denied it again. My heart pounded.

I started thinking of every single person it could be. My mind went to the worst-case scenario. *He's cheating on me. If I see the phone, I'll have proof.*

My body moved before I could stop it.

I walked over to Shane and reached for his phone. He stood up and quickly pulled it away, positioning it above his head with one hand and using the other hand on my chest to push me away from him. "Get the fuck away from me, Emily! You're crazy!"

Crazy. The word was venom on his tongue. It infuriated me. Blinded by rage, panic and insecurity, I slapped him across the face. As my fingers met his cheek, my heart stopped beating. I mirrored the open-mouthed expression on his face.

"I'm so sor –" I started to say, but a quick flash of pain silenced me as his open palm struck my own face. Stunned, I couldn't gather any thoughts other than my enduring need to see the phone. Tears ran down my hot cheek. "Please. Let me see it."

He shook his head in disbelief. "You're a fucking psycho." He eyed me like I was a rabid animal as he backed away. "You are a crazy fucking lunatic, Emily."

He turned and walked out the front door. I ran after him. Despite what had happened I couldn't get my mind off needing to see that fucking phone. I needed to confirm I wasn't crazy. I wasn't psychotic. I wasn't a lunatic.

But *fuck* if I wasn't acting like all the above.

He got into his car and pulled the door shut before I could reach him, locking all the doors. I pulled the handle sobbing before he put the car in reverse and began to back up.

"Stop!" I yelled. "Where are you going?"

He cracked the window so that I could hear him reply, "I'm not coming back until you calm the fuck down and stop acting crazy. Do not drive after me. Do not call me. You will only drive me farther away." And with that, he rolled up the window and drove off.

I fell onto my knees where his car had been and wept. My cheek burned, and shame began to engulf my body as I realized people in the apartment complex were probably staring at me.

Pitying me.

"Poor, crazy Emily. She's playing the victim again."

I hated myself.

I hurried back into the apartment. Sadie was waiting at the door, her tail wagging in a mix of excitement to see me return and concern over the yelling and tears. I collapsed into the couch, patting the cushion beside me to invite her to be close. She joined me, curling up in a ball beside me with her head on my leg.

I wept. What the hell was wrong with me? I *hit* him. I *slapped him in the face* because he wouldn't show me his phone. Self-loathing burned inside of me, a fiery storm.

Less than 15 minutes ago, Shane and I were comfortable on the couch together. My evening could have gone so differently if I hadn't started a fight. I despised myself for behaving like a child. I hated my actions.

Shame swallowed me as I realized I had – yet again – ignited another blowup argument.

And my needs were still unmet.

I never saw his phone. I was never reassured. Instead of reassuring me, he slapped me in the face and left. The reality of it all set in, and I didn't know what to do other than cry.

He slapped me.

What was I supposed to do now?

I folded into myself, blanketing Sadie with my body, and sobbed into her fur.

SHANE RETURNED AN hour later. He approached the couch and sat near me, keeping space between us as if I might attack at any moment. "Are you done?" he asked cautiously.

There was no point asking to see his phone now. Anything that was there earlier would be deleted by now. He wasn't an idiot.

But I was.

I gave a slight nod of my head. I had no energy to continue arguing.

He wiped a hair from my face, then traced a finger along the cheek he had struck. "You know I didn't mean to slap you. It was an involuntary reaction to you slapping me first. I couldn't control it. You know that, right?"

I said nothing. Slapping him was the wrong thing to do, but I also didn't feel like he deserved an apology.

He kept talking. "Em… You have these psychotic episodes where it's like I don't even recognize you. When you act crazy like that, it makes me not want to be with you."

Once again, he had come to tell me all the ways I was making it impossible for him to love me.

"You have it so good. You're married to someone who loves you so much, you live in a beautiful apartment in a beautiful country, and yet you're still so ungrateful…"

Ungrateful. I hated when he called me that. I had gratitude for the things in my life that were good. Did that mean I was supposed to turn a blind eye to infidelity and abuse?

"Emily?"

I looked at him, wondering how long I'd been lost in my own thoughts.

"Are you listening?"

"Yes."

"What do you have to say for yourself?"

I stared blankly. I had so many things to say… but I had no energy to speak. No matter what I said, he would refute it. No matter how much I argued my side, he would shoot me down. No matter how much I tried to hurt him, he would hurt me a thousand times worse. I shook my head. "Nothing."

"You have nothing to say?"

"I just… can't… argue anymore. I'm so tired."

Shane scooted closer to fill the distance between us. "Emily…" He put his arm around me. "I love you." He buried his face into my neck. "I want to move forward."

My body was rigid.

He kissed my neck. I pulled away, but he tightened his grip and kissed me harder. I pushed against his chest. "I don't want this right now."

"Babe," he cooed. His lips moved from my neck to my mouth. "Come on…"

There was no warmth on his lips.

I shifted uncomfortably, angling my face away from his.

He pulled me closer as a mischievous grin formed on his face. "I don't know why, but I get turned on when you're sad…"

A chill traveled down my spine as his disturbing words sunk in. "That's… fucked up."

"I don't know why it happens. You make me so mad that I just want to…" He chuckled. "I don't know, fuck some sense into you." He started to pull down my shorts.

I stopped his hands. "You shouldn't feel happy for making me sad."

"Then let me make you happy again."

He pulled my shorts off and rolled on top of me, forcing his mouth onto mine and kissing me fervently. And I was so tired – so emotionally exhausted – that I could do nothing. Fighting him would take energy I didn't have. This would only last a few minutes.

It wasn't like the makeup sex we'd had before. There was no electricity between our bodies. There was only pain and resentment. I felt his anger release inside me with every thrust.

chapter thirty-one

I sat alone in our dimly lit bedroom, weighed down by my persistent sadness. It was Monday. I had to start getting ready for the gym, but the heaviness left me wanting to crawl back into bed with Sadie.

Two weeks had passed since the sting of Shane's hand on my face, accompanied by the accusation that I was delusional. The physical blow was surpassed only by the assault on my already fragile self-worth. I felt small and insignificant, my mind whispering that I deserved this, that I was unworthy of love. Shane was not weighed down by sadness. He returned to his normal life while I lay ensnared in his web.

I couldn't leave… but I couldn't stay. How much more could I take?

I walked into my bathroom and gazed into the mirror. I no longer recognized myself. I had once been full of sparkle. *My sunshine girl*, my mom called me. Now, my reflection revealed a face etched with sorrow, eyes devoid of the glimmer they once held. It felt like I was staring at a corpse.

"What is it going to take for you to be happy?"

Shane's question echoed in my mind. I didn't know the answer. On paper, I had everything. I had a husband and a dog, I was traveling throughout Europe, progressing in my career… My social media posts painted a highlight reel of my amazing life.

"You guys look so happy together!"

"So great to see your smiling faces."

"What a wonderful life you have in Germany!"

The comments I received further invalidated my world of delusion.

I had no reason to be unhappy or ungrateful.

But I never told anybody about the fights.

I never told them about Shane messaging another girl asking for naked pictures.

I never told them about him slapping me in the face.

Why would you? I spoke silently to my reflection in the mirror. *You slapped him first. You started it. You're not the victim. You're just acting like one.*

I closed my eyes and took a deep breath.

When I opened my eyes again, I forced my reflection into a shimmering fake smile, almost convincing enough for me to believe it.

I pulled on my gym clothes and checked the time on my phone – 5:45 a.m. Shane was away on a work trip for two days and would be getting up soon to start his day, so I texted him something to wake up to.

Emily: *Good morning. I hope you have a nice day.*

I cringed at the message after I sent it. Not because of the words I spoke, but because of the honesty behind them. The truth was, I still wanted Shane to be happy. I still wanted Shane to feel loved. I still loved Shane. It didn't matter that I was crushed by my own delusional sadness. I poured whatever light I could still find in myself into him… in desperate hope that he would pour it back into me. Because what else did I have?

After I worked out at the fitness center, I headed to the locker room to shower and get ready for work. While I was putting on my clothes, my phone vibrated. I picked it up expecting to see Shane's reply.

Tom: *Hey, can you talk?*

My skin tingled. Jen was currently in the States visiting family, and Tom never texted me privately. The implied urgency was alarming.

Emily: *Sure, what's up?*
Tom: *Can I call you?*

I took a minute to hastily finish getting ready and walked to my car before responding and telling him to call. His name lit up my phone screen as it vibrated in my hand.

"Hey, what's up?"

"Hey. Are you alone?"

Am I alone? I frowned, puzzled by the question. "Yes, I'm in my car… what's up?"

"Em – look, I don't know how to tell you this, so I'm just going to say it."

My heart raced. Was Jen okay? "What do you mean?" I stammered. "What's going on?"

"Shane and Jen are having an affair," he said after a moment.

I heard the words, but I didn't understand. Those words didn't make sense in that order. Those words *couldn't* make sense in that order. It was impossible. "What do you mean?"

"They've been hiding it from us. I don't know any details. I just found out."

"How… did you…" I stammered.

"Jen's iPad. I can send you the texts."

The 30-something seconds it took for Tom to send me the screenshots were the longest of my life. My hands shook. My breath was rapid. My mouth went dry.

Finally, they arrived. I tapped open the conversation between my husband and one of my closest friends.

Shane: Hey beautiful
Jen: Hiiiii :)
Shane: I miss you so much.
Jen: I miss you too
Shane: I want to fuck you so bad
Jen: Oh really?
Shane: Really
Jen: You're bad
Shane: You make me this way
Jen: You make me blush
Shane: If you were here right now, I'd be doing a lot more than making you blush
Jen: What would you be doing?
Shane: Holding you and kissing every inch of your beautiful body
Jen: Well then I can't wait to get back :)
Shane: I am going to make you so happy

I stopped reading, nausea churning in the pit of my stomach.

It couldn't be real. I shut my eyes tightly and wished it away. This had to be a cruel nightmare. *Wake up, Emily. Please wake up.* I prayed to the universe that when I opened my eyes again, the texts would be gone.

But I opened my eyes and there they were – undeniable proof of Shane and Jen's betrayal, mocking my futile hope to escape them. My chest filled with excruciating pain as my heart shattered.

"You still there?" Tom had been sitting quietly on the other end while I digested the screenshots.

I looked at the clock on my phone. I was 10 minutes late for work.

I was never late for work. "I have to go," I said before I hung up.

I started driving to my office as tears streamed down my face.

This. Can't. Be. Happening.

I stopped at a red light and opened another screenshot from Tom of his conversation confronting Jen. She was apologizing, saying it was all a mistake.

Fucking two-faced bitch.

I thought she was my friend. My mind raced with memories of the four of us traveling, hosting barbecues, spending summer days at the lake. Hatred seeped through my skin. How long had this been going on? I needed to know.

I called her and she sent me to voicemail. I texted.

Emily: *Answer the phone*
Jen: *I'm sorry, I don't know what else to say.*
Emily: *Is this true? How could you do this to me?*

No response. *Lying backstabbing bitch.*

I called again, reaching her voicemail a second time, then a third time, and then she blocked my number. *Fuck.*

The light turned green, but I couldn't pull my focus from my phone. One hand on the wheel and the other on my phone, I frantically opened my Facebook Messenger app and found myself blocked from messaging Jen. I opened Instagram – blocked.

Within minutes, my world, my marriage, and my friendship had shattered simultaneously in one devastating blow, and she wouldn't even grant me the courtesy of a conversation.

My friend. My friend who had assured me that Shane loved me. My friend who I'd welcomed into my home more times than I could count. How could this be real? Pain filled every space inside my body, my heart screaming for the torture to end. I knew who I needed to talk to next.

I called Shane, who also sent me to voicemail. Jen must have warned him they were caught. I called again, and again, until he finally answered.

"Hello?"

"Please, tell me this isn't real," I choked, now crying so hard I could barely get the words out.

He acted confused. "What are you talking about?"

"Seriously, Shane? *Jen*?"

"Em, I don't know what you're talking about…"

His false innocence drove a surge of anger through me. "I've seen the fucking texts so don't pretend you don't know what I'm talking about!"

He paused. "How?"

"Tom found them." I pulled into the parking lot for my work building, parking around the back where nobody would see me crying. His silence fueled my rage. "How could you do this to me?!"

"I… It was only texts," he stammered. "I promise you *nothing* physical happened –"

"Bull*shit*," I spat.

"I swear to you on my life, Emily. Please, you have to hear me out –"

"My *friend*, Shane?" I emphasized the word. It was unbearable enough when Shane betrayed me for a stranger. Betraying me for one of my friends… it was incomprehensible. My entire body convulsed with sobs.

Shane's voice grew frantic. "Emily, I'm so sorry. I don't know what the fuck I was thinking messaging her. You and I have been fighting – you know, things have been so bad…"

"My *friend*…" I repeated, my cries suffocating me.

"Baby, we have to talk about this… please," he begged. "I have to go right now because of work but please talk to me about this in a little bit. Okay?"

I hung up without agreeing. I was now 20 minutes late for work.

I needed to pull it together. I looked at my reflection in the rear-view mirror. Black mascara covered my swollen cheeks. I dabbed at them with the sleeve of my sweater, but the tears wouldn't stop pouring. I couldn't do it. Although I had been practicing it for years, today I could not plaster a smile on my face and pretend I was okay. I could not hide that my world had stopped turning.

I texted my boss.

Emily: *Hi, unfortunately I'm experiencing a family emergency and I need to take a sick day. I'm so sorry for the late notice and the inconvenience.*

Boss: *No inconvenience here, Emily. Please take all the time you need. Hope everything is okay.*

I breathed a sigh of relief and snuck the back way out of the parking lot to avoid being seen by any of my coworkers.

I returned to the comfort of Sadie and my bed. The day continued while I lay stuck in time. I wept inconsolably, struggling to grasp at any possibility of our marriage bouncing back from this. I played out a million outcomes in my mind, trying to find one where we returned to our happily ever after.

But I couldn't.

We didn't.

I could not recover from this.

My entire body ached and throbbed and pounded.

Every time I had felt my gnawing intuition telling me Shane was unfaithful, he convinced me I was delusional. He convinced me I was losing my mind. But I wasn't crazy. *I wasn't crazy.*

I was *right*. Only, being right didn't mean I'd won – being right meant I lost *everything*.

The thought of ripping myself free from him filled me with dread. He had woven himself into the fabric of my existence. I didn't know what pieces would be left of me without him.

I lay in ruins as texts from Shane poured in.

Shane: *I love you*

Shane: *Please talk to me*

Shane: *I fucked up*

Shane: *I'm so sorry*

Shane: *I promise it was only texts. I love you so much and I would never want to mess this up.*

Shane: *Please talk to me*

Shane: *I need you, babe. Please*

Shane: *I'm losing my mind over here. I need to see you and hear you and know you're okay.*

Shane: *I love you more than anything in the world*

Shane: *We will recover from this. Everything will be okay, babe. I promise. I will do whatever it takes to fix this.*

I left his messages on read.

Sadie pushed her head into my arm. I wrapped it around her, my tears wetting her fur. It wasn't fair that she had to comfort me, over and over, attempting to repair a heart she didn't break. And yet she did it every single time. Desperate for someone to console me, I began to text Gina.

Emily: *I just found out Shane has been having an affair with my —*

I deleted the text before finishing it. I couldn't tell Gina until I was absolutely, 100% certain that Shane and I were done. It'd be strike three – she'd never forgive him for this.

I started to text my coworker Sharon, who I'd begun to form a close bond with, but who didn't know nearly as much as Gina when it came to my history with Shane.

Emily: *The reason I couldn't come into the office today is because I found out that Shane –*

I deleted that draft as well. If I told anyone, the decision would be made for me – I would have to leave Shane, and quickly. Word would spread, and I couldn't stay with him absorbing the pity of everyone around me.

Was I strong enough to leave him? Where would I go? Could I afford it? How could I possibly find the answers to these questions when my entire body ached so deeply? Every fiber of my being longed for someone to hold me and tell me I would be okay. I wept, and Sadie lifted her head to lick the tears from my cheeks.

Instead of confiding in someone personally, I snuggled closer to Sadie and opened my Facebook app to post a status. *I'm ready to come home*, I wrote, adding a broken heart emoji. It was vague enough to conceal the reason for my pain, but enough to let the world know I was hurting.

SHANE CAME HOME the following day to find me in the fetal position. I'd barely moved, except to feed and walk Sadie. He sat beside me on the bed, his face contorted with pity.

I hated him. I wanted him to die.

And yet I loved him. And I wanted him to comfort me.

And I hated myself for being so fucking confused about everything.

Tears cascaded from his blue eyes, then he threw himself around my body. "I will do whatever it takes to not lose you," he choked.

I crumbled in his embrace, the weight of my heartbreak crushing me.

How could he be the source of my deepest pain, and yet my only solace?

How could he be the thing that killed me, and yet the thing I couldn't live without?

Though I could not form the words, my shattered heart whispered, *I don't want to lose you either.*

chapter thirty-two

Our marriage hung by a thread in the days that followed. Shane begged me to tell him what he needed to do in order for us to move forward.

My first request was for him to text Jen, telling her he never cared about her and that she was a mistake. Selfishly, I thought hurting her would reduce my own pain… but it didn't. When I remembered the things he said to her, it broke me all over again.

My next request was for us to go to marriage counseling. He agreed and even went so far as to schedule the first appointment for us. The drive to the counselor was tense. I wondered what good this session would even do, what hope there was that a man I'd never met could repair what we'd broken.

We sat in an uncomfortably small room, Shane and I beside each other on a frayed leather loveseat and the counselor on a stiff-backed chair across from us.

"What brings you in today?" the counselor asked after introductions, his face impassive as he glanced between us.

My jaw clenched. I couldn't bring myself to explain Shane's infidelity. I hadn't told my friends or my family – how could I confide in a stranger? Embarrassment engulfed me. I felt so small. I looked to

Shane, silently pleading that he explain his mistakes so that I wouldn't have to repeat them out loud.

Shane nodded at me and I felt my tension ease. I scanned the shelves lining the wall behind the counselor's head, my eyes landing on a wilted orchid as I struggled to follow the words that were coming out of my husband's mouth. "Emily… has trouble trusting me because of things that happened before we got married, and because I have a friendly demeanor that she believes is too flirtatious."

My stomach churned. Telling Jen he wanted to fuck her was *friendly demeanor*?

"I see," the counselor nodded. "And does that cause issues between the two of you?"

Shane nodded in return. "She has these major insecurities that lead her to have panic attacks and lash out at me, verbally… and physically."

My breaths grew shallow. My fingers found a spot that was peeling on the loveseat and I ran my thumbnail under the flap of leather. I pulled it up and rolled it between my fingers into a ball. Shane hadn't agreed to come here to work through our issues. He was going to pinpoint me as the issue. I couldn't bring myself to look at him again, so I dragged my eyes up to the only other person in the room.

The counselor's thin-framed glasses rested on his nose, and behind them, his accusatory eyes narrowed in on me. "What are you insecure about, Emily?"

Where the fuck to begin? "Him being unfaithful," I muttered in response.

"Because of what has happened before?" he asked.

I shook my head as I glared at the counselor. "Because of what is *still* happening."

The counselor raised an eyebrow. He glanced at Shane, then back to me. "Can you tell me more?"

I shifted my focus to my feet on the stained linoleum floor. Shane placed a hand on my knee and applied the slightest bit of pressure. I resisted the urge to slap it off me. It would have appeared that he was comforting me; but it was a warning. He didn't want me to tell the counselor the truth.

"It's what she believes is happening," Shane answered for me. "I haven't been unfaithful to her since we got married."

I dropped the balled-up leather and chewed the skin around my thumb. *Why am I here? What is the fucking point of being here if I'm not going to fucking speak?*

"I know I don't always do the best job at comforting her," Shane continued in his most charming and understanding tone. "But a lot of these fights wouldn't happen if she didn't attack me for things I haven't done. She makes me feel like the bad guy – blaming me for situations she creates in her head – and it upsets me."

I listened to Shane paint himself as the victim, my own body covered head to toe in invisible bruises and scars, and tallied up all that he wasn't saying. He didn't mention Jen. He didn't tell the counselor about hiding his phone from me. He didn't talk about the bites, the time he threw my computer at the wall, or when he pushed a door into my face. But he didn't tell the counselor about the time I slapped him in the face either. It was a stalemate. If I tattled on him, he'd tattle on me.

I was frozen. There was no point trying. It was a lose-lose situation for me. To explain Shane's infidelity and abuse to the counselor would only cause a fight between us later, and I'd have to suffer twice – once through the humiliation of retelling that painful experience, then again in the storm of fury Shane would inflict upon me later.

I bit off a chunk of skin from my thumb and watched the blood pool in my nail bed.

"Have you ever been treated for depression, Emily?" the counselor asked.

I felt tears welling in my eyes. I stared at the popcorn ceiling to avoid his judgmental gaze as I shook my head.

"Do you feel sad often? Like you're always on the brink of tears?"

Right on cue, a traitorous tear fell down my cheek. I nodded.

"I'd like to refer you to a psychiatrist." He scribbled on his notepad. "There is medication we can prescribe for you – an antidepressant – that will help improve your mood. The boost in serotonin might help relations between the two of you. And Emily, perhaps we can continue one-on-one sessions to get to the root of your insecurities."

I watched my life play out as a movie, furious with the main character who couldn't speak up for herself. *Say something*! I screamed at myself internally. *Help*! I pleaded silently to the counselor. He didn't. Instead, he sent us along and told me the front desk would be in touch to schedule my psych follow-up once my referral was processed.

Shane and I drove home, neither one of us speaking. I felt crushed by defeat. He wasn't going to change anything to make this marriage work. Another hoax I'd foolishly fallen for.

When we got home, he began to get ready to leave for his midnight shift. Another night of sleeping alone for me and Sadie. At least she understood my pain in a way that the rest of the world did not. She witnessed it. She knew the truth.

Shane made me feel worthless. With each crushing blow, I was losing my will to live. The weight of his affair with Jen had placed such a heavy burden on my soul that I truly believed I would not survive another heartbreak. I would accept defeat and descend into nothingness. I would leave my world of pain and go where he could no longer hurt me – where nothing could hurt me – because my painful existence would cease to go on.

As I felt the ache of my heart, the death of my soul, my crushing self-hatred, and the desolate loneliness of the world around me, that nothingness called to me. And I clung to Sadie to keep me tethered.

chapter thirty-three

The psychiatrist prescribed me a daily dose of 150 milligrams of Effexor, which helped numb some of my heartache. I maintained neutrality in my relationship – celebrating Thanksgiving and Christmas with Shane as if we were on the mend – but at some point, that neutrality turned to apathy. I didn't care very much about anything anymore.

After the holidays, Gina came to Europe on a work trip, and we made plans to meet in Rome. Shane decided to come along, too. I didn't want him there, but he insisted upon it.

"Did you tell her?" he asked me during our flight to Rome. He didn't need to be specific – whether he was referring to Jen, or the slap, or the counseling – it didn't matter. I hadn't told her anything.

I shook my head and spoke quietly so the passengers around us wouldn't hear. "Can you be good to me this weekend?"

His brows furrowed. "What do you mean?"

"I don't want her to think we're having trouble." I held his gaze. It would be the first time I saw Gina in more than a year. I didn't want the trip to be tainted with arguments between Shane and me. I felt embarrassed by the thought of it. "I just want us to act happy."

He studied me. "It's *you* who isn't happy, Emily."

I looked down at my hands and rubbed the bandage around my

thumb. I'd chewed the skin so deep that layers of flesh were exposed. I pressed down on the gaping wound underneath the bandage until a faint red blotch appeared on top. "I will be happy this weekend."

He shrugged. "We'll see."

WE LANDED IN Rome and met Gina at the train station. I was ecstatic to see her – the first true happiness I'd felt in months – and nearly burst into tears when I threw my arms around her.

The next two days were full of sightseeing, all the pizza and wine we could get our hands on, coin tosses into the Trevi Fountain, and near-perfect behavior from Shane and me. Surrounded by incredible history and architecture – from the Colosseum, to the Vatican City, to the Pantheon – my persistent misery slowly shifted to excitement. Like a veil being lifted, I began to feel the lust for life that traveling awoke in me. I remembered the world wasn't only loneliness, pain, and heartache; it was opportunity, joy, and wonderment.

On our final night in Rome, we stumbled into karaoke. Entering the bar, Gina and I beamed at each other in excitement – karaoke had always been one of our favorite pastimes. It couldn't be a more perfect ending to our trip. We immediately rushed over to the DJ to put down our names for several songs.

The two of us ordered beers from the bar while Shane found a seat at a table in the corner. We took turns on stage. Gina belted the lyrics to "Blue" by LeAnn Rimes, and "You and I" by Lady Gaga; and I followed with the revengeful hits "Gunpowder and Lead" by Miranda Lambert, and "Before He Cheats" by Carrie Underwood. Although I hadn't consciously done it on purpose – they were both great karaoke tunes – I realized how fitting my song choices were as I performed them in Shane's direction.

Shane watched with a bored expression from the corner of the bar while Gina and I drank, sang, and danced. After an hour passed, he walked over to where we stood on the dance floor and placed a hand on my arm. "You ready to go back to the hotel?"

I widened my eyes. "Now? No! We're having so much fun!"

His lips tightened. "It's 1 a.m., Emily… I'm tired."

I glanced at Gina, who was shouting along the words to "Sweet Caroline" as she held her drink in the air. She clearly wasn't ready to call it a night either. It was our last night together and I wasn't sure how long it would be before I could see her again. I looked back at Shane. "Do you want to go back, and we'll meet you there in a little bit?"

He scowled. "Are you serious?"

"We won't stay out that much longer. Just another hour. Is that cool?"

He took a step back from me. "Wow, you're really going to do this…"

I could sense his anger and I didn't want to have a scene in front of Gina. "Shane," I warned. "Not here."

He shook his head disapprovingly. "Have fun," he said sarcastically over his shoulder as he began to leave.

"What's his deal?"

I realized Gina was now standing beside me, watching Shane walk out of the bar. The music was loud, so I didn't know how much of the conversation she'd heard. "He's tired." I rolled my eyes. "He's going back to the hotel."

She frowned. "Should we go?"

I shook my head. "No. Let's sing another song!"

I didn't care that Shane was mad. I could deal with that later. I wanted to enjoy the night with my best friend because I finally felt alive again in her presence. For the first time in months, I didn't feel heartbreak, pain, numbness, or apathy. I felt a reason – and a need – to be happy. I felt my sparkle.

After another hour of karaoke, Gina and I began our short walk home. We marveled when we reached the Trevi Fountain just a block before our hotel, lights illuminating the beauty of its ivory sculptures in the tranquil setting with no other late-night sightseers around.

I stopped in my steps to take it in. Tomorrow, I wouldn't be in Italy. I wouldn't be with Gina. I would return home to my cage. My heart begged for a few more moments of solace. "Do you want to sit here for a minute?"

"Sure," she agreed, choosing a center seat in the row of curved benches before the fountain.

We sat in silence and listened to the cascading water. Maybe it was the baroque glory before us, or the impending finality of our trip, or the Italian beer surging through my veins, but I suddenly felt compelled to word vomit all my troubles to Gina. "I have to tell you something," I blurted.

She shifted her focus from the fountain to me. "What's up?"

"Shane and I are not good."

"What do you mean?"

I swallowed. "He had an affair with my friend Jen three months ago. I've been trying to move forward. We went to marriage counseling, I started taking antidepressants, but honestly, Gina… I don't think I can move past this."

Her face transitioned from shock to sympathy, clutching her hand over her mouth as I spoke. I continued, telling Gina about how I sensed Shane was being unfaithful for the past two years, and how I had caught him messaging another girl during our first year in Germany. I told her about how Tom found the messages between Shane and Jen, and how I wanted to die when he sent me the screenshots.

She threw her arms around me and hugged me tightly "Why didn't you tell me all of this sooner?"

I returned her embrace as I stammered, "I felt like… if I told you… it would mean my marriage is over."

She pulled back to look at me. "Is it?"

I stared at the fountain and let the roar of the gushing water fill the silence between us as I considered my response. I studied the intricate marble art. And suddenly, it hit me.

I was 23 years old living in Europe. I had traveled to more countries in the past two years than I ever thought I'd travel to in my life. I was in Rome, sitting in front of one of the most beautifully renowned fountains in the world… and I had the *audacity* to let a man ruin that? I would let an unfaithful, manipulative, destructive person steal *my* happiness and opportunity from me?

The universe was throwing signs at me everywhere I went – every new city that awakened my soul whispering to me, *"This is the life you deserve. This is the life you can have."*

But not with Shane.

"It has to be," I finally said, looking at Gina. "Right?"

She shrugged. "You're the only person who can make that choice."

My throat grew tight. "Why is some part of me still afraid to lose him?" Tears began to fall down my cheeks. "How can I still feel love for him after seeing him for what he is? What the hell is wrong with me?"

She grabbed my hand. "There is nothing wrong with you. You are pure. He is not. He will continue to take advantage of your kind heart for as long as you allow him to, and it will never make sense to you because you are not the type of person he is."

A loud sob escaped my body.

"Emily, I know Shane is all you've known of love… but love doesn't have to feel like this." She squeezed my fingers. "Love doesn't lie to you and break your heart. Love is supposed to feel good. Love is supposed to feel safe."

Something deep within me ached. I remembered the safety I had once felt in Shane's arms so many years ago. That safety was gone. "I want that."

She nodded. "Moving forward, you need to tell me things. Don't be afraid of how I will react. I am not here to judge you. I'm your *best fucking friend*. Please, don't go through this alone."

I wiped my eyes and gave her a nod of agreement. "Deal."

THE FOLLOWING MORNING, Shane acted friendly toward us, but avoided direct interaction with me. After packing our bags, we walked Gina to the train station where we said our farewells and hopped in a taxi to the airport. As I hugged my best friend goodbye, I felt comfort knowing she was sharing the weight of my burden. I wasn't alone.

Shane and I rode silently in the taxi. As we neared the airport, I looked over at him and caught his eye. He shook his head.

"What?" I asked.

"Last night was pretty eye opening," he said bitterly.

"How so?"

He shrugged. "You're immature. You're not ready to grow up and have a family. You're still a fucking kid who just wants to party."

My skin grew hot. "Seriously? Gina is my best friend, and I haven't seen her in –"

"And I am your husband," he interrupted. "And last night, you had no regard for that. No regard for my feelings or what I was comfortable with. You did what *you* wanted. And I see it now."

"See what now?"

"That this isn't going to work," he snapped.

The taxi driver looked at us in his rear-view mirror.

I glared at Shane as I spoke calmly and clearly. "All I did was stay out at a karaoke bar for an extra hour with my best friend –”

"No, what you did was choose yourself. It's what you do every single time. You're selfish, you're immature, and I never should have married you."

I digested his words and waited for my tears to form; but they did not come. I searched for sadness within my body; but I could not find it. All I found was an overwhelming sense of agreement.

I never should have married him either.

Our taxi pulled up to the departures curb at the airport. I handed euros to the driver and grabbed my backpack from the trunk, an unfamiliar sense of empowerment brewing as the realization came over me: *My life doesn't have to be like this.*

"We can stay together for the next ten months or so until we leave Germany," Shane said as we began to walk away from the cab. "But once we're back in the States, I don't know if I see this marriage continuing."

"Fine," I replied, almost too quickly.

His eyes shot daggers at me. It wasn't the reaction he wanted. "Fine?"

"Fine," I repeated, as I shrugged my shoulders and walked into the airport.

chapter thirty-four

The trip to Italy was the beginning of the end. It wasn't the argument itself, but the entire scenario that had played out.

It was saying no to Shane and choosing to do the thing I wanted to do instead; and feeling no shame as he attempted to gaslight me into submission the next morning.

It was overcoming my fear of confiding in a friend, her acceptance of my truth, and her willingness to support me through it.

It was the small taste of freedom – the glimpse at a life I could have in an alternate universe – and it was enough to give me the most dangerous weapon against him: Hope.

Envisioning a world without Shane once seemed impossible. Now, Hope painted a brilliant version of me that could exist without his love, his anger, and his crushing betrayal. Hope told me that my independence was my power.

Hope lit a spark inside of me. As her flame grew, it engulfed my other emotions and shone light on my resentment toward Shane. I no longer felt ignited in his presence. My skin no longer burned under his touch. Instead, he began to repulse me. Somehow, I had gone from loving him to hating him overnight. Because Hope hated Shane, and thus, held by Hope's embrace, so did I.

On the heels of our return from Italy, my coworker Sharon invited me to go country line dancing at the western bar on a nearby Air Force base. She had invited me several times before, and I always politely declined because I knew Shane would get upset at the idea of me dancing at a bar without him. I studied her text.

Sharon: *Emily, come dancing with us tonight! You'll have so much fun, I promise!*

Shane was working the midnight shift again, and like a moth to a flame, I was drawn to the opportunity to feel the small sense of power – of rebellious freedom – I'd felt in Rome.

Emily: *Okay, I'll come :)*
Sharon: *YAY!*

Sharon had become one of my favorite parts of my job. Her positive attitude and zest for life were attributes I longed to embody, and although I hadn't confided in her about Shane and Jen, it comforted me to have another female lift my spirits in the crushing aftermath of my friendship breakup.

Sharon's husband Chad and his friend Roger joined us at the bar. Roger was tall, towering over me by several inches – opposite of Shane, who banned me from wearing heels due to his insecurities of me being taller than him. His smile was radiant, a straight white curve along a chiseled jawline. It was honestly overwhelming how handsome he was. As he introduced himself to me, I tried not to stare too long, for fear it might become obvious how enamored I was.

I mimicked Sharon's movements through song after song, the two of us laughing every time I fell out of step and cheering every time I got it right. I was having so much fun, nearly forgetting about the world outside of that dance hall. When the music slowed down to a partner dance, Sharon joined Chad, and I walked in the direction of the bar to get another drink.

A broad, strong hand reached for my arm, and I stopped in my tracks, turning to see Roger smiling at me. "Would you like to dance?"

My heart hammered in my chest, but I grinned in return. "Sure, but I don't know how…."

"Don't worry." He spoke with smooth confidence. "I'll lead. Just follow."

As we moved to the dancefloor with the other pairs, he placed one hand on mine and the other on the small of my back. I almost shivered in response. He led us through the foot motions, twirling me around in multiple directions, our arms passing overhead and around my waist, then ending in a sudden dip that took my breath away.

"Wow!" I laughed. "You're good at this."

He studied me as we continued to move in step with the music. "You've never two-stepped before?"

I felt shy in his gaze. "Never."

"Where have you been?" he joked.

I gave a small shrug. "At home with a husband who doesn't dance."

His soft brown eyes widened. "Wait – you're married?"

My feet lost rhythm with the music, and I took a moment to collect myself back into step. I immediately wished I hadn't brought up Shane. Even though I knew it was wrong, I had been savoring that moment with Roger. "I am," I admitted, my eyes moving to the ring on my finger.

His eyes followed. "Oh. Damn."

Damn? Was he upset? Was it possible he was feeling me the same way I was feeling him? *No way.* Roger was too handsome, too nice, and too perfect to be into me. I chuckled in return, brushing it off, and we continued our dance until the song came to an end.

After we parted, I made my way to the bar where Sharon was ordering waters for the four of us, having just finished her own dance with Chad. She smirked at me. "How was that?"

I blushed. "How was what?"

Her eyes shot to Roger, who stood talking to Chad only a few feet away. Roger looked back at us, the side of his mouth forming a smile when he met my eyes. "You know what," Sharon whispered. I only smiled in return.

Returning home that night, I couldn't stop thinking about Roger. For years, I had never let my thoughts stray from Shane like this. But I couldn't stop smiling thinking about that moment we shared. It was wrong. But I deserved happiness. I deserved to feel giddy. I deserved whatever this was.

My judgment clouded from too many drinks, I reached for my phone to text Sharon. My heart beat out of my chest as I hit send.

Emily: *Please tell Roger that I'd love to hang out with him again :)*
Sharon: *Tell him yourself ;) ;)*

I laughed. Then, I opened my Facebook app to send Roger a friend request. I put my phone on my nightstand and drifted to sleep as scenes of our dance together played over and over in my head.

THE NEXT DAY I opened Facebook to find that Roger had not only accepted my friend request, but messaged me, too.

Roger: *Emily :) Last night was fun. When will we see you again?*
Emily: *Soon I hope? I had so much fun!*
Roger: *Maybe beer pong at Sharon and Chad's next weekend?*

Emily: *I can probably make that work :)*

I heard the front door unlock. Shane was home from work. I swiped the messages off my screen and walked down the hallway.

He took a seat on the living room couch to remove his boots. Barely looking up at me, he asked, "How was last night?"

I rested casually against the wall across from him. "It was fine."

"Who was there?"

My breath grew shallow. "Sharon and her husband."

He gave an uninterested nod. "Cool." He walked past me into the kitchen to grab himself some water as my phone vibrated in my pocket, sending a chill up my spine. "I'm exhausted. I'm going to sleep."

"Alright," I said. It was Sunday, so I would be doing housework while Shane slept. "I'll be quiet."

He walked toward the bedroom, stopping to give me a half-hug in the hallway. My phone burned a hole in my pocket as his arm wrapped around me. He kissed me on the forehead, but it felt more out of obligation than kindness.

This is what our marriage had been reduced to. Lies. A lack of intimacy. An impending end date. I watched him walk into the bedroom, then hurried over to the couch where I pulled my phone out to read two new messages.

Roger: *Cool, I hope you can make it. I really liked meeting you. I'm bummed you're not single...*

Roger: *I'm sorry if that was inappropriate*

My heart raced. My fingers danced rapidly over my phone screen while I crafted my response.

Emily: *My situation is complicated… I won't be married much longer*

My chest nearly exploded as I sent the message. *Holy shit.* What the fuck was I doing? It was wrong, it was so wrong… but then:

Roger: *Oh really? Tell me more…*

Roger and I messaged back and forth for hours that day while Shane slept in our bedroom. I barely got any of my housework done. I knew I was stepping into dangerous territory, but I couldn't abandon the thrill. For the first time in a long time, I felt desired – and I wanted to see how far I could take that fiery feeling before getting burned.

Our conversation plunged deep. He wanted to know all about me, and I started to share. I told him about the troubled state of my relationship in detail. I even told him about Jen. It felt good to admit how miserable I was, trapped in a marriage which was delicately hanging by a thread. He was empathetic. He listened. He cared.

Roger: *I barely know you, Emily, but I promise you deserve more than that. You should be treated like a damn queen. Come to beer pong this weekend. Let's get your mind off it.*

Our messages continued for days. I took careful caution to only talk to him when Shane was sleeping or at work, and turned my notifications off when we were together so that my phone wouldn't vibrate and spark his curiosity.

The student had become the master.

The more I talked to Roger, the more I was able to break free of the manipulative chokehold Shane had on me. Each flirtatious message added fuel to the growing flame inside me. I burned with eager anticipation to drastically change my life – to make a move that would change the course of my future.

It only took one week of talking to Roger before a lightbulb switched in my mind: I was no longer afraid to lose Shane, and I wasn't afraid to hurt him either.

This was my out.

chapter thirty-five

The weekend of beer pong inconveniently fell upon Valentine's Day. Although our marriage was in shards that were barely taped together, Shane insisted we go out to dinner before his work shift. He presented me with my favorite candy and a rose, and I gave nothing in return – contrary to previous years when I'd showered him in love. I didn't want to pretend that our love was anything worth celebrating.

As I sat across from him at the Italian restaurant, I feigned interest in his attempt at conversation, swirling my spaghetti while my mind played out various scenarios in which I told him I didn't love him anymore. How would I do it? How would he react?

We had driven separately to dinner since he'd head straight to work after our meal. I strategically waited until we were in the parking lot to tell him I was going to Sharon's, knowing he couldn't hang around to argue.

He furrowed his brows. "Tonight?"

I kept a casual tone. "She wants to have a Galentine's night. Drink some wine, watch a movie. I'll probably end up crashing there, so can you come straight home after work for Sadie?"

He glared, as if he could see through my lie, but then replied, "Sure."

Phew.

I ARRIVED AT Sharon's house and rang the doorbell, running a quick hand through my hair and adjusting my shirt. I took a deep breath, the anticipation of seeing Roger again nearly swallowing me whole.

Roger answered the door. I drank in his tall, handsome body as his bright smile gleamed at me. He welcomed me in a hug. "Glad you could make it."

As his arms wrapped around my body, I had to bite my lip to contain my excitement. It was only our second time meeting in person, but after this past week of messaging I felt like we knew each other on a much deeper level already. His scent, the feeling of his body, his warmth – it rushed over me like a wave of comfort.

We began a round of beer pong, Sharon and me on one team and Chad and Roger on the other. I locked eyes with Roger from across the table, and he stared back like I was the most beautiful girl he'd ever seen.

Sharon and I lost to the boys, and we decided to switch things up for the second round. Roger joined me on one side of the table while Sharon left to join Chad. I sunk my first shot, earning a nod of approval from him, and when he sunk his own, I gave a gentle squeeze of his arm to return the support.

When I nailed my third shot, he hugged me, upping the level of celebration for each successful toss. As the game went on, and more alcohol flowed through our bloodstreams, our hugs began to linger. His hand rested on the small of my back for a moment longer than it should have. My hands explored the muscles of his back beyond a casual embrace. The tension between us was building, and I knew he felt it, too.

It came down to the final shot. If Roger was successful, we'd win the game. Sharon and Chad heckled us from across the table. I placed my hand delicately on his upper back as he aimed. His ball flew through the air and sank perfectly into the cup on the other end.

He turned to face me, eyes wide with excitement, and before I could say a word, lips pressed against my mouth. Foreign lips. Not Shane's lips. No… they were softer. They were delicate. But they were electric. They were thrilling. They were… everything.

In a blink, three faithful years of marriage ended.

Roger pulled back, the realization of what he'd done now hitting him. He studied my face with concern. "Should I have not done that?"

My heart pulsed rapidly, but my body consented. I searched for guilt, but it wasn't there. I felt *alive*. I wanted more. "I'm glad you did," I reassured.

A drunken cheer erupted from Sharon. "I've been waiting all night for that!" We laughed in response. She then yawned and said, "Alright… I think it's time to call it. I'm exhausted. Y'all can stay here…" She raised her eyebrows at me. "But I only have one guest room."

I looked at Roger, my proposition in my eyes, and he grinned back at me like a devil.

We retreated to the guest room and began to kiss with an intensity I hadn't felt in ages. He removed my shirt and grabbed my breasts, and I burned with desire at his touch. He was ravenous, his tongue moving from my mouth to my neck to my nipples. My body sprung to life with adrenaline as it recalled the forgotten feeling of being so wanted – so desired – and yearning for it in return. It was primal. It was everything. I gave in completely, abandoning regard for anything other than my need to fulfill that desire.

I WOKE UP next to Roger the next day. As I looked over at him, now sober, I reflected on the night before. Surely, I'd feel guilty without the alcohol impairing my judgment. I waited for reality to crash down upon me – regret, shame, panic.

But none of it came.

I inhaled a long, slow breath and held it for a moment. As I slowly exhaled, I realized the only emotion present in my body was liberation. I didn't need to live a life of misery, entirely dependent upon how Shane treated me.

I could make my own happiness.

My independence was my power.

I lay there, naked in bed with a man I'd only known for a week, with zero regard for my husband, and I knew it: My marriage was over.

Roger stirred beside me. "Good morning," he spoke sleepily.

I smiled. "Good morning."

He scanned my face. "How are you feeling?"

I noted the sensations within my body. No tightness in my chest. My breathing was calm. My skin was warm. My heart beat slowly. *Peace.* "I'm… actually… feeling great."

He grinned. "Yeah?"

"Yeah."

He reached out an arm, inviting me to move closer. I accepted and scooted toward him until my face rested atop his chest. He stroked my shoulder, and I could have spent an eternity in that moment, basking in the high of finally making it to the other side.

But I knew I couldn't stay there. Despite the way it felt, I wasn't really on the other side yet. I had a husband to return home to.

And I had a marriage to end.

chapter thirty-six

I returned home to find Shane in bed. He had been home from work for a few hours and was deep in sleep. I studied him from the bedroom door frame. Surely, the guilt would hit me now. But it didn't. I felt vindicated.

It would be several hours before he woke up, so I brewed myself a cup of coffee and sat on my patio with Sadie to think about my next steps. I pulled out my phone to text Gina – who would also be asleep due to the time difference – but at least it would help unload my thoughts.

I had told Gina about Roger after the first night we met. She was completely supportive of my secret flirtation with him, stating it was time to put my own happiness first.

Emily: Hey, let me know if you can talk on the phone when you wake up. DON'T TELL ANYONE but I slept with Roger last night and I'm freaking out!!! I don't even feel bad! Honestly, I woke up this morning feeling so free and invincible. I know for certain now that I don't want to be married to Shane anymore. I wish I could pack my bags and leave today. He leaves for work at 11 a.m. your time. Let's chat after that.

I deleted the text after I sent it for safe measure and pondered how

I would break the news to Shane about wanting a divorce. It shouldn't come as a shock; everything had changed since Jen. He knew I hadn't moved past his infidelity and was growing more distant each day. He was the one who had said in Italy that we could stay married for the remainder of our time in Germany and figure out what to do once we returned to the States… but I didn't think I could wait another nine months until our departure in November.

For so long, I had been afraid of the unknown. Shane was my sanctuary – my comfort, my safety, my familiar place. But he was no longer my sanctuary. He was my prison. And I needed to get out.

But where would I go? Back to California? I cringed at the thought of moving back to my hometown. I missed my family and friends, but the idea of returning home from battle defeated brought forth a shame I couldn't bear. I'd burned so many bridges with my stubborn adamance to be with Shane, and there I was – *a fool* – because Shane had done exactly what everyone expected him to do.

Could I stay here? Would I be able to support myself and Sadie? My managerial role came with a higher salary, my car was paid off, and the cost of rent was reasonable. I sipped my coffee while I watched Sadie absentmindedly rolling on her back, absorbing the sun rays on her black fur. It terrified me, but the prospect of forming a new life in Germany seemed brighter than returning to the place that was stained with memories of love and heartbreak.

I rehearsed my breakup speech while I cleaned the kitchen and living room to preoccupy myself until Shane finally awoke that afternoon.

He wandered into the kitchen where I sat at the table working on a grocery list. He yawned. "Good morning."

"Good afternoon," I replied. It was 4 p.m.

"How was Galentine's?" he asked sleepily.

I gave him a soft smile as I responded, "Good." I wondered if his instincts could pick up the scent of another man on my body.

He moseyed over to the pantry and took out a box of cereal. He poured some into a bowl, topped it with milk, and joined me at the table.

Every nerve ending in my body pulled me in the direction of staying quiet, of saving the topic for another time; but my heart – bruised, battered and broken from years of abuse – stood firmly on its ground. "You know what you said in Italy about us splitting up when we go back to the States?"

He nodded, eying me curiously.

"I've been thinking about it." I bit my lip to stop it from quivering. "I might not go back."

He studied my face for a moment while he chewed his cereal. "What do you mean?"

I took a deep breath. *Here goes nothing.* "I might stay here."

"You can't," he said flatly.

His eyes bore down on me, and at one point I might have faltered; but I maintained my confidence. "Yes, I can. As long as I remain with my current job, they'll sponsor my visa to stay in Germany and I'll just have to rent my own apartment off base."

He swirled the spoon around in his cereal bowl, not looking at me. "What about us?"

My voice was gentle as I said, "I think we both know where our marriage is headed, and we've just been too afraid to admit it."

His brows furrowed; but I saw confusion fall upon his face, not anger. "What changed?"

I fumbled with the pen I'd been using to make my list. I thought about Roger – the messages, the kiss, the sex. I wondered if Shane knew a cheater sat before him. "I've… been feeling this way since… Jen." I grimaced. Her name was bitter in my mouth. "I wanted to see if I could move past it… but I can't. And I think… you'd be happier without me –"

"Emily," he interrupted. "I could never be happy without you."

I exhaled a sigh. Why was he making this difficult? I was trying to give him an out. I shook my head. I had to be firm. "We bring out the worst in each other, Shane. We haven't been happy for a while. All we do is fight. We're both to blame, and we both know it's not getting better. We need to end it before it gets worse."

I froze in anticipation as I waited for his anger and retaliatory words to surface. Instead, he reached across the table for my hand and held it. I watched his fingers caress mine, then intertwine. We stared at each other in solemn silence for what felt like an eternity.

"If this is what you want… okay," he conceded softly. "But let's keep talking about it. Let's keep thinking about it."

I nodded and refrained from pushing further. His reaction was a hundred times calmer than I had expected, and I didn't want to push my luck.

WHEN GINA CALLED that evening, I told her everything about my night with Roger and my conversation with Shane. After momentarily losing her mind over the news, she asked, "What are you going to do if Shane doesn't agree to the divorce?"

"He can't stop me," I countered.

"But he'll try. You know how his manipulative mind games work."

She had a point, but I had Hope on my side now. I wasn't afraid of losing him anymore. "There's nothing he could say to make me change my mind this time."

"I'm so proud of you, Emily," she encouraged. "You are doing the right thing. Please know that no matter how messy this gets, no matter how hard it gets, you are doing the right thing. Do not be afraid to ask for help at any point."

Her words comforted me. "Thank you. I love you."

"I love you, too."

And Gina was right. I came home late from work a few days later to find yellow sticky notes lining our refrigerator. I began to pull them down, one by one, reading the words written in Shane's handwriting:

When things feel impossible, remember how much I love you.
You're still my whole world, no matter how difficult things are lately.
We'll always be stronger together than we'll ever be apart.

Irritated, I left the kitchen and walked to our bedroom. More sticky notes awaited me on my closet doors.

You're the most beautiful, amazing, intelligent, strong woman I've ever known.
You are my reason for living.
I would be lost without you.

I huffed. I peered into the bathroom, where even more sticky notes lined the mirror.

We can make it through this. I promise.
I will never give up on you. Please don't give up on me.
I love you, Emily. Now and forever.

The notes felt like little thorns in my heart, but I closed my eyes and reminded myself that this was Shane's manipulation at work. When things didn't go his way, he resorted to either anger or Machiavellian charm. He was wise enough to know anger would push me away farther right now, so he was trying to lure me into reconsidering.

I would not reconsider.

Since Shane would be away at work for the night, I drove over to Roger's for pizza and a movie. We'd been texting frequently since beer pong night, recounting the incredible time we'd had together and how neither of us could wait to do it again. Amid my excitement surrounding him and my resentment toward Shane, I became less careful ensuring all my tracks were covered.

I arrived at Roger's apartment, which was nestled into a small German town not far from the military base where Shane and I lived. He stood waiting for me on the front step. I beamed at him as he held the door open, ushering me inside before pulling me into him for a kiss.

"You doing okay?" he asked, his brown eyes scanning my face.

"Better now." I kissed him again.

Shortly into our movie, my phone vibrated. I glanced over, and my heart fell into my gut when I saw Shane's name light up on the screen. He didn't normally call me from work.

"Are you going to answer?" Roger asked, also noting the name on my phone.

I frowned. "It'll be weird if I don't." I accepted the call. "Hello?"

"Where are you?" Shane's accusatory tone blasted through the phone.

"At Sharon's," I quickly lied.

"Bull*shit*," he snarled. "Who are you really with?"

My chest tightened. "What are you talking about?"

"You think you're fucking sneaky, you lying cunt?!" he bellowed. My entire body froze. "Maybe you should do a better job logging out of your Facebook. I brought your laptop to work with me. I'm reading all your messages with *Roger*."

My laptop. I hadn't even noticed he took it with him to work because I hadn't used it when I returned home. *Fuck.* I thought about my messages with Roger. How much had he read? How far back had he gone? My hands began shaking.

"You fucking lying slut," he taunted. "You're really something else, you fucking hypocrite. You're such a fucking cunt."

I hung up the phone before I could hear another word. I looked over at Roger, my face hot with embarrassment as I realized he'd heard every word.

He stared at the phone. "Fuck." Then at me. "You alright?"

My entire body trembled as I shook my head.

"What do you want to do?"

I swallowed. I had no idea. I had never been in this situation before. Trying to think quickly, I opened my Facebook app and deleted my message history with Roger. I had no idea how much Shane had read but I didn't need him reading any more. I swiftly changed my password, then visited my history of logins and logged out everything except for my phone. Then, I turned off my phone. I needed to buy time to think.

"Do you want to stay here tonight?" Roger asked.

I nodded. "Please."

He placed an arm around me. I began to cry. I was so embarrassed that he'd heard Shane call me those names. I was mortified to be crying in front of him. But a comforting hand gripped my shoulder as he said, "You're going to be okay."

THE NEXT MORNING, my fingers trembled as I turned my phone back on. As expected, Shane had called and messaged all night. I had 17 voicemails and 53 texts. I skimmed through the rollercoaster of messages ranging from anger, to insanity, to hurt.

Shane: *Answer your phone or I will fucking kill you Emily*
Shane: *I will kill you and I will fucking kill him*
Shane: *You're going to be sorry for what you've done*

Shane: *Do you have any idea what you've done?*

Shane: *You're going to regret this*

Shane: *YOU STUPID FUCKING CUNT I WILL END YOUR LIFE IF I EVER SEE YOUR FACE AGAIN*

Shane: *How could you do this to me Emily?*

Shane: *Don't you have any idea how much I love you?*

Shane: *Why would you do this to us?*

Shane: *I'm going home when I get off work to pack my clothes and I'm moving into the barracks. Don't be home. I don't want to see you or speak to you.*

I stayed with Roger until later that morning when I deemed it safe to assume that Shane had come and gone from the apartment. I was driving along the two-lane highway toward home when a familiar vehicle approached in the other lane.

Oh fuck.

I panicked as Shane's truck inched closer. I hadn't waited long enough. There was no way off the road. Just my lane, his lane, and forest on either side of us. I had no choice but to pass him and pray he wouldn't turn around and follow me home. We were merely hundreds of feet away from one another when Shane veered his truck into my lane, as if attempting to crash into me head-on.

Screaming, I slammed on my brakes to try to avoid a collision. At the last moment, Shane recklessly maneuvered back into his own lane, missing me by seconds. I caught sight of his face as he passed me, and what I saw frightened me to my core. He was yelling, teeth bared, eyes bulging from his face with a level of rage I'd never seen before.

I had broken him.

I started to cry. With shaking hands, I guided my car to the nearest exit where I pulled off and reached for my phone. I couldn't take the chance of encountering him again. I dialed a number I had saved to use in case of an emergency – a number I never thought I would need until this moment. Shane's military supervisor answered on the other end.

"Sir," I pleaded through tears. "This is Shane Foster's wife. I need your help. Please."

I spilled everything. I told him I didn't feel safe with Shane coming home because I feared he would harm me, that he'd threatened to kill me via text, and tried to run me off the road. I requested a restraining order and a permanent room for Shane at the barracks. I was so grateful when he took me seriously, assuring me that Shane would not be coming near me unsupervised again.

I finished my drive home and scooped Sadie up into my arms, apologizing over and over to her. She didn't know it yet, but she had just lost her dad.

I RECEIVED A phone call later that Shane would be coming to gather more of his things, escorted by two military police officers to ensure no contact between us.

I sat on our living room couch as they entered our home. I watched Shane walk to the bedroom, rage seething from his skin. Sadie ran to greet him. He ignored her, and my heart splintered. After a few minutes, he came back down the hallway toward the front door. He said nothing as he glared at me, flanked by the two soldiers on either side.

His dark brows furrowed over eyes that unleashed an inferno upon me. The creases of his nose were filled with hatred. His lip curled in disgust. And although he did not speak, I knew what this moment meant: things would never be okay between us again.

I was in the deep end now, and there was no safety net. There was no turning back to the life I had once known. It was time to sink or swim.

chapter thirty-seven

A month after Shane found out about Roger, Sadie and I moved into our own apartment, and I filed for divorce. I made four significant mistakes as I began to forge my new path.

By the time I moved out, Shane's boiling rage had cooled to the point where we had exchanged a few neutral text messages and he reluctantly agreed to assist with moving some large, heavy furniture items to my apartment in his truck.

Letting him know where I lived was my first mistake.

As hard as it was to believe, it was the end. Some days it hurt painfully when I came across funny things I wanted to share or exciting news I wanted to tell him. I'd lost my best friend, my partner, my roommate, my family, my confidante, and my future – all at once. My bones ached for the parts of him I missed.

Other days, I felt relieved. I could see a light at the end of the tunnel of heartbreak, and it shone brighter than ever before. I was strong for leaving Shane; and I didn't care how messy things had to get to reach that point. All that mattered was I got out.

But the loneliness of each night alone was an aching pain that begged for relief. Even with Sadie by my side, and Gina a call away, I yearned for the comforting distraction that only human contact could bring.

I searched my phone for an answer to my heartache as I lay in my new bedroom. My fingers hovered over Roger's name, but my heart sank knowing I couldn't call him. We'd hung out three more times since the night Shane found us out, and in trying to fill the void of losing my husband, I began to grow emotionally attached.

I tapped open our message thread, reminding myself of our last conversation.

Roger: *I think we should take a step back from what we're doing and just be friends. I'm not looking for a relationship and I don't want you to feel like I'm leading you on.*

Emily: *I'm not looking for a relationship either, but I thought we were more than friends? Why did you pursue me in the first place if you weren't interested?*

Roger: *It's my fault. I shouldn't have crossed the line with you. I thought we were on the same page about just hooking up. I didn't mean to be an asshole.*

Emily: *The way you acted toward me didn't imply that you only wanted to be friends. I can't help it that I ended up liking you as much as I do and you don't feel the same. It sucks.*

Roger: *I'm sorry. Hopefully we can be friends whenever you're ready.*

A sharp sting of rejection made my chest tighten as I reread the conversation. Of course he didn't want to be romantically involved with someone in the middle of an unstable divorce. Chasing a married woman had probably been a fun pursuit, but the resulting mess wasn't something he signed up for.

I felt stupid.

I rubbed my forehead. I needed to immerse myself in something other than real life for a little bit. Looking around my room for a solution,

I spotted the iPad sitting on my dresser. I had gifted the iPad to Shane on his birthday last year, but I pocketed it when we split. I never saw him use it, so I figured he wouldn't miss it. Downloading an eBook sounded like the perfect distraction.

I hopped back into bed and pressed the home screen to wake up the iPad. I hadn't even looked at it since bringing it over to my apartment. A series of notifications greeted me as the screen lit up. *Wow, I guess he actually did use this thing.*

Wait. My breath caught in my throat as I realized some of the notifications were from Facebook. There was no way. He wouldn't be stupid enough to leave his Facebook logged in on a non-password protected iPad, would he?

I tapped open the Facebook app. *Holy shit.* The iPad was logged into Shane's Facebook. The thing I'd asked – no, *begged* – to see for the last few years. Did I dare check it now? My curiosity took over.

And that was my second mistake.

I started by looking at his status updates, which had been hidden from me since he blocked me after finding out about Roger. He had posted about me cheating on him and that being the reason for our divorce. As comments poured in from people expressing their shock and sympathy, he'd responded that I was lying to him the entire time and he was heartbroken. Playing the victim at my expense – no surprise there.

Next, I went to his messages. Girl, after girl, after girl in his inbox. My stomach turned. He must have been talking to any and every possible girl he could get a response from, shooting his shot in each conversation I opened. My "husband" had been away from me for a month and was acting like I never existed.

I skimmed conversation after conversation, the hair on my arms standing as my blood began to boil beneath my skin. Then, a message stopped me in my tracks.

Shane: Hey beautiful. I've been thinking about you, and I really want to come see you again.

April: What makes you think about me after all this time?

Shane: I'm no longer married.

April: Oh wow, what happened?

Shane: She cheated on me.

April: I'm sorry to hear that, but I don't think it's a good idea for us to see each other again.

Shane: Why do you say that?

April: Last time we slept together, you didn't tell me you were married until after and it made me feel horrible. Then after you went back home to your wife you stopped contacting me all together. Why would it be any different this time?

I reread the last message two more times.

Last time we slept together, you didn't tell me you were married...

My heart became a brick inside my chest. *Who the fuck is this?* I clicked on her profile. She lived in Grafenwöhr, where Shane had been sent for work during our first year of marriage.

The place I went to visit him with Sadie.

The place where he made me feel missed, wanted and secure.

I struggled to breathe as the significance of what I was finding sank in.

Up until this point, although I had suspected it, I had never found hard evidence of Shane being physically intimate with another woman during our marriage – he had always denied it and swore that his bouts of weakness were only words exchanged. Here was proof that Shane had slept with another woman all the way back in our first year of marriage.

How many others have there been?

Panic. Icy panic coursed through me. *It shouldn't matter, he doesn't belong to me anymore.* I tried to push it out of my mind. I tried to let it go.

But I couldn't. I needed to hear the truth. I needed to know.

Calling him was my third mistake.

"What," he answered curtly, letting me know my call was unwelcome.

"How many women did you sleep with while we were together?"

He scoffed. "What are you talking about?"

"How many were there besides April?"

"What the fuck are you talking about?"

My throat tightened as I spoke, tears forming in my eyes as a byproduct of my rage. "Stop treating me like a fucking idiot!" I hated how weak I sounded. "I'm looking at your messages with her right now. Were you fucking her the whole time you were away?! Was it before or after I visited you?"

Shane paused, then his anger filled the silence between us. "How the fuck are you in my Facebook right now?!"

"Answer my questions!" I demanded, tears now streaming down my face.

"No – you answer my question and get the fuck out of my Facebook right now!"

Overwhelmed, I hung up the phone. I frantically searched for more evidence before he could reset his password and lock me out. My phone vibrated. I declined his call. It vibrated again. I hit the red button. He kept calling, and when I didn't answer, he sent a text.

Shane: *I'm driving to your apartment.*

I jumped out of my bed as the shock of his message stopped my sobs. *He's coming here.* I paced back and forth in my room, my hands shaking. *What do I do? What the fuck do I do?* It seemed like only minutes passed before he appeared at my door.

My fourth mistake was letting him in.

I don't know what I wanted from Shane. Our marriage was over – I didn't want him to try to save it – but part of me wanted him to at least *attempt* to dispel the information I had just uncovered, because it was too much pain to handle. I felt like my whole body might crack into pieces from the relentless throbbing in my chest, and I desperately needed him to at least *try* to hold me together.

He stormed into my apartment. "How'd you get into my account?"

I stared, speechless. This man… this man I once loved so much. I envisioned him in bed with another girl. I thought about him coming home to me. Lying.

He walked the short distance from my front door to my bedroom, where he spotted the iPad on my bed. I could do nothing but watch. Frozen. Heartbroken. "Fucking psycho," he muttered before turning to face me. "Thought you could just take this?" He motioned toward the device.

"You weren't even using it!" I shouted as I followed him into the bedroom. "You didn't even notice it was gone!"

"So, your idea was to just keep tabs on me? Stalk me from a distance?" He moved toward me until we were face to face. "*You* moved out, Emily. *You* fucked another guy. *You* filed for divorce. What the fuck right do you think *you* have to be upset here? You selfish, crazy bitch."

Rage swarmed inside me. "You fucking lied! You fucking cheated on me! The whole fucking time!" I wailed, and before I could get a grip of my emotions my arm swung in the direction of his face.

He caught it before it could make impact, gripping my forearm tightly as he smirked. "Here I was thinking I missed you, but you haven't changed one bit." His fingers dug deep into my forearm.

I swung my other arm in his direction, but he was too fast. He caught that arm too and held me stationary as an evil smile spread across his face. "And yet, somehow, seeing you cry still turns me on."

With swift motion, he spun me; wrapping his arms tightly around my body so that my own were pinned to my sides. Using his weight behind me, he pushed me onto my bed. His heavy body landed atop mine. On my stomach, I writhed under his weight attempting to roll him off. He pressed an arm firmly across my back and used the other to pull my shorts down far enough for him to force himself inside. My entire body tensed in an effort to reject him.

For a moment I froze while my brain sorted through what was unraveling in real time.

My husband, cheating on me and lying to me.

My husband, gaslighting me to believe I was crazy.

My husband, who I am divorcing.

My husband, who I no longer live with and who is having sex with other women.

My husband, who is having sex with me right now.

No.

Not this time.

I swung the back of my head up with as much force as I could muster. It collided with something hard – his chin, his forehead – I didn't care.

"Fuck!" he snarled in pain, lifting his upper body off mine to avoid another blow of my head.

"GET OFF!" I bellowed, loud enough for the neighbors above me to hear – loud enough for the entire street to hear. I would take no more. "I'll report you for violating our no-contact order!" I threw an elbow at him and dug my knees into the bed, launching my hips upwards, sideways, anything other than still. "I will end your fucking career!" I shrieked.

It was a promise. My words dripped with hatred and rage.

Shane retreated, pulling up his pants. I rose to a seated position on the bed, pulling up my own. He shot me a repulsed glare, rubbing the bottom of his lip where I assumed my head had collided. "So fucking *dramatic.*"

He shook his head. "How long are you going to play the victim here?"

If my eyes could throw daggers, he would've bled out on my floor. "Get the fuck out of my apartment," I ordered as sweat dripped from my forehead.

He grabbed the iPad and walked out of my room toward the front door, pausing to look back at me. "To answer your question, there were too many others to count." He pulled my front door open. "If you actually believed all I did was *talk* to Jen, you're a fucking idiot."

Fury. Burning hot rage at my fingertips. Fire on my cheeks. An inferno in my chest. I erupted, and vitriol spewed from my heart through my throat as I made every attempt to wound – to kill – his ego.

"You think I give a fuck about that now?!" I stood from my bed and marched toward him at the front door. "I have zero regrets about cheating on you with Roger! He fucked me better than you ever could because guess what? He can actually last longer than two minutes!"

His lip curled.

"Best sex I've had in my life and all of it was worth it because it made me realize I don't need *you*!" I jabbed my finger into his chest. "I don't love *you*. You brought *nothing* to my life. You were a waste of my fucking time. You are a piece of shit, and *no one* will ever love you."

He sneered. "And *no one* will love you either, Emily. Sooner or later, everyone in your life will see you for the miserable bitch that you are."

And with that, he walked out the door.

My body convulsed with shaking breaths as I watched his car pull away. Anger. Shame. Hurt. Fury. Panic. I sank to my knees on the tile floor of my apartment and wept. It all hurt so much. When would it stop hurting?

I retreated up the hallway to my shower where I stripped my clothes and stepped into hot water, my skin feeling filthy from where his body had been only moments before.

I lathered shampoo into my hair. I hated the craziness he had instilled in me. Always looking over my shoulder for the next threat, terrified to open messages on my phone. It drove me mad, and he blamed me for it. But the threat was real. I never wanted to live in fear caused by someone else's infidelity again. I rinsed it clean.

I washed my face. I hated the anger that spewed from me unto him. I hated the rage that boiled within me, the abusive behavior that only he provoked. I never wanted to act like that with anyone ever again. Stroking my temples and my cheeks, I cleansed my pores of it all.

I scrubbed my shoulders and arms. I hated the burden he made me carry. My body was exhausted with the weight of the blame. I didn't want to blame myself anymore. I scrubbed it away.

I lathered my midsection and legs. I hated the way my growth had been stifled. He shrunk me to a version that fit within his narrative and then he stopped watering me, stopped feeding me, to ensure I would not grow beyond my confinement. With upward strokes I encouraged my body to once again stand tall.

I brought hot soapy water across my backside and the region between my legs. I hated that these sacred parts of me were violated by his touch. He had stolen them for years. With gentle circles I washed them as I reclaimed ownership.

I scrubbed at the hurt and I rinsed off the anger.

Lather. Rinse. Repeat. Lather. Rinse. Repeat.

Even though it was hard to do while my heart was bleeding, I showered myself in the love I needed.

Finally stepping out, I wrapped my hair in a towel, pulled on fresh pajamas, and hopped into bed with Sadie. *Sweet Sadie.* Immediately, I was overcome with guilt. I buried my face in her fur as I began to cry, this time for her. Because she never deserved any of this. But she licked my tears and rested her head on my arm to tell me it was alright. Her eyes, one brown and one blue, bore into mine, letting me know she loved me through it all. I held her closely, silently vowing she'd seen the end of this nightmare. Suddenly, I realized what I needed to do.

I hopped out of bed and went into my closet, pulling out a box. When I had moved out of our apartment, it was too painful to throw away all the photos of Shane and me. Instead, I'd shoved them into a box along with the Tiffany's bracelet and diamond heart-shaped necklace he'd given me, the letters he wrote me from basic training, and the sticky notes he'd placed throughout the house. I'd tucked the box away in my closet to deal with another day. Today was that day.

I took the box outside and emptied its contents into my trash bin, saving only one wedding photo in my hand, then placed the bin on the curb for pick-up the next day.

I brought the photo to my kitchen sink. I grabbed a lighter from my counter and ignited its flame. I watched the flame, mirroring the one that Hope still burned within me. And Hope – she instructed me what to do next. My hands followed her instructions as they lifted the photo from the sink and set fire to one corner.

The flame spread up Shane's body, consuming him in its fiery path. It devoured his midsection, obliterated his chest, and crept toward his face. As fire engulfed his face, I watched his expression contort as the photograph disintegrated before me. I tossed it in the sink. The flame consumed me next, erasing the version of me that was Shane's lover, his wife. The photo burned until it was gone and the flame, with nowhere else to go, went out.

But my flame, Hope's flame, burned even brighter.

I got back into bed with Sadie and stroked her head as she nestled up beside me, her head on my belly. Her body radiated warmth.

Any trace of Shane would be gone by morning.

And I would finally be clean.

chapter thirty-eight

A bird can't fly with clipped wings.

Shane had been clipping my wings since I was 16 years old.

I thought it was love. In the early days, that's what it resembled. The attention, the excitement, the sweet moments shared together, the sacred oath of our commitment to one another – I was desperate for it, and with rose-colored glasses on I ignored flags that were so obviously red.

He was strategic. In the beginning, he clipped my wings only enough to prevent me from flying away. I could still move gracefully; I could rise and fall without his assistance. The limits he placed on me were for my safety – an act of love – because he cared.

He clipped them further as our relationship progressed. Despite my efforts at flying away, I could never make it far enough to escape his reach. As dependency upon my caretaker – or my captor – increased, the ability to escape – or even the belief that I could – diminished.

But the good thing is, feathers grow back.

And birds relearn to fly.

SHANE AND I didn't speak again after that night at my apartment. I blocked his phone number, but I wouldn't know if he even tried to contact me. When our divorce was finalized six months later, the papers were sent to the post office box we shared, for which I no longer had a key. I had to contact him to ensure he sent me a copy.

At this point, the only way to reach him was via email. My mind flashed back to three years prior when he had done the same to reach me in a time of desperation. Only this time, I wasn't reaching out to reconcile; I was reaching out to tie up loose ends.

He responded to my email saying he would mail the papers to my German address. He closed with one last goodbye, the final words he spoke to me:

Shane: *Go ruin someone else's life, you fucking cunt.*

I studied his words, but I didn't find validity in them. I didn't ruin his life. Looking back on the last seven years, I had given him love, acceptance and forgiveness when he didn't deserve it. And what I received in return wasn't love. Love doesn't manipulate and abuse. Love doesn't kick you when you're down. Love doesn't drag you to the depths of hell and back.

I looked down at my thumb. Tough skin had formed over where I'd chewed layers of flesh away, year after year. Though the wounds were no longer open, the thick scar tissue was visible.

I turned my gaze to Sadie, who lay on my bed, and sighed. "It's just you and me now, sweet girl."

Sadie wagged her tail in response even though she had no idea what I was saying. I could tell her anything and she would still wag her tail. That's why I loved her so much – because she supported me unconditionally.

I deleted the email from Shane – I didn't owe him a response – and looked at myself in the mirror. My reflection stared back, and I realized how tired I looked – way too tired and worn down at only 23 years old. I looked like I had lived 100 years. I thought of my mother and the mask of depression she had worn throughout my childhood. I saw it in myself.

But then I thought of her glow – the way she came back to life when she recovered from the heartbreak of her divorce. The way she accepted love into her life again, and how the right kind of gentle love made her vibrant.

A single tear traced a path down my cheek, carrying with it the weight of my pain. I knew the time had come to reclaim my worth, finally free from Shane's suffocating grip. Free to begin a life where love didn't equate to suffering and where my worth would never be questioned. I knew, one day, I would be vibrant again.

With clarity, I made myself three promises.

"I promise to never let Shane back in," I said out loud to my reflection.

There was no question mark at the end of our relationship, only a solid period of finality. Full stop. What was once a golden brick road between our two hearts now lay in rubble. I couldn't erase Shane from my life, but I could ensure his chapter was over, and no future chapter would ever contain him.

And the chapters that lay before me were filled with opportunity. I could travel the world and awaken new pieces of my soul in an endless pursuit to absorb it all. I could change the course of my career trajectory. I could be whoever, and whatever, I wanted to be.

"I promise not to settle for less than I deserve."

The beginning of my new life would start here in Germany. Shane was moving back to the United States and although the Army would pay to move me back as well, I didn't want to go home. What would I be going home to? The town where Shane and I met and fell in love, the family and friends who warned me not to marry him? I couldn't face it. I had to do this alone.

I thought about the person I was before Shane. Could I be my old self again? Was there still a version of me that existed separately from him? Or would the new me simply be a phoenix, rising from the ashes and born anew?

I hadn't put myself first in years. I had neglected the things that made me happy, that made me feel alive. I had blamed myself for all the wrongdoings that had come my way. I explained away Shane's temper as the response to my behavior, and his infidelity a byproduct of my shortcomings.

It stopped today.

From this moment, and in every moment yet to come, I would be the partner the girl in the mirror deserved. I would hold her in high regard. I would take care of her. I would listen to her needs. I would not allow her to shrink under the weight of anybody else. This, I promised to her in one single sentence.

"I promise to be better," I said.

And I meant it.

And Sadie wagged her tail.

acknowledgements & author's note

Thank you to my friends, family and every person who took the time to read this novel – my catharsis.

Thank you to those who encouraged me to keep sharing, and those who shared their own darkest stories with me. No longer will we silently shoulder a burden that was never rightfully ours to carry.

Thank you to my husband, who patiently supported me through a three-year process of diving deep into my memories and resurfaced emotions. As awkward as it may have been to watch me spend hours upon hours writing about an ex-lover, you never made it feel that way. You remain my biggest fan.

After I left my toxic marriage in 2014, it took me seven years to go to therapy. When I finally began processing my trauma I struggled to recount stories due to memory gaps, a common symptom of PTSD. My therapist encouraged me to write down what I could remember, and then fill in the rest. And thus, *I Promise to Be Better* was born.

This novel is not intended to be a hero's tale nor a stellar example of how to navigate an abusive relationship – it is neither; but it is raw, and I chose to share it with you for its vulnerability and complexity.

According to the CDC, 1 in 4 women and 1 in 7 men will experience physical violence by their intimate partner at some point during their lifetimes; and about 1 in 3 women and nearly 1 in 6 men will experience some form of sexual violence. If you find yourself within those numbers, know that you are not alone. If even one person benefits or finds healing from reading this story, then it was worth every minute I poured into it.

And should my ex-husband ever come across this book – I have forgiven you, but I will never forget. Do better.

Be better.

about the author

Erinn Keala is a self-published author who believes writing is one of the best forms of self-expression. She has more than a decade of experience in marketing, journalism, and blogging; but this is her first – and perhaps only – novel, written from the depths of her worst memories in an effort to bring healing to herself and others.

Erinn lives in Hawaii with her husband and dog. In her free time she enjoys traveling, hiking, going to the beach, fitness and food.

www.erinnkeala.com
Connect on Instagram: @erinnkeala